FOR

Mum and Dad

ACKNOWLEDGMENTS

Thank you for believing in this.

GOLD AND SILVER CHAINS

Hannah was furious. Her dad wasn't due home from prison until Christmas. Now he was to return in July, right in the middle of her French exchange. Hannah knew that the French exchange was even more of a surprise to Jean than Harry's return from prison, but that didn't lessen the blow.

'He's not meant to be home until December. If I'd known, I wouldn't have arranged it.' Hannah fumed.

Jean placed her hands on her hips. 'Let's rewind a second, Missy, I didn't know anything about this French exchange. Did the school not think of consulting me?'

'Methodist College has nothing to do with it!'

'Who the hell is arranging it then?'

'I saw a poster and applied.'

'Well, that was clever of you. But why didn't I have to sign any forms?'

'You did.'

'I did not.'

'Your signature is on the forms. You agreed to everything.'

'Not again, Hannah!'

Hannah softened as she tried hard to suppress a smile, 'Mum, let's face it, I've been signing forms for so long now that your signature is mine.'

'Oh f...for god's sake.'

'You were going to use the F word again, weren't you? You'd better not teach Etienne such poor English when he gets here!'

'Ate what?'

'Etienne, mum! Et-ee-en!'

'How the hell am I going to remember that? Hang on, you said he.'

'I did.'

'That's a boy.'

'It is.'

'Holy god.'

'Stop blaspheming!'

'Where are we going to put a he?'

'Well, I was thinking Shelley and I could move into your bed with you, but now that you've landed this bombshell on me, I don't know what to do!'

'It was meant to be a nice surprise. Your dad was going to come through the door and you and Shelley were going to jump up and down and cover him in kisses,' said Jean.

'Mum, we're not children anymore. I don't even know what I'd say to the man.'

Hannah watched as Jean's face turned to dust. She started up the hoover with her customary cleaning face, attacking the living and the dead on the skirting boards that bordered the blue and pink flowery wallpaper. The propulsion of this tiny machine of a woman did not mask the fear in her eyes. Hannah wondered what had unsettled Jean. Was it the French exchange student? No, she would still be mid-tirade about that and Hannah knew that she would secretly enjoy having a French boy in the house. It would give her something to tell the neighbours for the next few years. Could it be that Jean too would not know what to say to her Harry after almost nine and a half years of his absence?

The power cut abruptly. Jean catapulted words towards her daughter. 'If you are going to have a French exchange student stay in this house for three weeks, then you can help me tidy up! This place needs renovated badly. The wallpaper hasn't been changed in three years. Ate-at-ten can stay in your room. You and Shelley can sleep down here on the pull-out sofa. I want this house cleaned from top to bottom and all that junk in your room packaged up and sent to the attic or the skip, do you hear me?' Jean looked around the room, her eyes narrowed in a visionary calculation. She flicked her eyes to Hannah again, 'Here, tell me this. Who paid for this exchange?'

'I did!'

'What with?'

'Mum, haven't you noticed I've been working twenty hours a week in Top Shop and babysitting every weekend! There's just the small matter of spending money.'

'How small?'

'Well, I can't do many hours in the shop while he's here. Could you give me £300?'

'No.'

'£200.'

'No. Hannah, I have bills coming out of my ears.'

'Will your man be able to work when he gets home?'

'He'd bloody better. I fancy a holiday to France too when I think on it. How do I get myself on one of those exchanges?'

'France wouldn't be big enough for your big mouth!' Hannah laughed, hopping swiftly as the hoover clipped her legs, 'Hey, watch out!' she cried.

'Don't you be so cheeky mademoiselle. You're not too old to get a good hiding!' said Jean with a twitch of the head and a broad smile.

***

Two letters in one day, one hand-written in the familiar faltering scrawl of her husband, and one succinct electronic message from a friend. The former narrated news of an early release, 'I'll be home by July.' The latter was a souvenir of a walk, 'You reminded me of home.'

Jean kneaded the reality of Harry's release from prison into a tight ball and gripped it firmly in her hand. Her husband, her own intimate stranger, was coming home after nine and a half years. Jean looked around the room and tried to picture him seated by the fire. She searched for him by the TV or walking through the door. He wasn't there. She tried to capture something: his footsteps, his legs stretched out across the rug. Nothing. His voice came from the back of the house, but not his face. Why? Why couldn't she see her husband in her mind's eye? A thought dropped from her mind and landed on the floor with a thud. She released her hand and looked around.

She could not see her husband in her own living room because he was never there when she needed him to be there.

Jean went back upstairs. She looked around the tiny box room and inhaled the heady scent of the past. There was Robert, a little four year-old boy with a drum around his neck and two drum sticks glued to his fingers. Jean had had to pour him into bed after the Twelfth of July parade when he had stood tall among the men of the Argyle Temperance Flute Band, pride beaming from his red cheeks, his skinny legs racing to keep up with the wide stride of the bandsmen.

His face. Jean saw him on the bed again, his face soft and shining, a slightly upturned nose perched delicately in the air. She smiled and turned to the screen.

She read the email again, slowly this time, line by line. She stopped at the last line and read it three times, 'I thought of Robert today. I know you will wish me to always think of Robert and I will. He was like a son to me.'

Jean closed the email and turned back to the bed. A drum around his neck tied up with ropes.

Ropes around his neck.

She fell into her own hands, a painful sound emerging as her body collapsed on the bed. Tears drenched the cotton of her son's pillow. Robert. She huddled into herself and fell again. She allowed herself to fall freely in the silent walls of her home, heaving sounds from the pit of her stomach and tugging them from her body to release the pain. She needed to feel it again. She wore it like a heavy woollen coat and wrapped herself in every fibre of it. She would never give it away. It was her consolation.

A year and a half had passed. Each day, she found herself awake and alive, and so she lived. Each night she wanted to be in the same place as her son.

***

Hannah tipped back her head and felt the moist spring rain settle on her cheeks. She was in Botanic Gardens. She looked around and recollected Jean perched on a picnic mat in her raincoat, handing out sandwiches wrapped in clingfilm, oblivious to the drizzle and the fact that no one else was having a picnic to celebrate the peace. Everyone else had ignored the passing of the peace agreement, Hannah realised, except Jean Adams from Snugville Street.

Rachael glided down the hill by Hannah's side, her long tanned limbs glistening in their ambivalence towards the elements.

'Rachael, does your mum celebrate the peace?' asked Hannah.

'What peace?'

'The peace here in Northern Ireland, dummy.'

'No, why would anyone do that?'

'Jean does.'

'Jean is amazing,' smiled Rachael.

'Shut up. She's a header.'

'Well, we can swap then,' said Rachael. 'You take my stuck up cow for a week and I'll take your mum.'

'Ah stop it. Your mum's just a wee bit posh. She's a good woman. Anyway, Jean brings us here for a picnic on the anniversary of the referendum for peace.'

Hannah felt the weight of Rachael's eyes on her. 'You're kidding me. She's a laugh. Is tonight cabbage night, by the way?'

'You and your cabbage. Yes it is. What's the big deal about cabbage anyway?' Hannah asked, knowing the answer well.

'Oh you'll never know how lucky you are to get home cooked meals,' said Rachael.

'Oh shush. Catriona makes nice things like lasagna and pasta. Jean wouldn't know a plate if there wasn't a spud on it.'

'Catriona wouldn't know a cooker if it was turned on.'

Hannah laughed at her friend's constant tirade of vitriol towards her

4

mother. 'You should give her a break, Rachael. She works hard. I think what she has done with her life is impressive. I'd like to do something like that one day. Imagine running your own company and driving around in a Mercedes! And to live on a house like that in Windsor Park. It's so lovely.'

'You'd hate it,' said Rachael.

'How do you know?'

'She wasn't always like that, you know...so into her fancy show home. When we lived in East Belfast, we had a normal house. It was cosy. And it was a nice street. We played hopscotch, rounders and skipping. There were no kids playing on Windsor Park when we moved there. I can't even sit on a seat without her ruffling a cushion under my bum. She's obsessed.'

'Maybe she is,' replied Hannah, 'but it's nice that she made it like that on her own. You have to admire her for that.'

'She took half of dad's business, so technically she didn't make it on her own,' said Rachael.

'She owned half of your dad's business, so technically she did. And she backed the right horse in the end with a tech company.'

Hannah liked Catriona and the unusual spelling of her name. She'd visualised Katrina in her head until she had seen it written down. The scarcity of the Irish language on Snugville Street had contributed to this error, and Hannah regretted that her acquisition of French, Spanish and German had been so swift, when her knowledge of the language of her ancestors was negligible. Catriona spoke Irish and French fluently and she practised French with Hannah at every opportunity. It was Catriona who'd given Hannah the leaflet for the French exchange and Hannah always felt the hand of friendship in her presence. Perhaps Catriona knew where to look for the respect that eluded her in her own home, and found affirmation in the heart of her daughter's friend.

'Rachael, let's go for a walk in the Museum, there's something I need to tell you.'

Hannah had never mentioned her father at school. *My mum is alone* was code for *please don't ask any questions*. Once, Rachael had been direct and asked Hannah if her dad was alive. 'Yes,' was her answer. Hannah then turned away. None of the other girls dared inquire. Hannah knew that she was a little more streetwise than her friends at Methodist College: it was a useful skill when mixed with academic ability. She had never felt the need to play up or cause trouble, but retained the esteem of her fellow pupils because they knew that her address was just off the Shankill Road, a heartland of violence during the thirty years of the Troubles.

School had been easy for Hannah, and lying was an instinct. *No, I don't remember the Shankill bomb. My brother died in his sleep. My mum is a single mother.* Shelley attended secondary school near the Shankill, so she was out of the way. Hannah had warned Shelley that when her friends visited

Snugville Street, she was never to speak of their father. 'I'll get crucified if anyone ever finds out. They'll look down on me. Don't ruin it for me.' Shelley always followed her big sister's lead. Despite having a foot advantage in height over Hannah, she shrunk away from confrontation.

Hannah walked up the steps of the Ulster Museum. The bleak modernist left-hand side of the building emerged from the grey stone classic right-hand side like an architectural centaur with the head of a stately home and the behind of a concrete horse. Somehow, it worked, the cubic projections of concrete giving Hannah the impression of something free, of a Belfast that was not immersed in the past.

'Let's sit down.' Hannah motioned Rachael to a seat in the foyer. 'Okay, so this is difficult.' Hannah said.

'Oh God, you're not up the duff are you?' asked Rachael, her face strained.

'No, don't be daft! I'm not pregnant!' she exclaimed. 'If I could find a boyfriend, that'd be a start.'

'What is it then? You're making me nervous.'

'It's my dad.'

Rachael's eyes rested, as though a flicker of movement would deter Hannah from speaking.

'I lied to you,' Hannah continued.

Rachael remained still.

'He and mum didn't split up.'

Hannah sensed that Rachael needed to breathe. 'Open your mouth, would you, before you pass out,' said Hannah.

Rachael exhaled a swift breath, 'Go on.'

'He's been in jail since since the end of 1993.'

Rachael didn't flinch. Hannah tried to detect a reflex. Had her green eyes practised this reaction before?

'Did you already know?' asked Hannah.

'No. I...'

'Oh, it's just you look a bit off colour.'

'I don't know what to say. That's almost ten years. What did he...Did he do something bad?' asked Rachael with a minuscule voice.

'Yes, he did. Look, Rachael, I couldn't ever tell anyone at school. It's hard enough going to a school like that if you live on the Shankill. It would have changed people's perceptions of me. Imagine if Conor Simple found out. He'd have me for dinner.'

'He's an idiot. Nobody listens to him anyway,' Rachael said.

'I know, but imagine if he knew. He told the entire school about Lacy Hamilton being pregnant and she's his own cousin!'

'He's a shit, but why didn't you tell me before now?' asked Rachael, her eyes sympathetic, her voice gentle.

'I wouldn't have minded you knowing, but I was scared that your mum would...I like your mum. Imagine if she knew. She wouldn't let me in your house anymore.'

'Oh, nonsense. That woman has more skeletons in her closet than shoes, and that's saying something! Anyway, your dad. What did he...what's his name?'

'It's Harry and he...' Hannah took a deep breath. Heat burned through to her bones. She knew that her pale freckled cheeks would be scarlet by now. She tried to speak again but the words got caught in her oesophagus and broke up into whispers as fine tears blurred the edges of Rachael's perfectly proportioned face. 'Right, deep breath. Here goes. When we were kids, we were playing on the street.'

Rachael's head began to move up and down. Hannah watched as she shifted her hands to the side of the seat, as though predicting the only possible outcome of a child playing in the street in the Shankill.

'You know, it was safe to play there. We played hopscotch and rounders and skipping there too. The only problem was the traffic. My mum used to try to keep us on Snugville Street in case...Anyway, Shelley was six and I was eight. She ran away from me...' Hannah stopped speaking as her nostrils widened and her face filled with the pulsating fever of a memory buried. She climbed the white cubic atrium with her eyes and inhaled deeply. Her mind borrowed the order of the wide minimalist space and she continued, her eyes still hitched to the summit. 'She ran away from...She ran into the bomb and a shard of glass cut through her. She lost her foot.'

She'd said it now and her body restored itself. She felt composed. Hannah looked at Rachael whose eyes had now assumed Hannah's pain. She was silent. 'Daddy walked...' Hannah paused as she recalled the word daddy. She hadn't said it in many years and its enunciation took her to another time. 'Dad was angry. He punched a guy. Mum said there was no excuse for it, but Mrs McAdam told me that the man he punched was a terrorist. It doesn't matter either way. The man died when his head hit the ground and dad went to prison.'

Hannah bathed in the bright light and looked around the ceiling, unable to face her friend. She took in the enormity of the space and sensed that Rachael was overwhelmed by the vastness of a secret uncovered. She was attuned to the ciphering in Rachael's mind. Rachael would be counting all the times she'd wondered, but dared not ask. She would be eliminating theories, registering them one at a time and filing them away in her mind. Hannah's heart was thudding so loudly in the silence that the whiteness around them was flickering like a screen.

She felt her friend's hand, warm and firm on her own. Rachael spoke, 'Come on, let's get you a cuppa.' Hannah walked towards the cafe, restful in the resolve of her friend's hand, unburdened from almost six years of lies.

***

Jean's workshop was busy with the resonant drilling of a needle on a zip.

'Shit!' Jean said as she reached down to gather up sequins from the floor.

'Talking to yourself again, Mum?'

Jean looked up to find her youngest daughter at the doorway, a small shadow growing over her face as she entered the room.

'Ach, hello there love. Is it that time already?'

'Yes, mum, time for a cup of tea. Stretch yourself now or you'll end up in pain again.'

She instinctively rubbed her hands together and stretched her fingers. Carpel Tunnel Syndrome had brought Jean a tingle in her fingers and a trickle of money into her bank account. She could barely feel the sequins of the dress in her hands. She had been providing West Belfast with handmade Irish dance dresses for five years and was unprepared for the sudden shift from embroidery to glitter. 'These bloody sequinned dresses are a pain in the arse,' she said. 'I'm going to put a sign up saying "No more bling!"'

'Mum, you really should. I told you before, you need to stick to turn ups and adjustments. Better money, less pain.'

'Would you listen to you? You're getting as bossy as your sister!'

'Don't say that! She scares the life out of me half the time!'

Shelley smiled and walked to the kitchenette in Jean's workshop. Jean heard the click of the kettle and the silence of something unsaid. She worked on the zip again, with one ear dull to the sound of the machine and the other acute to the absence of her daughter's shine.

Jean feared fifteen for her children more than any other age. It got her at fifteen. It grew like a cruel plant and tightened around her in knots. She had set up a system in her mind and knew how to fight it, but it had caught her mother and taken her away, leaving two children alone. Jean had been fifteen, and her brother, Robert, eight. Jean had managed, but Robert dipped and then plunged headlong into its obscure and opaque depths. No one could rescue her brother, just as no one could rescue her son.

Her son, named after her little brother, had been happily working one day in Holland, and the next it took him. There had been no signs. Only Jean knew why. She had watched it grow inside her only son like the soft, serrated edges of a stinging nettle. Jean had learned its healing compounds and she thought that Robert had started to understand. She had taught him to grab it firmly and hold it tight: to touch a nettle leaf with soft fingers was to welcome its bite.

Hannah had been fine, Jean reflected. She was always insolent and

8

autocratic, an academic girl with the simple mind of her father. But what about Shelley? Where was she? Could the traumatic events of her life have impacted on a vulnerable mind?

People in Belfast had started to talk about depression. Jean's neighbour had set up a support group and the press had fed off the gloomy statistics. They said suicide was now an epidemic in West Belfast and that it was filling graves as fast as the bombs that had torn the city apart.

They said it was the hallmark of a post-conflict society, but Jean knew that depression and suicide were stitched into the DNA of the people. Suicide had always been there, masked in alcoholism and hidden under bowed heads. It was a family's shame in Ireland's past, when ministers hailed it as a sin from the pulpit.

She peered at Shelley again, 'Are you okay love? You're not your usual sunny self.'

Shelley looked up with wide eyes, 'I've been thinking about Daddy.'

Jean moved her hands away from the machine. Shelley's daddy. She'd pushed thoughts of him away. Less than three months. She didn't want to face it, not yet.

'What about your daddy?'

'I know he did a really bad thing, but I was thinking about all the things he missed. It's not fair in a way.'

Jean listened. She hadn't considered Harry's pain. She had refused to think about it. It was part of the sentence she had imposed. Her heart could not make up for the limits of her mind.

'Imagine never hearing your children argue,' Shelley continued.

'Argue?'

'Yeah. That's what people do, isn't it? Daddy only ever saw our happy faces.'

'I suppose.' Jean looked at her daughter and saw more beauty in her face than ever. Her long fair hair had started to darken, but her blue eyes were deep and full of Harry.

'He didn't see us lying on the sofa in our pyjamas,' Shelley continued.

'We were always in our Sunday best.'

Jean looked at her daughter and softly responded, 'I hadn't thought...'

'You used to get us to take our school books to him to show him what we'd done, but he never did our homework with us. I can't stop thinking about all the things he never got to do.'

Jean tried hard to touch the sympathy of her daughter, but Harry wasn't real anymore. He was a body she went to see once a week, sometimes once a fortnight. He was a shape and a voice. He made her laugh sometimes, but he never incited sympathy. She would smile and chat furiously to hide an overwhelming sense of nothingness. She didn't know what to say to Shelley. She lifted her tea and walked towards her to the sofa opposite the sewing machine.

'What do you think of this French boy coming over? Hannah says he's seventeen. I wonder what he looks like!' Jean said, changing the subject.

'I don't like the idea of a smelly boy in my room. Can I go to America instead?'

'No, you can't and you're a geg. One minute you'll all tears and sympathy for your father and the next you're on a flight to America!'

'I know, but Annie said that when I was old enough, I could be an au pair for the summer.'

'You're not old enough.'

'I'll be sixteen this summer,' Shelley protested.

'You're still too young.' Jean said.

'Annie said she'd pay the flights.'

'When did she tell you all of this?'

'By email, of course.'

'Email indeed! She sends me letters with old fashioned handwriting that take days to get here and you get emails! She told me she liked the tradition. She's always been away with the fairies, that one. Wait 'til I talk to her!' Jean laughed.

The letters from America were one of Jean's greatest pleasures. The minute life became too fast, a letter came through the door to take her on a slow walk with her friend. There was no better feeling than tearing through an envelope, unfolding the contents and then reading over the words that had been written with so much care.

Jean's mind blackened in a recollection of guilt. Annie would never understand the emails that Jean read at night. She could never explain to her friend that part of her existence.

***

Mr Barker, the head of Sixth Form, was a tall and elegant man, a no-nonsense creature who hailed from the past. He coasted across the stage, the black silk from his cloak spraying behind him.

He spoke swiftly, 'Today, you have an important task. You will be asked to vote for next year's prefects.'

He paused and scanned the assembly, as though identifying the accused from his pulpit.

Mr Barker's speeches were decorated with just enough encouragement to motivate, but always delivered with a knowing warning against the misdeeds that were lurking in the minds and lockers of his students.

'You might be tempted to vote for your best friends.' His head lowered as his eyes policed the room.

Hannah's darted back to the grey-haired man with the soft grey eyes and pleaded. *Guilty.*

He plucked his head back out of his neck and added, 'This would not be wise. Methodist College must retain its reputation for endeavour, talent and academia. Please ensure your friends demonstrate at least the first item on the list. This voting system is new and you have been entrusted to ensure that it delivers. Do not disappoint yourselves. Do all the good you can.'

A stream of black silk indicated his departure.

Hannah turned to face Rachael, 'I tell you what, you vote for me and I'll vote for you.'

Rachael smiled, 'Agreed.'

They walked along the corridor towards their French class. 'Bloody double French with Miss Walker on a Friday afternoon,' said Rachael. 'I can't bare the thoughts of it. Fancy sneaking off to the common room for a cuppa instead?'

'No chance,' Hannah replied and trailed her friend by the arm. 'You are going to get through this A Level French exam. I'll make sure of it.'

Hannah felt responsible for her friend's poor A level selection. She had sold a vision of two friends working in Brussels in the European Union, dashing around Europe at the weekends and sipping wine in the evenings in town squares bustling with cafés and good looking men. It had been a great pitch until Catriona had taken Rachael on a weekend break to Brussels at the start of the school year. She returned to report that most people in Brussels spoke Flemish, the town squares were freezing and the men were all pushing buggies over cobbled streets that were impossible to navigate in heels. Her mum had met up with an old friend who worked at the European Commission and who spoke French, Dutch, English, German, Spanish and Italian fluently, but who was really struggling to get her Chinese up to an appropriate level. Rachael had thrown her hands up at that point and surrendered her future job to one of those continental European types married to the men pushing the buggies, and decided she had more hope of finding an engineering job and a handsome rugby player at home.

Hannah still had the dream.

'Hannah, I have zero interest. All she talks about is Simone de Bloody Beauvoir. That's hardly going to get us an A, is it?' Rachael complained.

'I like her stories.'

'I know you do. We all want to learn French while you two sit and talk a load of rubbish. I mean who cares about feminism anyway? Is it not a wee bit passé?'

'*Passé?* See, you do love French. You can't get away from it!'

Miss Walker held the kind of beauty in her voice and in her eyes that made people stop and simply watch. Her skin was olive with fine lines that betrayed her age. Hannah had the sheet white skin and freckles of her mother and was in awe of anything darker than peach. Miss Walker's smile was ablaze with the natural sheen of an old movie star and she paced the room with her nonchalant silk scarf floating behind her. Hannah tried to calculate her age. Late forties? But no, she was in France as a student in 1969. She must be in her fifties. Miss Walker lifted her copy of *Thérèse Desqueyroux*. At that point, Hannah knew that she was all hers.

The truth was that Hannah did not understand *Thérèse Desqueyroux*. Thérèse, who had tried to kill her own husband, was like a dark shadow of a human being kept alive by convention. Hannah didn't have any deep insight into the novel, but she knew how to engage with her teacher. Her strength was her response; conversation her friend.

Miss Walker stood at the table, supporting herself on the plinths of her hands, 'So, tell me, why would a woman try to kill her husband?'

Hannah waited whilst Miss Walker echoed the silence of the room. Hannah refused to move a muscle as she furtively glanced at the other girls and one boy in the class. No one stirred. The usual frustration mounted. Hannah experienced an unexplained empathy for her teachers during and after a long silence. She couldn't bear it. She held back for another minute. Miss Walker was not yet ashen, but the tension was tightening and draining the blood from her claret cheeks and lips. Why wouldn't they speak? They were smart girls, much smarter than Hannah. Come on! Help the woman!

Hannah sliced the silence, 'Because she had to live with him.'

Three girls in the corner giggled. Hannah didn't mean to say those words. She wasn't quite sure where they had come from, but now that she had aired them, she started to think about them. Perhaps the reason why her mum was the life and soul of Snugville Street, was that her husband was behind bars. Jean Adams, who had lived trauma throughout every step of her life, sucked up unhappiness like a hoover. If she didn't say 'cheer up, love' a hundred times a day, she said something beginning with f.

Hannah, pleased with her philosophising and the laughter she caused throughout the room, had Miss Walker in her hands again, 'Well, Miss Adams, you are quite the insightful young lady, aren't you? But most husbands and wives do have to live together. What made her do it?'

The only thing that had caught Hannah's attention when she had read the novel was the term Thérèse had used to describe the unborn child that she did not want. *Créature inconnue. Unknown creature.* It sounded almost hollow in English, yet it was eloquently cruel in French.

Hannah looked up. 'Depression,' she said.

'Ah beh oui! La dépression! Bravo Mlle Adams! Let's explore the theme of depression.'

'Miss, we've done la drogue, le sida and le chômage. Is there anything about French A level that would inspire us to stay on the course?' asked Hannah.

Miss Walker held her lips firm and looked around the room where repressed laughter faintly hummed from the bowed heads. Finally a smile emerged, large and radiant, dispelling any worry of chastisement for Hannah and hope of learning for the other pupils. Hannah had overcompensated and had come up with a word that was ripping her apart on the inside. *La dépression* had left a terrible scar on her family. A flash of Robert's face appeared and Miss Walker smiled, 'You're right, Hannah, it's a Friday afternoon. Let's talk about something other than depression, drugs, aids and unemployment. I'm looking down the list of topics here and I think Miss Adams has a point. The only thing that's not depressing is religion. Right, tell me about religion in France, Rachael.'

Hannah laughed as Rachael held her head in her hands and beamed colours that said clearly to everyone in the room, 'Transport me to a chemistry laboratory now, please!'

***

'For fuck….In the name of goodness, Han…Hannah, darling, would you be awfully kind and remove your files from the table?'

Hannah laughed and continued her discourse in mock eloquence, 'Why, of course, Mother dear. Where would you like me to put them? It's just that there is the small matter of my French writing exam coming up and I am trying to revise. Your other daughter has taken up residence in the bedroom and I am currently limited as to spaces I can occupy. I can't fit all these files on Robert's wee desk.'

Jean flicked a tea cloth over her daughter's head. 'Is there no way you can study in a more organised way? she complained. 'Look at the mess you're making. How can you read five opened lever arch files in one go? See, that's where you're going wrong. Your mind is full of the clutter.'

'Oh, is it indeed? And since when did Jean Adams become an expert on revision?'

'I did your homeworks with you for years. You wouldn't be where you are today if it weren't for me!' said Jean with a pout and roll of the eyes.

Hannah smiled, 'Mum, do you think you could help me again? I'm trying to remember all this vocabulary, but I keep jumping around. Look here, I've written the English words down this side and the French down the other. Could you help me?'

'Certainly.' Jean sat down with a feeling of purpose and picked the first word that jumped out at her.

'Deprivation.'

'Déprivation.'

'Wrong!' Jean swiped the tea cloth across her daughter's head.

Hannah ducked and held up her arms, 'Mum!' she exclaimed. 'What was that for?'

'You got it wrong.'

'No I didn't.'

'Are you questioning my French?'

'Yes.'

'It's privation.' Jean elongated the first vowel and made her best attempt at a French accent.

'Ooo, check out your accent.'

'May Wee! Right, next one, Housing Estate.'

'Cité or HLM'

'Wrong!' Jean flicked the cloth again as Hannah moved her seat away from the table, 'Oh wait a minute. Say the last bit again. Did you say HLM in French?'

'Yes!' Hannah screeched.

'Okay, keep your knickers on! Drug Dealing.'

'Le trafic de drogue,' Hannah instinctively moved her hands up to her face.

'Correct! Unemployment benefit.'

'L'allocation d'aide au retour à l'emploi.'

'Correct. Show off!' Jean scanned the rest of the page, 'Here, is this not a wee bit dull, love? I mean, I thought it was meant to be the language of love. What's romantic about all this?'

'Flip me, you're as bad as Rachael. And what's with the hitting me on the head?'

'That's how my mum taught me. Every time I got a spelling wrong, she whacked me over the head with the spelling book.'

'Did it work?'

'It did. It was worse in school. We got cracked knuckles with a ruler for getting something wrong.'

'Mum, why do you never talk about her?'

'Who?'

'Your mum.'

'I do.'

'You don't'

'I thought I did.'

'You don't.'

'What do you want to know?' Jean stalled for a moment, worried that she might not remember anything at all.

'Tell me something about her.'

'I can't just tell you something. Ask me a question.'

'Was she smart?'

'Very!'

'Did she work?'

'Yes.'

'What did she do?'

'She worked in an office in the mill before we were born. I don't think she was so prepared for babies.'

'Could she sing?' Hannah asked.

'No. Sorry, love. You can search for that gene and you'll never find it. We've all got high chests and flat voices!'

'Did she smile a lot?'

Jean's body filled with warmth. Her mother's smile was a gift, and Jean rarely got gifts from her mother. She tried to think of the best way to describe it. 'My mother's smile was like a candle burning when the electricity was out.' She sensed her daughter's lack of understanding in the weighty quiet.

'What was her middle name?'

'Her middle name was Theresa.'

'Anna Theresa. That's nice.'

Jean watched as Hannah's face came alive with something.

'We're doing a book in French with a Theresa. Or, should I say Thérèse. I didn't even like the name before now. Anna Theresa. That's lovely. Anyway, this Thérèse woman, she's a wee bit bloody depressing, as you would say.'

'Funny that...' Jean stopped. She had never discussed it with Hannah.

'Funny what?'

Jean scrunched the tea towel into a tight ball, 'Hannah, love, Anna Theresa...she took her...she died of an overdose. She was depressed.' Jean wanted to look up or to the left or right or anywhere but Hannah's face. It was like stealing away a fairytale from her daughter and giving it an unhappy ending.

Hannah's brow creased, 'Like Robert and our uncle.'

'Just like them. Your granny didn't die young, though. She had me when she was thirty-five. She was fifty when she died. It's young, but not like her son and the grandson she never knew.'

'Mum, do you think...Is it in the family? Could you... Could I...Could me or Shelley...'

'Love, I don't want to lie to you. It's something you might... If...if it happens, you need to take control of it.' Jean's knuckles were white. Her voice was shaking. 'It's an illness. Imagine you were diabetic. You'd take your insulin every day wouldn't you? It's like that only the sugar is a sadness. After Robert, the doctor gave me some medication. There's no shame in taking medication.'

'Miss Walker said she had it in the seventies.'

'Did she now? It's good that people talk about it now. It's good. What else did Miss Walker have in the seventies?'

'France, travel, boyfriends, feminism.'

'Feminism?' repeated Jean.

'Yes, feminism.'

'Did she run around burning bras?' laughed Jean.

'No,' Hannah choked. 'Why would she do that?'

'I never could figure it out. You'd be knocking seven bells out of Belfast with anything above a C cup.'

Hannah rolled her eyes, 'Mammy! Were you not a feminist then?'

'Feminist? What for, love? I was out working from the age of fifteen. What would I be doing with feminism? I had a brother to raise. There's no such thing as sexual liberation if you're stuck in the house every night with a child.'

'I'll mention that to Miss Walker. I'll maybe gloss over the bra burning.'

'You do that.'

'What about your dad, my granda?' Hannah asked.

'I thought we were being all miserable and French?'

'Did he not help?'

'He did. Your granda was a good man, but he worked on building sites in England so we didn't see him much. He sent us some money over. You know, I got to tell him I was pregnant with Robert before he died.'

Jean looked at her daughter's tender face and saw a flicker of her father. 'You have his blue eyes...like mine.' She watched her daughter's eyes drown in some elapsed space in time. She hadn't seen seventeen with her own mother, but she remembered times like this, sitting at the table, asking questions about how they used to live. Jean's throat started to fill. She swallowed and looked at the page that now had her finger and thumb prints stamped on it, 'Right, back to work. Gross Domestic Product.' Hannah watched a moment longer. Jean unravelled the towel again, 'Come on, GDP. I've got to get the spuds peeled for dinner.'

***

The ambition hadn't been there until the results came in on Monday morning. Hannah blushed when Rachael pointed out the obvious implication of getting more votes than any other student in the prefect's election. 'Just think, you could be head girl next year,' she had said.

Hannah did not at all want the extra burden and duties of head girl. Next academic year was important to her. She needed three As to do French and Spanish at the University of Edinburgh. The prize had been laid before her, though, and she was within its grasp. The other female contender was Rebecca Dunne, an all-rounder, who had as many skiing and tennis trophies as Hannah had pay-slips. No sooner had Hannah introduced her ego to the idea of it, than it was snatched away from her. One vote in the head girl race. It didn't add up, not until Friday, the day after the positions were announced.

A comment from Conor Simple in English Lit was stated in such a casual manner, that it barely felt like a slight. *I hear daddy is coming home.* Hannah was so unaware of what was happening that she laughed, half expecting the punch line to follow. The silence from the other pupils, who were united in collective whispers moments before, had more impact than the words from Conor's pimple-stippled face. Hannah slowly turned around, opened her book and started to read the blurred swirls on the page.

Mrs Henderson entered the room, unsuspecting Mrs Henderson with her ill-fated teacher words. 'Hannah, as you are the only person with the book open, could you read the first paragraph on page 577 of *Great Expectations.*'

The corners of words came into focus, and Hannah read the mechanics on the page with a quivering voice as her heart valves tried to shut down. 'Crowding up with these reflections came the reflection that I had seen him with my childish eyes to be a desperately violent man; that I had heard that other convict reiterate that he had tried to murder him; that I had seen him down in the ditch tearing and fighting like a wild beast. Out of such remembrances I brought into the light of the fire, a half-formed terror that it might not be safe to be shut up there with him in the dead of the wild solitary night. This dilated until it filled the room, and impelled me to take a candle and go in and look at my dreadful burden.'

Hannah stopped reading. She looked back over the page and pieced together the passage. A teacher could not have known what cruelty was contained in the words. Hannah's body convulsed. She pressed her knees together and dug her heels into the polished floor. The room chimed with the quiet censorship of voices choking on their own disparaging taunts. Hannah, already the smallest person in the class, shrank again.

Mrs Henderson was tuned into something now. Her eyes moved back to Hannah as her question fell into the lair, 'Why does Pip not feel safe with the convict even when it is revealed that he is his benefactor?' She coughed after an unbearable pause.

Hannah could not save this teacher. Mrs Henderson continued, 'Take a look back through the language that is used to describe this meeting. "The wretched man, after loading wretched me with his gold and silver chains for years." Why isn't Pip grateful? Is it just because this man is a convict?'

The words bounced off the taut silence.

'Okay, so it's Friday morning and we're a bit tired. Working alone, write down a few lines to describe how you would have felt if you'd been

17

Pip. Conor, could you step out of the room for a moment?'

Conor slowly followed Mrs Henderson. Hannah wrote one word. *Shame*. She stopped. Her hand shook. She waited for the inevitable. Mrs Henderson returned without Conor. 'I would like you all to pack up your things and quietly make your way toward the library. If I hear a report of a sound, there will be serious repercussions. Please leave the room.'

Hannah didn't move. She knew she wasn't included. By now her eyes were brimming and water had dispelled the word on the page. The humanity of the woman before her was etched in her brow. She placed a chair opposite Hannah and spoke, 'Hannah, I'm sorry. I wouldn't have asked...No one...I didn't know about your father.'

Mrs Henderson was a mist of blue and green. Hannah remained silent. The teacher's voice was tender and kind. 'You are a very talented pupil, one of the best.' Look at this.' She pulled an essay from a pile and pointed. 'You know, most of the people in your class will get an A or B in their English A level. It's a smart class, but this is the only essay to have ever got me here.' Mrs Henderson was holding a fist to her heart.

Hannah looked into her teacher's eyes and crumbled. She sniffed and breathed deeply as pride and shame churned through her tears.

'I'm going to leave you here,' said Mrs Henderson. Read through your own work one more time. Read the comments at the bottom of the page. Breathe deeply and walk into your next class with your head held high. Don't ever answer them back.' She stood up and walked towards the door. Hannah desperately wanted her to stay, but needed to be alone. Her eyes smiled when Mrs Henderson looked back.

Hannah read her own words. She understood. It was a good essay and she had put her heart into it. Did it make up for the fact that she didn't get a single vote? She didn't know. She was a prefect and she knew she would learn to be happy with that honour. She stared out the window and crowded up her own reflections.

Why did all of Harry Adam's children have to serve his sentence? Would no father have been better than one who had loaded her with chains of shame?

MOONLIGHT SERENADE

It was day time again. Harry enjoyed the nights, the dreams, the escape, but dawn opened up like a merciless reminder of the beauty of life. There was the routine of prison life; an enhanced regime for good behaviour. Then there was the survival routine that came of his own making. He awaited Nathan, as he did every day, for their nine o'clock meeting in the library; an empty library packed with discarded cells of knowledge.

Later, he would use the gym. At the age of fifty, his body remained strong, despite the tugging of time and the synthetic nature of the exercise he took. He would run on the treadmill and dream of colour and the scents of freedom: the hills around Belfast would be there, green and black. He would climb the Black Mountain with Hannah and Shelley in his mind and do all the things he had never done with them, running faster to blot out the reality that he had done nothing at all: their childhood had passed him by.

Hannah. A strain in his abdomen still played on him from her last visit. She had wielded the might of her silent eyes and struck him painfully. The walls and polished floors were cold enough without losing the warmth of his daughter's smile. What had happened? Whatever it was, she mustn't have told Jean. Jean would have said something.

Jean too had been storing her own silences, casting new clouds in the windows that narrowed as Harry's youth slipped away. Only Shelley made the daylight brighter, removing the harsh images he had painted in his mind for almost ten years; images of a small girl trapped in the debris; images that were conjured up through second hand stories and photographs in newspapers. Harry's memories had been created to mask an uncomfortable truth: a stranger had reached out his hand and pulled his six year old daughter from the rubble; a stranger had helped his wife save his child from a bomb that killed nine people and injured more than fifty; and a stranger had picked up a dusty child, his child, with blood pouring from her severed body, while he had walked through a park in East Belfast holding Linda's hand.

Harry hadn't heard the bomb. Harry had heard the crunch of papery brown leaves as two souls moved in tandem.

By day, Linda was there with him in her suit in the bank where he'd met her. She was slender and gentle. She would place her hand on his cheek and smile a thousand quiet words. Her voice was her touch; her courage contained in the impalpable movement of her limbs. Harry could not shake Linda from his mind each day. He had told her once that he would divorce Jean and he'd promised her things that could never be delivered; it had all seemed so easy before a bomb stole his illusion in a loud awakening bang.

Harry had realised too late that he had a family, a perfect family. Why didn't he know that at the time? In a hospital waiting room in the middle of an October night in 1993, he'd seen it clearly. Dozens of people had moved in and out looking for relatives, but he couldn't find Jean. He had desperately wanted to find his wife, who'd grown from her diminutive self to someone saintly. When he had finally broken through the chaos of the relatives and victims, he had found her all over again. She had sobbed in his arms and his chest had expanded.

He had absorbed her pain. Harry had absorbed Jean.

Yet, here in this prison of his mind, as the sun cut tunnels through barred windows, Linda's fragmented face fell on him like lace.

And he lived it all again: the crushing beep of Shelley's heart as she lay on a bed tied up to machines, crying by her side for everything he'd done, watching over her for three days and three nights, going home to see the shadows under the eyes of Robert and Hannah, and sobbing, endlessly sobbing when he saw the faces of the dead lined up on the front page of the newspaper.

He had driven to Linda, resolved to tell her how wrong he'd been. She'd already heard about Shelley, and the shame of walking through a still park under a brilliant sky with Harry had swept her to the ground. Linda had had her own cross to bear, that of a Christian woman who'd sinned. Harry's family needed all of him and yet he was in East Belfast, his heart still belonging to a woman who was hysterical, believing that her punishment for her sin was a bomb.

A sickening anger had cut through him. Harry couldn't explain to Linda that the IRA had caused the bomb because it would have been a vindication of his own crime, yet he didn't want to watch her bleed. Morally bereft, he'd caused destruction in every direction he'd turned, and the ruination of so many lives choked him.

Harry recalled tightening the slim silver chain around his neck after seeing Linda, as though its light grip might strangle him. But his children had bought him that chain and he let it go.

He had walked from the Shankill and kept walking, moving through side streets where painted kerbs turned from red, white and blue to green, white and gold. He had punched a man outside a republican bar and then walked away in silence through the broad lit streets, calmly showing his driver's licence at an army patrol, patiently waiting whilst his details were recorded.

Harry could have walked on to prison, knowing that he had expelled the nihilism of his mind.

Harry was in prison and he imagined a small living room with a portrait of a family hanging over a fireplace, and the colours of peach and pink. It was there in his home where he could touch Jean and love her: he knew he could love her, and he could live in the daytime again because his children would forgive him.

But they could never forgive him, not all of them, not Robert.

Harry looked up as a twenty-five year old man arrived by his side in the library. He shook his hand, 'Sit down, Nathan, son. I want to show you this book about the Docker's strike in 1907.'

***

'Why don't you get yourself a proper computer desk?' said Hannah as she walked into the room. 'What are you up to anyway?'

Jean wasn't sure if it was Carpal Tunnel Syndrome, a state of panic or an incurable combination of both, but she could not manoeuvre the mouse fast enough to minimise the window. She stood up, cracked her knee on the wrought iron of the sewing machine table, lifted the keyboard with the edges of her hands, tipped it over, and rattled the life out of anything lurking between the keys.

'These bloody things are a health hazard!' she said, swiftly swiping at the contents of the keyboard that lay scattered across the table with the duster from the pocket of her apron. She then moved around the table in a roving warrior pose with the duster attached to one hand, her body at all times disguising the email that was still fully visible on the screen.

'Using ancient furniture won't help you in your efforts to keep a clean house. Mum? Mum! What on earth are you doing now?'

Jean was on top of the table, her bare feet cold on the flat metal plate that contained the sewing machine. Her legs were covering the computer screen.

'There's a spider web in the lampshade,' she said. 'My granny would turn in her grave. And that table's an antique. It was my great granny's. There's not a chance that we're getting rid of it.'

'Oh for goodness sake, get down before you end up in the grave with your granny. If that machine's as old as you say it is, it might not be a good

21

idea to climb up on top of it. And besides, have you thought about redecorating in here? It's a bit...'

Hannah stopped speaking as Jean turned and looked at her daughter. She rested her eyes for a moment on a space beyond Hannah. It was the face of a young footballer from Robert's childhood. *Ryan Giggs*. Robert had loved Ryan Giggs.

'Sorry, Mum,' said Hannah. 'Ignore me. It's too soon. I shouldn't have...'

'No, no. It's okay, love. Those posters. Look at them. They're starting to fade. I should put them in a box.'

Hannah didn't respond. She stared at the wall and then lowered her head. A small voice came from her lips. 'Maybe. Maybe keep them for a little while longer. There's no rush is there?'

'No. No, there isn't,' sighed Jean.

'I'm off to work now.'

'Okay, love.'

Jean's feet remained on the table as Hannah walked away. Her duster fell to the ground and her hands melted again. The table shook. She looked down. The heavy wrought iron supports were as sturdy as they were when they left the Singer factory more than one hundred years ago, but Jean's legs were trembling.

Jean climbed down from the table. She read the email again.

17 May 2003

Dear Jean

I took a walk around Leiden on Friday night after work. The Van der Werff was packed with people sitting outside. I was alone and took a seat by the window overlooking the canal and watched the water. I thought of how you wanted to bottle up the picture of the canal with the weeping willows and windmill and take it home. You said it would be like bottling up a small piece of Robert. Please smile as you read this. It is a happy story.

When Robert moved here, we went out for a drink to celebrate his seventeenth birthday. It must have been around 1998. Robert met a girl in the Van der Werff that night.

There's beauty in an eighteen year-old girl, a deep beauty that shines through the skin. As features become more refined and the eyes become deeper, it is replaced with something more rehearsed. Majella still held that purity on that night that she met Robert.

Robert had a few bierjes before plucking up the courage to speak to her. She was from Cork and the accent she had was almost musical. I found it hard to understand her against the noise of the bar, but I was happy watching Robert react to her. He tried his first ever Dutch sentence and it was fortunate that she wasn't a Dutch girl. We had told him that 'How are you?' was 'Ik hou van jou,' and so, he spent his first week in Holland telling everyone he met that he loved them. Anyway, after he'd told Majella that he loved her, she explained that she was on holiday, that she was looking for her cousin, and didn't speak a word of Dutch. She was only there for a month, but they saw each other almost every day.

I approached Majella on Friday night and explained that I had met her through my son five years ago. I don't know why I said it like that. It was quicker than explaining to her that he was my son's friend and the words had stayed with me since I wrote them in the last email to you. I took the light out of her eyes when I explained that he'd died. Maybe I shouldn't have told her, but I wanted her to know so that she would understand and remember. She said she'd lost touch when she went back home and was curious to see if he'd still be there. She is moving to Holland to work here.

I was thinking, as I talked to her, that you live a whole life before the age of nineteen, and I want you to think of Robert in that way. Robert may have been taken from us, but the story of one so young is worth telling.

I know that you will be smiling because Majella remembered. Robert left something behind.

Jean, I want to talk to you and see you again. I know it's difficult, but it might be the last time.

Take care,

Roy

***

Mrs McAdam was seated by the fire in her padded, red, velvet dressing gown. Shelley was certain she'd never seen anything like it in a shop. It was like an old boat that had yet to be retired, and it could be seen sailing around Snugville Street at any given time of day carrying a pedalo of a lady with pink curlers in her hair.

The Shankill Road served as a border of decorum. Never would Mrs McAdam set foot beyond it without being fully dressed, and then she would be spectacular with a formality that had passed by every generation since Mrs McAdam stepped out in the 1930s. Shelley focused on the dressing gown again and marvelled at how its length allowed for the most expansive parting of the legs. Whilst women across Belfast clasped their knees, Mrs McAdam's were set adrift under red velvet, her stockings wrinkled around her skinny ankles and her feet anchored into matching red, velvet slippers.

This dear old lady with nostalgic watery blue eyes was in charge of Shelley and Hannah during the period of their mother's absence. Shelley knew well that it was Jean's way of ensuring that someone was there to watch over her oldest friend and neighbour. Mrs McAdam was family in every way but blood, yet she remained Mrs McAdam. It was a forgotten observance that was shared with Mrs Small, Mrs Rainey and Mrs Lloyd, the other three octogenarians on their row of red-bricked terraced houses. The 'Adam' in her name helped forge the bond. It amused Shelley as a child that the Adams lived next door to Mrs McAdam.

The musty perfume, the brilliant shine of her false teeth and the soft layers of her folded white skin, all enveloped Shelley's senses like unconscious memories from the cradle. Mrs McAdam's stories were like breathing, even though she had lost each decade since the 1970s. Memories of the lifetime of Shelley and Hannah came in wide strokes, yet she could paint the war years with a fine brush. She could depict the Belfast Blitz, when the Germans bombed the city, in harrowing detail, whilst the dances and the music halls came to life in splendid colour with her red lips, always shining with lipstick, regardless of the stage of her attire. Shelley relished spending time with the only remaining link to the family she never had. Each hour with Mrs McAdam was like time spent with an unseen past.

Whilst Shelley and Hannah slouched on the sofa facing the fire and the adjoining wall of their house, Mrs McAdam was seated upright on the wooden framed chair closest to the fire, the chair where she would sleep with her eyes open throughout the afternoon. Positioned to her left was a small crystal glass of sherry, and to her right an ashtray. Smoke fumes swirled throughout the tight space, dancing off walls and resting in the lungs of Shelley and Hannah. Shelley breathed in deeply, immersed in the vapour. She waited until Mrs McAdam started to doze before addressing her sister. 'Is mum staying with Roy or in a hotel?'

Hannah glared at her with blue eyes that appeared black with indignation.

'Oh. Did I say something I shouldn't have?' Shelley fumbled.

'It's not that you said something you shouldn't have said. It's what you didn't say! What were you thinking?' exclaimed Hannah.

Shelley's skin burned with the sting of Hannah's words. 'I wasn't thinking anything. I just never understand why she stays in a hotel and wastes all that money when she could stay in Roy's flat. She stayed with Annie when she went to America.'

'If there was something going on, surely she would stay with him,' whispered Hannah.

'I didn't think there was something going on! What on earth made you say that?' said Shelley, stunned that her own words had led to this unexpected interpretation.

'Sorry, I thought you meant...'

'Now, now girls. You mother is visiting the place where Robert died and spending time with the man who looked after him. Don't let your imaginations run wild. Your father will be home soon.'

Mrs McAdam frequently feigned sleep for long enough to surprise everyone. Shelley should have known.

'Sorry Mrs McAdam, I didn't think...' said Shelley.

'I had a secret love once.'

It was the voice of Mrs McAdam. Shelley sat to attention.

'Oh aye, you didn't expect an old lady like me to have a past did you?' She flexed her right toe into an arch and held it out by the fire. 'I wasn't always like this, you know. I used to have the finest ankles in the Shankill.'

Hannah smiled. Shelley looked back at the old lady, knowing that she had eclipsed the present, and waited.

'When I was a girl, we used to go to the dances. It was Big Band music. Oh it was wonderful.' Shelley watched with a smile as Mrs McAdam's eyes drifted around the dancehall of her memory, her fine ankles, no doubt, moving to the rhapsodic sound of saxophones and trumpets. 'What lovely times!' she said. 'They used to say sweet sixteen, but seventeen was the sweetest time of all.'

Shelley understood. Mrs McAdam was bringing Hannah into her world.

'It was a Moonlight Serenade at the Plaza dancehall on Chichester Street. You should have seen the style! We'd set our hair on a Thursday night and wear a scarf all day Friday. The minute the siren went at the mill, we'd rush home through rain, and take out the curlers. Oh and we were gorgeous. Young girls nowadays don't make half the effort.'

Shelley laughed. 'Mrs McAdam,' she asked, 'what about this Moonlight Serenade?'

'Oh aye, I was saying...the girls would line up along the hall and the fellas would come along and ask you to dance. I never got asked. Week after week, I waited. I don't know why with these ankles of mine.' Mrs McAdam grinned mischievously and revealed her assets with a turn. 'Well, one Friday night in the summer of 1939, I was swaying to the music and didn't I catch the eye of the saxophonist! Oh what he was doing with that brass, I can't tell you.'

Shelley giggled and looked at Hannah, who was mesmerised. Mrs McAdam continued, a spell of flames bouncing off her eyes, 'Let me tell you, he was all chiseled chins and eyes the colour of the Irish sea! I sat alone and swayed to his music for the rest of the night. When the music ended, he waved me over to the stage and played the Moonlight Serenade just for me. I was the envy of every girl in the Plaza. Then, he walked me home, right to this street.'

'And what was the secret?' came Hannah's voice, hard against the misty dreams of Mrs McAdam's past.

'You youngsters are too impatient. Well, I was going to tell you anyway. His name was George. He was from over the border in the Free State. Bands used to travel up and down in them days before all the trouble.' Mrs

McAdam leaned in now, 'He was a fenian, you see!'

Shelley and Hannah gasped in tandem. Hannah spoke in a cracked throat that was busy mixing remonstrance with shock, 'You can't use that word, Mrs McAdam!'

'Well, what's the modern word, then?'

'It's not a word people use,' Shelley clarified, not quite sure how to approach the subject of political correctness with a women who had lived in a world that had bypassed appropriate speech in favour of hearty tales. Fenian, a word Shelley had often heard as a child as a slur on Catholics, was now seen by anyone with any sense as a foul diatribe. The light departed from the eyes of Mrs McAdam. Shelley added, 'Maybe it wasn't such a bad word in your day. Go on, Mrs McAdam. Tell us about this George.'

'Well, we walked for miles. I had to be home for eleven or my father would have taken his belt to me, but I got home at half past midnight.'

'Oh no! What happened?' Shelley asked, enveloped in empathetic fear.

'Well, I got my first kiss, the longest kiss. It was the best night of my life: soulful music, a moonlit walk, a long kiss from a Free Stater, and a good hiding!'

Hannah laughed, 'A good hiding from your dad?'

'No, from my mother. She caught me first. Luckily, my father was drunk and asleep. Oh she took the brush shaft to me and told me I wasn't too old for it! Wee Anna next door heard the whole thing. Says I to Anna, "It was worth every bruise for that kiss."'

'Was it Anna, our granny?'

'Yes it was indeed your granny. Oh here, Hannah, your mammy said about the French boy coming over. Did you know that there's French in your mother's line?'

'What, French knickers on her washing line?' Hannah laughed.

'No, Hannah, don't be so cheeky,' interrupted Shelley. 'Mrs McAdam's right. Mum said that her granny told her that there was French in the family.'

'Jean's full of it. What a load of nonsense! Right, well, Mrs McAdam, I'm going back next door, Mademoiselle Shelley will be here to keep you company. Thanks for the story. That kiss sounds like something else!' Hannah winked in Shelley's direction and kissed Mrs McAdam's cheek goodnight.

'It was Anna's mother, Sally, who told me about the French blood. No wonder you're a good linguist,' added Mrs McAdam.

Hannah lingered at the door for a second longer and looked into Mrs McAdam's eyes, 'Thanks Mrs McAdam. I'll see you both in the morning. I'll get the buttermilk for the soda before going to school. Goodnight.'

***

Belfast women poured out of Departures with perfect hair and the hope of Amsterdam in their eyes. Roy marvelled at how small they all seemed. He had lived in Northern Ireland most of his life and it hadn't occurred to him that the entire country was so modestly built, like the neat rows of red-bricked terraced parlour houses that once crisscrossed the city. Jean was embedded among them, several inches smaller than the smallest, and yet she stood out like a narrow house with scrubbed steps and shiny windows. Her smile was a bright lamp, her teeth perfectly aligned and her blue eyes alive with an energy that came from leaving her guilt on the plane.

Roy knew that this was Jean's escape, her chance to live out the existence of her son, her time to feel the physical touch of someone who loved her in a way that slipped through the boundaries of what was acceptable and real.

This was the fifth visit and each greeting he gave was awkward, the range of a hug too complicated in the dimensions of their bodies. He reached down, kissed her on the cheek and took her bag. She smiled and walked in silence past the tulip stalls and wooden clogs, casting her eyes up and down from the gleaming tiles of the airport towards his face.

The train breezed away in the easy hush of a light whistle. Roy rehearsed Jean's eyes, two deep blue tears that smiled effortlessly on the white porcelain of her face. Her freckles were hidden under a light layer of makeup, but he remembered them. He had learned them. He awaited her voice. He awaited her essence.

'Thank you for coming,' he said.

Jean's face brightened into a wide smile. She reached out for his hands and held them in her own. Her silence prevailed until she caught a glimpse of a woman passing by, a woman with her head shaved on one side and blue hair protruding from the other like an electric shock. The woman's blue jeans were ripped meaningfully into threads, leaving two ivory buttocks shimmering down the train. Roy watched as it built up and then it happened: resplendent words formed in an instant, designed to make him laugh.

'Holy God. Did ye ever see the likes of it? She'll end up with piles. If she'd let me shave off the hair on the right side, I could do a nice wee job stitching it onto her bum and the world would be less blind. What do you think?'

Roy was thankful for the woman with the inky head and wide hips and held Jean's smile, 'Jean, while you're busy bottling up memories of Robert, I would love to bottle up all your words and keep them. I keep telling you. There is a poet in there somewhere.'

'Oh, don't you be starting with poetry now. I had enough of that from...from Annie.' Jean's eyes fell on her hands with a splash.

Roy tightened his grip, 'Jean, we can't think about all of that. I told you many times that Annie wouldn't mind. She's my ex-wife, remember.'

Jean blinked at something and smiled again, 'I know, I'll be okay. I'll enjoy the weekend, I promise. I have to. It's the last one.'

'Yes, I...'

'Come on,' said Jean, 'Chin up! I've got my walking shoes on.'

'Can I still not convince you to go on a bike?'

'No, love, not on those cycle lanes. Not again. This arse was not crafted so perfectly to suffer on a saddle.'

'Well, there's something we can both agree on!' smiled Roy.

Jean's eyes shone. She was with him again.

'What about a boat?'

'What kind of boat?' asked Jean.

'We could hire one of those rowing boats and take a tour of the canals.'

'Maybe, we'll see.'

Roy already knew the answer. Jean would not do anything that spoke of romance. She wouldn't do anything to create memories other than those of her son, and yet, holding her hand on long walks, drinking in cafes and talking about Robert had somehow been more than romance to him. Roy loved Jean. He loved all of her, but she could never be his. She was a prisoner's wife, and until he had lifted her collapsed body from the ground after her son's death in Leiden, she had had a faithful marriage to an unfaithful man. Until he had wrapped her in his own sheets and held her in bed on her second visit, she had never touched another man.

Roy had taken Jean on a journey through the last years of her son's life. She had met the people Robert had befriended, and she had seen the bridges Robert had climbed at work. Roy knew that eventually the memories would run dry. One day, they would have nothing to say about Robert, except to repeat the same adages. Jean's destiny was with Harry, and it tortured Roy to think of her with another man.

Roy led Jean out of *Leiden Centraal*, where hundreds of bikes surrounded the station like a glistening moat.

'It never fails to amaze me,' said Jean.

'What?'

'The bikes. They're nice to look at all piled up there.'

Roy smiled. Jean's love of Leiden meant something to him, despite knowing she would never share it with him.

'Do you fancy a wee vodka?' Jean asked, smiling at Roy and nodding towards the Van der Werff, a prize of rest and sunshine at the end of a short walk in the cool shade.

'You're the only person I know who drinks vodka in the early afternoon,' teased Roy.

'You're the only man I know who drinks like a woman. The men of

Glenarm would have something to say if they saw you with one of those half glasses!'

Roy smiled at Jean's accurate slight, 'Glenarm, eh! You know I haven't thought about Glenarm for a long time.'

'Was it as nice growing up there as what Annie said? I used to envy the life she'd had. All that freedom and fresh air!'

'There's no better place than the heart of a glen,' said Roy, his mind resting on a memory of a young woman dancing in a bar. *Annie.* Annie was lost to him now and here he was with another woman whose love would pass him by. 'That's what I miss when I'm living here,' he continued, treading over the thoughts, as they approached the bar. 'The mountains and hills are too far away. Anyway, talking of Glenarm, did I ever tell you about my abduction?'

'No!'

'Well, you see. My mother was a Catholic from the Glens and my father was a Protestant from here in Leiden. She turned, as they say in Glenarm. My granny was still alive at the time when I was born and she was quite a strict Catholic.'

'Oh, I think I know what's coming.' Jean smiled.

'Granny was not happy at all about the Protestant situation, and the story goes that three days after I was born, she took me from my cradle and went to the priest in the Catholic church. Four weeks later, I was baptised again, this time in the Protestant Church of Ireland round the corner.'

Jean laughed as they entered the Van der Werff, 'God, when you think of the wee country we live in from this distance, it really is a strange place!'

'Full of great yarns, though,' smiled Roy.

'If there wasn't so much tragedy, it would be the funniest place on earth,' said Jean.

***

The damp gaze of Rachael's distant eyes didn't bode well for the holiday. School had finished for the year, she'd finally dropped French, and now she was going on her first trip to Croatia. What on earth did the girl have to be unhappy about? Catriona daren't have asked. The airport was too packed for her to withstand a swipe from her daughter.

Catriona smiled instead in the direction of a little boy who had just reached an obstacle in the journey his Woody doll had taken. Woody had gleefully hopped along his mother's legs, over the table and then onto another set of legs. He hesitated and looked into her eyes. Catriona smiled, pointing to her knees, 'Hello Woody, would you like to pass over these bony ridges?' The boy continued over the obstruction until he reached Rachael. Catriona watched as her daughter's eyes came to life. Rachael was smiling as she watched the boy play. He handed her his Buzz and she swooped it down and crashed it into Woody.

Catriona was grateful for the small boy and his toys, the mood in the airport typically setting the scene for how the holiday might unfold. She often worried that she had raised a spoiled daughter, but as she watched Rachael play with the little boy, she knew that she had accomplished something. When the boy was out of sight, Catriona spoke, 'You're good with children, you know. That's a special talent.' Rachael blushed and Catriona reproached herself for not spending more time praising her daughter. It was an inbuilt reticence resulting from her upbringing: affection was the reserve of grandparents in the countryside where she had been raised. It didn't come naturally to Catriona, or indeed her own mother. The holiday was still on a precipice, but she dared to push a little deeper, 'I think you'd make an amazing teacher some day.'

'Teacher?' Rachael repeated.

'Yes.'

'But you told me to aim higher, that I could be a chemical engineer or something with more money.'

'I was wrong,' said Catriona. 'Teaching is a fulfilling job, and you need your heart lined more than your pockets.'

Rachael choked, 'Mum, have you been drinking?'

'No! What made you say that?' Catriona smiled.

'You don't often talk about hearts and fulfilment.'

'I don't often have time to talk.'

This was Catriona's opportunity to switch off. She had her blackberry packed in case of emergencies, but despite its five stars, the hotel in Cavtat didn't have internet connection in the rooms. The idea of a real holiday in a completely new place gave her a welcome feeling of letting go. She was determined to let go: twenty-five years of anxiety had taken its toll and she needed to forgive herself. That's what Terence had said, 'It's time to forgive yourself, Catriona.'

Catriona recalled the hatred Rachael had demonstrated over the affair, and she wanted to win her daughter back again. There had been no affair. She and Terence had accepted the stigma in order to avoid any media speculation about the truth. Two weeks ago, they had agreed by email that it was time to tell people. Rachael's dad, Frank, had always known. She would tell Rachael in Croatia.

Rachael interrupted her thoughts, 'Mum, I've...It's Hannah.'

Catriona shook herself free of the dusty web she had entered and caught up with her daughter again. 'What about Hannah?'

'She's not speaking to me.'

'Why on earth not?' Catriona was seventeen again and living life through the mind of her daughter. What could be worse at that age of seventeen than losing your best friend? They'd never fallen out in all the years Catriona had known Hannah.

Rachael smiled again as Buzz Lightyear flew over her head. 'She thinks I told a secret about her.'

'What secret?' asked Catriona.

'I can't tell you. It's not my secret to tell, and she thinks you won't let her in the house if you know. I didn't tell anyone at all. I haven't breathed a word.'

'What makes her think you did it?' asked Catriona.

'The whole year knows and I'm the only person she told. She'd been lying about something for years.'

Catriona knew instinctively, 'Was it about her dad?'

Rachael's eyes flashed against her mother's, 'Did you know?'

'Yes, I did, and I also know that he's coming home near the end of July. We'll be back by then. That's why I...'

'What?'

'That's why I wanted to go in July this year. I wanted to be there when she...'

'Why didn't you tell me anything?'

'It wasn't my secret to tell.' Catriona smiled at her daughter and looked deep into her eyes. 'I can understand why Hannah lied. People can be judgemental. I know you never believed me when I told you that Terence was a friend, but I promise you he was. Anyway, we can talk about that later over a cocktail by the pool. When did this all happen with Hannah?'

'It was after the exams. She was in an English class and a boy made fun of her.'

'Was it Conor Simple?'

'Yes. How did you know? asked Rachael with confusion in her green eyes.

'His dad's a prison officer at Maghaberry prison. He would know about Hannah's dad.'

'He said his dad was a civil servant.'

'Yes, that's code in Northern Ireland for police or prison officer.'

'Why?'

'To protect them from attack,' Catriona explained.

'Did prison officers get attacked?'

'Yes, they did and they still get threatened even now in peaceful times. Hundreds of people in the security forces died during the Troubles.'

'But why?'

Catriona was impressed and appalled by her daughter's naivety in equal measures. Catriona and Frank had purposely afforded Rachael a sheltered life. They'd sent her to a private preparatory school and avoided talking about politics when she was around. Catriona often wondered if she'd made a mistake, especially given Rachael's friendship with Hannah, a self-sufficient girl who paid for her own holidays, pursued her own academic path and built her own walls of self-preservation. Catriona gathered her thoughts and responded, 'They were British and seen as the enemy by Republicans and the IRA.'

Catriona spoke, 'Rachael, we should all be grateful for the times we live in. Hannah was in the Shankill bomb. Did you know that?'

'She told me. I can't even imagine what that was like. She never mentioned it once, not until recently when she told me about her dad.'

'I'm not surprised. People don't want to be locked up in the past. Hannah doesn't want it to be a symbol for her or where she is from. It's great that Jean is taking on the French exchange student. I would never have thought...'

Rachael laughed, 'Me neither, can you imagine? It's a shame I won't get to be part of it.'

'Sorry.'

'Don't worry. We need a holiday...anyway, she isn't speaking to me.'

'I hope the girl is nice,' said Catriona.

'What girl?'

'The French one.'

'It's a boy!' exclaimed Rachael. 'His name's Etienne.'

'*Etienne.*' Catriona repeated the word and placed her hand on her chest, her face still with her daughter; her mind frozen. The background noise became a commotion of disjointed words. Only the voice of the young boy was clear. Catriona's eyes moved around the waiting lounge, a sea of hospital green and blue with stained ceiling tiles and cobwebs idly dangling like rumours.

Her eyes were thudding; her heartbeat racing. Rachael's head was moving now. The disquiet shrieked to a halt. Blurred images came back into focus.

An announcement. *Dubrovnik*. Rachael's hand on her leg. 'Mum, Mum, let's go. It's our flight.' Catriona shook her head and stood up, following her daughter. For the first time, her daughter showed her the way, and it all came back to Catriona again.

MAY WEE

The sun dipped in and out of the bunting that was strung from each lamppost on Snugville Street. Jean stood in the middle of the road with her head tipped to one side as triangle shadows swayed in the breeze. Her windows were adorned with small, square French tricolors that she'd made with paper and lollipop sticks, and the window boxes were crammed with red and white pansies that were bursting with plump leaves in the early July sunshine.

Jean smoothed down her blue and white striped top and placed her red beret on her head. She was adjusting the onion wreath that was suspended from the doorframe when Edith Piaf emerged like a crescent of voice and soul from Mrs McAdam's house. Jean turned to her right and saw a small ankle emerge in a blue patent shoe from the doorframe. She smiled when Mrs McAdam's voice joined the record that was crackling from an old record player in her living room. '*Non, Rien de rien, Non, Je ne regrette rien.*' The elongated body of Mrs McAdam then followed in a patterned red dress with a pulled in waist and three quarter length sleeves, her white hair shining in an elaborate do of curls and waves, and a cigarette poised between her fingers.

'Bonjour,' Jean called over, 'And don't you look like something from a Paris catwalk! Come here and do a twirl and give me a closer look at them ankles of yours!'

Mrs McAdam laughed, a joyous spectacle of gleaming false teeth, and made a royal wave in the direction of her neighbours across the road.

Mrs Rainey was first to take a closer look, 'Oh my good Lord in the heaven's above, if it isn't Dame Vera Lynn!' she called, as she crossed the road.

'Edith Piaf, if you don't mind,' Jean responded, her voice lost in the rhapsodic crescendo in the background.

As the final note sounded out, the women joined together in a chorus of 'Toi' and laughter and took up residence in striped deck chairs under the sun.

Jean had lost a stone in adrenaline and sweat in the weeks preceding Etienne's arrival. The living room and kitchen were now decorated in a compromise of white and pale blue; white to meet with Hannah's insistence that minimalism was the fashion; and blue to make Jean feel that she still had some control over decisions in the house that she'd paid for with her own earnings. Inspired by their Breton visitor, Hannah and Shelley had gone to the beach to collect stones for their candle jars and driftwood for the walls, items that Jean collectively referred to as 'dust gatherers'.

Jean concentrated on soft furnishings, her machine pounding away past midnight every night for three weeks. Hannah demanded a white chair, and Jean assured her that if anyone ever sat on it, they would bleed from the welt of the driftwood on their legs. Its position against the window guaranteed that it was unlikely to be occupied: ever since Harry had been arrested, fear of a revenge attack meant that no one ever sat down near the window. A vase on the window sill, the size of a small human, was a further line of protection. Hannah also demanded wooden floors and left Jean to fight with a sander and varnish. She finished the job that morning in the early hours.

'Daddy will think he's at the seaside when he comes home,' Shelley had smiled. Shelley was the only one smiling.

A small crowd had gathered at the house. One woman had 'May Wee' painted across her T-shirt and children waved flags and sang 'Frère Jacques'. By the time the car rounded the corner from the Shankill Road, their arsenals of French cultural knowledge were almost extinguished.

Shelley and Hannah emerged from the car first. A head was apparent like a shadow in the front passenger seat, skin not quite discernible in the shade. Shelley opened the car door as the women and children of Snugville Street cheered and whistled. Jean stood back and looked upwards.

Etienne, the seventeen year-old boy, loomed black against a blue Shankill sky, rendering the crowd silent.

It was neither Etienne's impressive height nor his dark attire that caused Jean to hold her breath: hair grew from his chin as black as a stallion and as thick as turf, and hair flowed from his head in a long mane of undulating black.

The overall effect was of something uniquely untamed, and sublimely poetic.

Jean walked towards Etienne, looked up, shook his hand, swallowed the expletive that was now stinging her tongue and clumsily uttered, 'F...Son.

You're not who I was expecting.'

Hannah glared and narrowed her eyes towards Jean and the string of onions. Shelley smiled at Jean. The welcome committee's silence eventually gave way to raucous laughter as handshakes were delivered to an equally bemused Etienne.

'Welcome to the Shankill,' Jean added.

He reached down and kissed her once on each cheek. As she was about to turn towards her audience and wink, his mouth continued towards her cheeks. In the confusing foray of kisses, she bumped her nose off his in a painful collision, assuming that the final kiss had been pledged.

Hannah explained, 'Four times in Brittany, mum.'

Jean, now flustered, confused and slightly inebriated by the adrenaline, reached up to Etienne and started kissing him all over again.

'Fook me,' he said to Hannah, 'your sister is very romantique, non?'

The laughter flowed like loose bunting in a Belfast breeze as Etienne sat down on a deck chair and revelled in the spotlight of Snugville Street.

'What would you like to drink, love?' Jean asked as the welcoming committee began to disperse. Etienne, who revealed some intricate celtic artwork around his sleeve as he stretched, answered with confidence in a clear English accent, 'A beer please. Thank you, Miss.'

Jean looked at Hannah, who shrugged her shoulders and then to Shelley who immediately offered to go the the off-licence, 'I'll take Mrs McAdam. She likes it when they ask her for ID.'

Etienne looked around the street with an air of great satisfaction, as though his accommodation met the number of stars offered in the holiday brochure with precision. 'I like,' he said, gazing towards the concrete Benefits office, the most utilised building in a two mile radius. His lips remained in a straight line, 'It is the place of, how to you say...le peuple?'

'The people' retorted Hannah, who seemed equally mesmerised by his deep analysis of the street.

'Miss, I have a gift for you,' he said to Jean.

Jean smiled and curtsied, her nerves now throwing up unexpected reflex responses.

He opened his rucksack and pulled out some black and white cloth. 'This flag is of La Bretagne.'

Jean unfolded the black and white striped flag and glanced back to her paper French flags with confusion and embarrassment.

'It's okay. The French flag is good. You make good flags.'

He smiled, and for the first time Jean could see a seventeen year-old boy through the mat of hair surrounding his lips. His hands searched in the bag again and this time he offered Jean a bottle of red wine. Jean's eyes widened and met his as he said, 'Ah, you like? I have many more.' He produced five more bottles and several bags of Breton sweet treats.

'These are from my parents. I wanted to bring more, but too heavy, sorry.'

Jean peered into the half empty rucksack. 'Son, what are you planning to wear for the next three weeks? It's just that my clothes aren't going to fit you.'

Etienne smiled and shrugged his shoulders, 'The soul is clothed in the fruit of the vine and music.'

Jean caught Hannah's eyes and pressed her lips together, trying hard to contain the noise that was lodged in her throat.

Etienne stood up and walked towards the boot of the car. He lifted out a case and returned to his seat in silence. Shelley and Mrs McAdam were making their way by when a loud sound like a breathless animal emerged from under Etienne's arm. Etienne was pumping what looked like a tethered bird with four erect legs: one falling from the belly, industrious with Etienne's entrancing fingers; two set in rigor mortis over his shoulder, filling the Shankill with sound; the third connecting to his mouth like a pipe. The overall effect was painfully loud, yet quietly nostalgic. The bird was repeatedly crying out for freedom as Etienne's arms pumped feverishly against its flight. Jean was so highly strung by now that her head shook in tune to the entrapment of green velvet. Etienne's right foot was tapping and his neck filling up with air, but Jean could not remove her eyes from his swift fingers. When he arrested his hands, the instrument continued to exhale its strangulated, but compellingly mesmerising symphony.

'What the fuck is that?'

The voice came from across the road where a teenage boy in a tracksuit stood with his hands over his ears.

Etienne replied, 'It's a cornemeuse.'

'Wha?' the boy replied with contempt.

Jean's body swelled up and she responded, 'It's a bloody bagpipe son. What did you think it was? A dead bird?' The boy scarpered and Jean congratulated herself on another triumph of French.

Etienne's voice, now dry and throaty, came again, 'You like my bloody bagpipe?'

Jean smiled, aware that every word uttered was addressed to her and not to Hannah, as though she were the only person present. 'Oh aye, son. The dead in the Shankill graveyard will need a wee nap after that, but you did a lovely job. Come on. Time to go inside before Mrs Rainey reaches for her gas mask.'

***

Etienne looked out of proportion and in conflict with the dressing of the living room in Snugville Street. Hannah, cognizant that her mother's nerves were in a precarious state, had to compel Jean to sit down with a cup of tea.

'Why did you choose Belfast?' Hannah asked.

It would be the first time that he had spoken to her since they were in the car, and even on that journey he had his head turned towards Shelley most of the time.

Etienne looked around, 'Moi?' he inquired.

Hannah sighed inwardly and contemplated that she was one hour into a six week trial. She turned to Jean for help and it came like a duster in the eye.

'Yes, toi! Can you see any other tall, bearded Frenchmen in the room? I'll teach you a new word, son. It's eejit. Can you say it now?' Jean rhymed 'Eejit' along with Etienne.

'And what does it mean, this word?'

'It means idiot!'

'Ah!'

'So, why did you to come to Belfast?' Jean repeated.

'I like to learn about Lira.'

'Who's Lira?' asked Jean.

'Mum, he means the IRA,' Hannah explained. She contained her laughter and averted Jean's eyes. When she finally turned back, she saw that her mother had swallowed her own chin. Confounded into a rare silence once again, Jean was clearly trying to come up with some kind of coherent response in her best English. Hannah waited, knowing that her mother's words would slice through his error like a guillotine.

'You've come to the wrong place, son,' said Jean.

Etienne's brown eyes were maelstroms of wonder.

'Come here,' directed Jean, leading him to the front door. 'Do you see those little red, white and blue triangular flags?'

Etienne was nodding.

'They weren't put up to celebrate the storming of the Bastille, or the Easter Rising, for that matter!'

Etienne smiled, 'You make very good jokes. What are these flags?'

Jean spread her arms wide, 'The United Kingdom, son. This is British Belfast. The Irish Belfast is less than a mile that way and that way.' She pointed to the right and then to the left. 'You'll not meet any Lira folk here!' Her neck was purple; her arms taut.

'Lira fook?'

'No, Lira folk. Say it with me. "Folk". It's another way of saying peuple'

Hannah was startled at her mother's recall of the word peuple. Jean turned back to Etienne who was about to speak.

'You say this is British. I understand. This is the street of the colonists.'

Hannah repressed a smile and watched Jean's hands move up to her hips.

'The what?' said Jean sternly.

'The British have oppressed the Irish for many centuries. I have read it.'

'That's one theory, son. That's one theory,' said Jean with consternation set in the folds of her brow.

'Yes,' Etienne continued, 'Like the French oppressed les Bretons.'

'That's a shame. I never did like the French. Shelley, take them wee flags down, love, and put the Breton one up.'

Hannah watched as a smile emerged from Etienne's face. Jean was now on fire. 'Etienne, you need an education. Come on out and I'll show you. Over there. City Centre. Catholics and Protestants boogie together, get drunk and have fun.' Jean shook her bottom and poured an imaginary pint down her neck. Etienne laughed and nodded, while Hannah stood at the door and rolled her eyes. 'To the left and to the right, Catholics boogie with Catholics. Here, in the Shankill, Protestants boogie with Protestants. Got it?'

'Mais oui.'

'May wee, indeed. Now, most Catholics want everyone to boogie together in Ireland. One big united Ireland with a huge dance floor the size of thirty-two counties.' Jean drew a picture of Ireland with her hand.

'Yes, yes.'

'Most Protestants want everyone to boogie together in the United Kingdom with Scotland, England and Wales. They want a dance floor that goes all the way across the Irish sea. They only want to dance in Dublin on holiday.' Jean moved her arms like a symphony orchestra conductor, painting an impossible picture of the United Kingdom.

'D'accord.' Etienne was nodding his head energetically.

'Does that make sense, love?'

'Yes.'

'Now, Lira. In the past, they used their guns and bombs.' Jean's arms extended into artillery as she wiped out the Benefits office with her imaginary weapon.

Etienne laughed.

'It's not funny, son.'

Etienne was motionless.

'Lira is not popular here in the Shankill. They killed civilians here. There are other paramilitary groups. Can you say that? Para-mil-it-ary?'

'Bien sûr, paramilitaire.'

'Not bad. You'll find them near here with their big cars. UVF. UFF. UDA. You'll see their pictures on the walls.'

'So, you like these paramilitaires?'

38

'No, I do not indeed, son. I don't like a single one of them. I don't like Van Gogh either, but I can describe one of his landscapes.'

Etienne's mouth was still open as they returned to their seats.

Hannah attempted to engage her exchange student once more, offering to take him on a bus tour of Belfast. He agreed with a simple, 'Yes,' but Hannah understood instinctively what Etienne was looking for. A new breed of tourist had emerged in Belfast and it was avaricious for a taste of the war. They came like bloodhounds in search of symbols of tension: political murals, rubble filled barren landscape, rundown buildings and images of a depressed people.

Hannah had witnessed visitors with long lens cameras jump out of black taxis on the Shankill Road, quickly snap the murals and then photograph everything from the trainers on the feet of the unemployed, to the vicious looking dogs on the ends of strings. They would stop at the worn out shops and snap their dilapidated fronts, as though their crumbling exteriors were leftovers from a riot. Hannah knew what a cleared bombsite looked like and the tourists would find nothing there but space. Hannah also knew that many of those same shops had thrived during the Troubles and were now under attack from a new, and more shiny enemy, lurking on the outskirts of the city in the form of family friendly shopping centres with car parks the size of small towns.

The Shankill Road looked like it was dying, and even though the population had dramatically shrunk since the days of the textile mills, it was still alive and re-emerging in a new way. Rarely had Hannah ever seen a tourist walk along a side street of the Shankill. There they would find the pride of a people who spent their days washing and caring for their new redeveloped homes. They would see the women who competed with each other for the most illustrious window display and garden ornamentation, and they would learn stories about an old community that preceded the Troubles, that preceded Belfast even.

Etienne looked into Hannah's eyes for the first time. 'I would like to see something. He rooted around in his bag again and pulled out a brochure, 'Tiens, I would like to see this.'

Hannah caught the familiar images of political wall art on the Falls Road, a neighbouring nationalist area where Hannah had yet to see anyone boogying, and nodded. The Falls was undeniably the stronghold of the IRA during their active years. 'Okay,' she agreed, her voice betraying the despondency that lagged in her drooped shoulders. The murals were spectacular in their art, but controversial in their message. Vitriolic brush strokes painted out harsh messages against Israel, Britain, America and President Bush. Support of a United Ireland, the IRA martyrs, Cuba, revolutionaries, Palestine and Iraq, meanwhile, were explicitly and implicitly portrayed.

Hannah, who resented the circus of wall art and political symbolism, was disillusioned by the predictability of Etienne. She had hoped, after seeing his long hair and strange bagpipes, that there might be a glimmer of originality to him. She thought about Jean's peace visits to Botanic Gardens each year and smiled inwardly, understanding for the first time the ritual of this politically ambivalent woman. Hannah wondered, as her mother had done many times, why there were no celebrations on the street to mark the cessation of violence; why there were no bronze statues of peacemakers; and why there were no festivals to join all the various communities together in shared songs and dances.

She placed her head in her hands and counted the long weeks ahead with Jean's new best friend. A firm feeling that Etienne did not like her scraped against her like a blunt razor. The feeling was not as depressing as its consequences: she wasn't so fond of Etienne either.

A stronger suspicion that the French exchange was a huge mistake, meanwhile, knocked her over like the melancholy echo of la cornemeuse. Images of what lay in front of her awoke a latent fear that she had suppressed. In two and a half weeks time, her dad would be returning from working in his horticulture job. No lies had been told: her father had grown green fingers in preparation for his release. The dynamic of her dad in the same room as Etienne, his bagpipes and his politics was too much to take in. Hannah looked around the room with its two armchairs and small sofa and tried to envisage them all there like an explosive version of the nuclear family. It was inconceivable.

Hannah knew enough about France to suspect Jean's six o'clock routine might be a couple of hours too early for Etienne to eat. He went to his room to unpack his half empty rucksack, during which time Hannah realised that she had no room to go to. She needed somewhere to breathe.

'Mum, I'm going to lie down in your bed. Can you shout on me when dinner is ready?'

Jean placed her hand on her left hip and pushed it out to one side.

'You look like you're about to sing I'm a little tea pot!' Hannah smiled.

'Very smart Missy. There wouldn't be a chance of you helping me peel the spuds, would there?'

Hannah felt a wisp of guilt for long enough to give her mum a beseeching face, but swiftly turned on her heel and made her escape upstairs when she saw Shelley walk towards the kitchen. She needed time to herself.

Etienne seemed unsure where to look during dinner on account of all three women in the room staring at his ears. He had gone upstairs, unpacked, and had, somewhat unexpectedly, tied his hair back in a ponytail. It was clear to Hannah that none of them really understood what they were looking at. The right ear was much easier to discern. It had a long green feathered earring that skimmed his shoulder. His shoulders were narrower now with his jacket removed and hair tied back. The left ear was a mystery. Jean had her head cocked to one side as she analysed its proportions. Hannah felt Shelley kick her leg under the table to alert her to do something with Jean.

'Mum, what do you think of the wine?' asked Hannah.

'Oh the wine's gorgeous.' Jean sipped and stared again. 'Tell your mum and dad thank you for that, won't you?'

Etienne casually raised his glass and said, 'Thank you. It's good wine. I like it also.'

Hannah knew how many seconds would pass before the subject of the left ear would be raised. She sipped some wine and tried to acclimatise to its initial vaporous smack on the palette. She moved it around her mouth and counted to five.

'Son, tell me this, if you don't mind?'

It was the voice of Snugville Street, thought Hannah.

'Yes?'

'What's that in your ear?'

Hannah exhaled with relief. Her mother was gentle for once, and her words did not inflict any obvious damage.

'This?' Eitienne held out the feather.

'No son, anyone can see that's a feather. What's going on there on the left?'

'Ah, this? It is how do you say, airing?'

'Yes, earring, but it's the hole in the middle, love. It's a wee bit bigger than the average piercing.'

'Ah, yes, I have had my ear stretched. You like it, Jean?'

'I like it,' lied Hannah too swiftly. Her lie didn't receive a blink. Etienne was fixed on Jean's expression.

Hannah watched as her mother contained something and waited again for the inevitable overspill. A fine stream of laughter started to seep out from between Jean's lips. Etienne didn't react at first. Seconds passed, dimples gathered in his cheeks and his shoulders started to move. Jean and Etienne locked eyes until Jean finally lost her will. Unbridled laughter raced from her mouth. Shelley, who was also clearly simmering, freed herself from the emotions she had been containing. Hannah was the last to join them. They laughed until tears streamed down their faces. Etienne, who eventually slowed his down to a trot, immediately set off again when his eyes met Jean's. It was contagious.

As the last shrieks of laughter left them again, Etienne recovered himself enough to speak, 'Ah Jean, you fooking don't like my ear.' He touched his heart and lost all his h sounds as his voice struggled to piece itself back together. 'You 'urt me 'ere.'

Jean stood up and walked to his side of the table. She placed her arm around his shoulder, 'Sorry son. I didn't mean to 'urt your feelings, but that's some size of a 'ole you 'ave there!'

Hannah scanned the small kitchen, from Shelley to Jean and back to Etienne and remembered something: a table set for six people, three small plates and three large plates. She could see her brother's smile as he looked at an American guest with awe. Hannah was a young girl and she was laughing at her dad.

Her eyes, already blind with tears of laughter started to fill again with something more saliferous. She blinked it back and took a longer sip of wine. She held it in her mouth and savoured it. She had searched for so long for a piece of her father, and he had been in the kitchen all along, his memory suppressed as years of uncurbed laughter perished behind their own bars.

Hannah was grateful to Etienne. What had been missing at dinner for many years, was this. Hannah's father had never been there in any other sense in her life except as an effervescent and happy presence in the kitchen. She could see all of him there, all that she had ever known. He had been a force of strength and playfulness, everything a child had ever wanted from a father.

***

Shelley was dreaming of bagpipes and a boy with long hair. He was looking at her with his deep brown eyes as he played, and she knew that it was all for her. He dropped the bagpipes by his side and pulled Shelley towards him. And then the dream disappeared and she became aware that morning had already dawned on Snugville Street. Shelley hid from the light and pulled the duvet over her eyes. She needed to return to the dream to see what happened next, but the brightness was in her face and the dream was now dark. The duvet was pulled back in a swift movement and a draught cut across Shelley's bare legs. Her sister was standing over her, fully dressed in a pair of brown bootcut trousers and a white vest top.

'Get up lazy bones!'

Hannah's voice was harsh against the weightless ease of morning.

'Get lost!' Shelley moaned and escaped back under the covers.

'I need your help!' Hannah demanded.

'What for?'

'I need you to guard me in the bathroom.'

Shelley smiled. They had been so busy redecorating for Etienne's arrival, that they had overlooked some key DIY tasks that had not been addressed in many years. They'd made a list of all the things they had to do, but the business of fixing the bathroom door had been relinquished in favour of purchasing fancy soap dispensers and matching towels. And so, their open door bathroom policy remained in place. Prior to Etienne's arrival, it was not unusual for Shelley to rush to use the bathroom while Jean was soaking under perfumed mist in the bath. It was the only way that three women could function with one set of facilities. In particularly challenging situations, and if they all had to get ready to go out at the same time, there were often three levels of concurrent activity going on in the four metre squared space. During Etienne's visit, the agreement was that Hannah and Shelley would use a basin in the kitchen for washing and a guard system would be put in place for use of the toilet.

'And Shelley.' Hannah's voice was softer, more pleading.

'What?'

'I need you to go into the bedroom to get my work badge out of the top drawer. I forgot to get it last night.'

'No way!'

'Yes way!'

'No! I'm not going in there,' Shelley protested.

'Well, obviously I can't go in. He doesn't seem to like me anyway. It would be better if he woke up to your pretty face.'

'Nice try. No. You'll have to get Jean.'

Shelley followed her sister upstairs. Hannah stopped at the top and looked towards their bedroom. She turned swiftly, her hand clasping her mouth, before running downstairs and straight out the front door. Shelley, perplexed by her sister's strange behaviour, continued to the the top of the stairs where she took in a very foreign sight.

There, in her freshly painted bedroom, with its white walls and white duvet covers, lay a naked French boy.

She swallowed and narrowed her eyes at a set of long, muscular legs, completely matted in black wiry hair. Somewhat blinded by France in all its liberty, her eyes then travelled up his torso, over his thick black neck, and onto a face bathed in light with deep red lips set like ridges on the contours of dark skin. She breathed in deeply and stared until a rattle at Jean's door startled her. Shelley scurried down the stairs and straight out onto the street, where Hannah was standing in a haze of light rain, her hand still restraining words from her mouth.

Shelley, who was outside in a short nightdress with no shoes, looked Hannah in the eye. As the drizzle turned to rain, and the sun jostled against the clouds for attention, tears of laughter started to run freely down Hannah's face. Jean arrived in her gingham blue nightie and fluffy slippers. Her eyes were wide. Her face beamed deep scarlet.

Mrs McAdam, who spent much of her life monitoring the activities on the street, waved them all in to her living room. Shelley dried her face with her hand and watched as Jean crossed herself three times, a habit she had picked up from a an old Catholic friend, and one that she frequently used in times of severe stress. 'Holy God in the Heaven's above! I think I need a seat!'

Mrs McAdam assumed a look of bewilderment. 'What's the matter, love? Is it the wee French man?'

Shelley watched Jean's face turn from red to white as her body gyrated on the seat. She stood up again. 'Wee French man! Wee! Mrs McAdam, there's no wee about it. There's a bloody Eiffel tower in my back bedroom!'

Shelley felt heat rise up her cheeks and she blushed and shook and tried to hide her face from the other women.

Hannah, ever practical in the face of hysteria, stated the facts. 'It would seem that our French friend likes to sleep naked with the blinds wide open, the door open and faint wind blowing over his parts.'

Mrs McAdam took a slight turn in her eye as the facts began to register. 'Oh holy god,' she said. 'And thon's a big fella too.'

Jean's motor sputtered and choked in laughter and the voice it emitted was barely decipherable. 'What in God's name are we going to do? I can't have Shelley and Hannah waking up to that every morning.'

'Excuse me! La tour Eiffel might not have such a positive effect on your nerves!'

It was Hannah again.

Shelley smiled and pretended to be part of something when her mind was focused on the red lips of a wild, bearded French boy.

'What are we going to do? Hannah, love, you'll have to talk to him!' Jean said, calmer now, but still with a tremor of something.

'I beg your pardon, I won't be taking any part in this. He doesn't like me anyway. Shelley, you do it,' Hannah replied.

Shelley awoke from her daze and felt her cheeks burn intensely. 'No way!' was all she could muster.

Mrs McAdam rubbed her hands together. 'Here,' she said, 'while you're all thinking about it, can I go in for a wee peek?'

'No!' came all three voices at once. Jean added, 'Flip me, this is probably illegal. I mean he's only seventeen and I'm in my forties and I've seen things I shouldn't have seen.'

'You could tell him that we get quite a few raids around here from the police and that he should keep his door closed.' Hannah's eyes widened with a demeanour of self-satisfaction at her own resourcefulness.

Shelley spoke up. 'But will that not scare him?'

There was a rap at the door. Shelley panicked. 'It must be him. We'll tell him Mrs McAdam is making us fresh soda for breakfast.'

Shelley opened the door. 'Good morning, Mrs Rainey,' she said. 'What are you doing up so early?'

Mrs Rainey's white hair was unusually disordered, and she too was still in her dressing gown, a similarly powerful dressing gown to that of Mrs

McAdam, only in royal blue.

She pushed past Shelley and stepped inside. 'Girls, I need your help. It's our Nena.'

Shelley watched as Jean returned to reality and acquired a look of concern, 'Is she alright, love?'

'No, she's in trouble with the police. There's a whole load of stuff in her house. We need to get it shifted.'

'What kind of stuff?' Jean's face became more serious and Shelley marvelled at how her mother could move through emotions like one continuous stitch on several textures of fabric.

While a commotion about stolen cigarettes was unfolding around her, Shelley lamented that her dream of kissing Etienne was now tainted and destroyed by the realisation that he was a man, and that she was barely sixteen, and completely unprepared for the hormones that were now racing around her body. She sat down on the sofa and tried hard to listen to a debate about whether Mrs McAdam should hide the cigarettes. Shelley was still embarrassed by the dream about Etienne, which now took on a whole new shape in her mind. She had never seen a naked man before, at least not a real one. She had dedicated many hours at the age of eleven to looking at the male underwear models in the Kay's catalogue, so she understood the general lay of the land. She did not, however, expect to feel an emotion so foreign in a mind that had yet to see the possibilities of those regions.

Etienne was in the living room when they all returned to the house, Jean having declined the offer to harbour stolen cigarettes on behalf of a disappointed Mrs McAdam. In Shelley's eyes, the boy with the long hair and hole in his ear was like a picture of pure sanity in the midst of the madness of Snugville Street.

'Good morning Shelley,' he said. 'I tidy your bed. I hope it is okay.'

Shelley thought that she might faint as she eyed the stowed away sofa bed with its folded sheets and recalled the dreams that she had had on that spot. Etienne was inspecting her closely, and she could not shake the impression that he was staring approvingly at her legs. The thought dispelled when she realised that he was probably looking at her prosthetic foot.

Jean entered the room and greeted Etienne with a wide smile. 'Bonjour!' she called out as she passed him. 'Scrambled egg and saus...' Swallowing the word, she looked back to Shelley and blinked. 'Scrambled egg and bacon this morning okay with you, Etienne?' She couldn't disguise the last notes of a giggle.

'Of course,' came Etienne's voice as he followed her into the kitchen, oblivious to what had just occurred and unaware that he would be denied sausage for his breakfast because he chose to sleep naked with the door ajar.

***

11th July 2003

Dear Roy

I never imagined a French exchange student could create such a frenzy. The entire community has fallen in love with him. He has appeared on the front page of the local newspaper with a headline, 'French student says "May Wee" to the Shankill.' Underneath, he is standing tall with his arms folded beside a black and white mural of a street scene from the Troubles. He said it was his favourite of the murals in the Shankill and I think he liked it before I told him that it was special to me. There are two little boys in the picture, one with a band stick and one with a drum. Behind the boys is a black and white scene of devastation after street riots in 1969. Etienne said that it demonstrates the poetry of the people of the Shankill. It's not often anyone talks about us in poetic terms. I can't help but like him. Mrs McAdam would say he's a boy who's been here before.

On Saturday night, he went to the Royal bar at the end of the street. He likes being on his own and had been asking if he could go out to a bar alone since he got here. I warned the barman that afternoon to look out for him. He did. Every man present bought Etienne a drink, and they ended up carrying him home at one in the morning and pouring him into bed. I really do hope his parents don't mind him drinking, as he won't be eighteen for another eight months.

Since the last time I emailed you, Etienne has become familiar with the dynamics of Belfast. I spent the day with him yesterday when Hannah was working and we walked the length and breadth of West Belfast. The strange thing is that I have started to see Belfast from a tourist's eyes. The first thing I noticed was the beauty of the place. The Black Mountain can be seen from nearly every street off the Shankill and yesterday it was filled with colour.

We passed the Edenderry and Brookfield Mills where tens of thousands of women in the Shankill worked. Fond and fear-filled memories of the loud droning sound came back to me. I worked at Edenderry from the age of fifteen until I got married. Etienne seemed to enjoy my stories. I'm relieved his English is so good, but I have taught him some bad habits. He says 'Fook me' frequently.

When we were at the top of the Ardoyne Road, I tried to explain our complex history: how millworkers in mixed streets, all living in equally rundown houses, had to move when it became unsafe to stay in their own homes in the early 1970s. Catholic families on one side of the Crumlin Road would swap houses with Protestant families on the other side. He called it ethnic cleansing. I was there when it was all happening. I saw families drag sofas and suitcases across the Crumlin Road and helped them carry their possessions. You don't really think of it as ethnic cleansing when you're carrying the sofas.

In a week's time, Harry will be home. Etienne has been a welcome distraction from everything, but I have been delaying what is inevitable. I don't know how long we can email each other. I said goodbye to you in Holland and we found ourselves writing to each other again. Things are more difficult than they promise to be when you put them into practice. I will miss you.

Love,

Jean.

CHILDREN'S LOVE

Although she couldn't see them, Hannah was aware of the resonant presence of marching bands. She walked back from the flower shop under a clear sky with a tray of fresh corsages. Mrs McAdam, who liked her orange lily to be freshly purchased on the morning of the Twelfth, opened the door in a pageant of powder and perfume. She was eighty-one years of age, but she'd always added a year to the number of Twelfth parades she'd attended. This would be her eighty second. Her mother had taken her to hear the bands when she was nine months pregnant. On the Twelfth of July in 1922, Mrs McAdam had kicked to the music in the womb until finally her mother's waters had broken. She was born the next day.

Mrs Rainey and Mrs Lloyd were gathered at Mrs McAdam's house. They were dressed to the nines with their orange sashes beaming like sunshine around their dainty necks. Hannah admired their hair and enjoyed watching them swim in her praise as she told them, 'You all look gorgeous, ladies.' Hannah had seen them prepare their hair every Thursday night since she was a child. She would sometimes help them apply their setting lotion with its rare scent of solvent and flowers and then carefully hook the slim rollers into place. Hannah had been there to help again on the Eleventh night, serving tea from Mrs McAdam's Royal Doulton tea set after the rollers were all fixed in place. In the Belfast of the past, it was the working family's prerogative to look as groomed as their middle class counterparts on the Twelfth of July.

Hannah had volunteered to drive the three ladies to the meeting point. She had found herself volunteering to do many things since Etienne's arrival. The number of people in the house was exceeding the number of possibilities for privacy. It was easier to leave.

It had been a few years since Hannah had partaken in a Twelfth parade.

She had stopped after seeing the shock on faces at Methody when the matter of the Orange Order parades was raised. 'An organisation that upholds the Protestant Ascendency is, by definition, bigoted', one boy had said. The idea that anyone might assume that the three ladies beside her now were bigots, left Hannah with a feeling of shame for her decision to ignore the tradition, just as being from such a loyalist part of Belfast often consumed her with the same force. Shame was her inheritance and she didn't know how to fight it.

As Hannah waited in Mrs McAdam's living room, she could hear the music of her childhood. She pictured Shelley in her handmade summer dress and pristine white socks and sandals swinging a rope in tune to the drumbeat. Each year until their father went to prison, they had both walked in the parade, clasping ropes from the ornate banners of the Orange Lodge.

They had all become spectators after 1993.

Hannah didn't know how to address the issue of Orangeism with Etienne. How could a free-thinking, French, left-wing atheist ever understand a fraternity that was created to celebrate and protect Protestantism; and that embodied the spirit of King William III, a Dutchman, who fought in a battle against his father-in-law in order to save Europe from a despotic French King in the year 1690? It was impossible to explain, so Hannah didn't bother. She left Etienne in the computer room in front of the Orange Order's website and told him to make his own conclusions.

Mrs McAdam and her friends were now in the car and ready to go. The first words from Mrs Rainey were delivered like a nostalgic song, 'Isn't it a Glorious day?' The ladies all responded in chorus, *'Glorious.'* Hannah smiled and imagined how different the feelings might be a few hundred metres away as a contentious parade passed through an area in which the Orange Order was as foreign as Etienne's stretched ear. Nothing was ever straight forward in Northern Ireland.

Hannah parked as close as she could to Clifton Street. The feeder parades from around Belfast had yet to arrive, but the ladies had their deckchairs and flasks packed in the boot and were content to wait with blankets wrapped around their legs until the parade commenced. A limousine had been arranged by the Orange Order for them as it was unlikely they would be able to complete the six mile walk around the route in their heels in varying degrees of arthritis. They looked like members of royalty when they waved goodbye. As Hannah walked away, she was consumed by the beauty of Belfast's past, and slightly repelled by some of the undeniably baneful elements in the parade. The minority of men and women who were unashamedly connected to paramilitaries looked at once at odds with the men in bowler hats carrying their silver swords and banners, and out of proportion to their actual number on the street.

Somehow their presence was magnified by being present at all.

Hannah returned home to find Etienne in a complete state of black and Jean in unconditional white. Hannah was in a good mood. She looked at her mum from behind as words bounced from her lips, 'Mum, you can see your knickers in those white Jeans. Is that a thong I see?'

Jean jumped around the kitchen batting her backside with her hand, 'You're kidding me! I sewed a lining into these. There's a full blackout blind around the ass. You can't see anything, can you?'

Shelley stepped in quickly, 'Mum, Hannah's winding you up. You look great!'

Hannah winced as a slap on the arm from Shelley took her by surprise. She watched Jean collect her belongings and move towards the door.

'Right, girls, Etienne,' Jean directed. 'Deckchairs at the ready! By the left, quick march!'

Hannah smiled as Jean led them all out onto the street with her deckchair over her shoulder. The parade wasn't due to start until twelve and it would only take them half an hour to walk into town, but they joined the great, the good and the intoxicated of the Shankill as they descended the long road to the city centre at eleven o'clock sharp.

Hannah watched Etienne's eyes alight on a woman clad in a Union Jack dress. 'It's a Spice Girl!' he exclaimed, sending Jean into convulsions of laughter. Hannah stared at the woman, who was as wide as all of the spice girls combined, and who held a tin of lager in one hand and a deckchair in the other. She smiled and started to enjoy the wonder and the absurdity of her past and present. There were so many people to watch and to enjoy, and Hannah realised that these people had set themselves up precisely for the bemusement of spectators. Why not laugh with them?

Hannah smiled as she watched Etienne and Shelley walk ahead. They almost glided together despite Shelley's awkward foot. Etienne may have made every effort to be different in his appearance, but his taste in females was as conventional as every other man's in Belfast. Heads turned when Shelley walked by. Her long, sunny hair was the perfect accompaniment to the charm of her pale face and sky blue eyes, and an intangible wisdom breezed through her like a soft fragrance. Despite the fact that Shelley was two years younger than her, Hannah knew that she emitted a deeper understanding of the world around her. Seeing her own life through a cloud of dust and blood in the Shankill bomb had perhaps left the mark of a deeper place or time. Whatever it was, Etienne hadn't missed it. He was as fascinated by Shelley as he was entertained by Jean.

Hannah's connection to Etienne was more raw than friendship. He pulled against her like the circular bound current that brought them both back to Jean and Shelley. His antagonism was as natural to Hannah as Robert's had been. Etienne gave her the fond memory of sibling rivalry with her brother.

***

The parade had been passing by for over an hour and Jean's companions had now started to wilt like spent lilies: Etienne was laid out on his deckchair with his head tipped up to the sun, Hannah was sleeping, and, although Shelley's eyes were on the parade, they were vacant and belied her weary spirit. Jean felt like taking a nap too. The initial thrill of something new was now replete with repetition as one flute band followed the next in an array of colours and ceaseless chorus of chirping.

Jean recalled the parades of her childhood when the bands were spectacular in their variety and their music. It was clear that the Twelfth festival had been hijacked in Belfast by flutists, and it wasn't the concert flutists of the Argyle band. Some bands still had their smart military uniforms, but others snubbed any effort with their loose t-shirts and dummy flutes. Jean thought about the infamous 'Kick the pope' bands. They smashed any chance of Catholics joining in the celebrations, whilst concurrently banging out some of the best sounds of the day. How would Jean explain that phenomenon to Etienne, the Catholic atheist who was now catching flies through his gaping mouth as he dozed?

The Pride of the Ardoyne was before them now, in tune with Jean's thoughts. The leader of the band was a teenager with his hair shaved and a mohican dyed in red. Behind him walked three flag bearers, with tattoos up their arms and dark sunglasses, all packed into a tight triangle.

Jean caught some movement to her left. Three drunken women, who were wrapped around one giant Union Jack flag, danced on the footpath, while small children with their band sticks and drums marched on the spot to the music. For the most part now, the entertainment was on the sidelines.

Jean spotted the Shankill ladies in a passing limousine and alerted Hannah and Shelley. They both stood up and waved before they even knew why they were waving. The Shankill Road Defenders followed with neat rows of shining uniforms and white drums adorned in flowers. Jean smiled as each man raised his white drumsticks to his lips like a mechanical toy. She recalled Robert copying them as a child. Two leaders in shiny boots intricately moved their long silver band sticks with art and deftness.

Jean looked to the right and caught a band man kissing a woman on the footpath. They held hands for an extended moment and parted swiftly when the band moved off again. Jean stared and understood the timid smile that was now spreading across the woman's face.

The music continued, but the people faded to colours as Jean's mind marked time.

It was Harry.

He had played the bass flute in a concert band. He had seen Jean, stepped out of the band, kissed her, smiled and returned to his music sheet.

The music ebbed into the distance as Harry's tune played in the fore of her mind. *Children's Love.* Jean blinked back a tear, the first tear she had shed for Harry since she had seen him crouch down beside Shelley's bed with his hands on his head. She had forgotten the music, just as she had forgotten so much of her husband. The only thing that Jean ever knew with any certainty about Harry, was his love for his children.

The music stopped suddenly as Jean watched people fold up their deckchairs and make their way to the field. She wiped her eyes and turned to see that Shelley and Hannah had already packed up.

'Well Etienne, what did you think of that?' Jean's eyebrows were raised.

'It was good, yes.' Etienne's face was straight.

'Was it good like your ear ornamentation or good like the wine?'

'It was an education. Thank you,' he replied as they began walking.

'I thought there might be the odd pipe band to show you, son. Sorry about that. It's all flutes nowadays.'

'Don't worry. I will see pipe bands tomorrow with Hannah and Shelley.'

'You know what Dickens said when he came to Belfast?' Jean asked.

'Dickens?' repeated Etienne.

'Charles Dickens. Famous author,' she explained.

'Ah yes, what did he say?'

'It's a fine place with a rough people.'

Etienne laughed. 'He didn't see the Shankill, then. It's a rough place with a fine people.'

Jean placed an arm around Etienne's waist. 'You know, Etienne, If we could keep you, we would. You have a home in Belfast.'

'Thank you. You also have a home en Bretagne. All of you.'

***

Harry was home. Hannah observed him from the corner of her eye, seated awkwardly on the blue chair by the fire. Hannah was squeezed uncomfortably between Etienne and Mrs McAdam on the blue and white striped sofa, and Shelley was sprawled out on her legs across the oatmeal rug by the hearth. The white chair remained vacant. Jean, meanwhile, hovered on the edge of the sofa close to Harry, not quite sitting, not quite moving. They each held a cup of tea and stared at the empty bars of the grate as though watching a boat roll through the tide. The tea had given them all some focus after one hour of rearranging the dynamics of their lives. Only Mrs McAdam and Etienne had remained stationary, both enthralled by Harry's presence.

Hannah thought back to the forty minute journey from Maghaberry prison. She had been silent, concentrating on the wet road. Through the rearview mirror, she could see Harry's eyes move from Shelley to the watery view through the window. He had insisted that Jean take the front seat, despite the length of his legs. The Peugeot 105 had been crammed with people and breath. The windows had steamed up and Hannah could not keep apace with the condensation and the deep reflections in the car as the fan exerted itself like the mechanics of their minds.

Etienne had guessed that something was amiss. He didn't say anything, but Hannah could read his thoughts in his eyes. He was as attuned to the atmosphere as they all were, and the atmosphere was like the swathe of black mist that had cut across the Black mountain on their journey up the Shankill Road.

Etienne was the first to break the silence. 'Harry, tonight I make a traditional Breton dinner for you all. It is my leaving gift. I will go now and start preparing. Do you like les moules marinières?' Etienne's eyes checked with Hannah for a translation.

'Mussels.' Hannah spoke quickly and nervously.

They all awaited a response. Harry smiled, his thunderous voice sounding a low initial rumble. 'Son, I couldn't tell you what a mussel tasted like. It would be a pleasure.'

Etienne was on a roll. 'I also make some traditional galettes with ham and egg,' he said.

'Savoury pancakes.' Hannah explained.

'It sounds great. Thank you, Et...'

'*Et-ee-en* dad,' Shelley annunciated clearly, as though the name contained her world.

Etienne stood up and moved to the kitchen. The door closed.

Mrs McAdam leaned towards Jean and spoke in a loud whisper, 'Jesus Christ Jean, the man hasn't had a home-cooked meal in ten years and you're going to give him eggs and the dregs of the sea. Harry, son,' she continued turning in his direction, 'if you'd come home to me, you'd have got a big steak and a warm kiss, I'll tell you that for nothing.'

Everyone smiled at Mrs McAdam. Harry stood up and walked towards the kitchen. He kissed Mrs McAdam on the cheek on the way and said, 'It's a date then. I look forward to one of your steaks. I'm going to help Etienne.'

Jean looked stunned, 'You what?'

Harry laughed and the room quivered. He leaned down and kissed Jean on the cheek. 'I learned to cook.'

Jean wafted away the kiss as her cheeks reddened, and her head started to move like a hen.

The first crack of lightning had sliced through their home and only Hannah and Jean had seen it. Harry had learned to cook in prison, while Jean had been cooking in her own prison of spuds and cabbage for years.

The four women sat in silence again before Shelley erupted, 'He won't know where anything stays!' Hannah jumped up and moved to the kitchen.

'I'll be your sous-chef,' offered Hannah. The words were directed at Harry, but he didn't turn around. She added, 'Dad.' He looked towards her and smiled.

'Thank you, Hannah. Now, could you lift out all the utensils and bowls and set the table.' Harry looked at Hannah and winked.

Hannah moved through the orderly cupboards lifting items she thought they might need, not knowing exactly due to the fact that she had never prepared a meal in her life. She re-played a moment in her mind. It was the wink. She was a small child, but she couldn't place it among the graveyard of buried memories.

Etienne was working swiftly with his sleeves rolled up and hair tied back. Harry hadn't taken much notice of the ear situation, and Hannah knew that her dad would only look beneath the skin. She remembered the faces of the inmates in the visitor's area of the prison. There was nothing to mark them out as criminals: some had their heads skinned and tattoos growing up their muscular arms like invasive plants, but most of them looked indeterminately ordinary.

Harry had once had a full head of mousy fair hair, but it was thinner around the crown than Hannah recalled and more grey at the sides. She watched him move around the kitchen and realised that it had been a long time since she had seen her father in motion. She was seeing him from angles that had been curbed, yet understood that he had always been free to move around inside: it was his children's eyes that had been locked up in a vision of a stationary man. Hannah knew that he was handsome, charismatic even. It would have been easier to resent a less charismatic man. His blue eyes were still crystal clear, his long perfect features, reflecting a mix of Shelley and Robert. She searched for herself in his face, but she wasn't there. Harry's entire frame had shrunk from the colossal man embedded in her memory since childhood, but he was broad and tall, and next to Etienne in the small kitchen, Hannah had the impression of twin spires. She felt suddenly very small.

'How do you know how to cook like that?' she asked Etienne.

Etienne stopped what he was doing and looked at Hannah with insipid eyes, 'My mum and dad work, so we cook.'

Hannah understood, and bowed her head a little as her father looked at her, gauging Hannah's response. Hannah had evaded every household task that had ever been put before her. Jean had cooked and cleaned and done everything in between, and it seemed that Etienne had noticed.

'I do lots of other things,' she replied defensively, whilst acknowledging her own inherent domestic idleness with an internal smile.

Etienne looked and waited. Her father kept moving, knowing perhaps that he was too apart from the routine of his own family to throw any stones.

'I drive,' she said.

'You drive.' Etienne replied flatly.

'I study too! And...and I work at least twenty hours a week in a shop...'

Etienne was smiling now and Hannah realised what was happening. Her French adversary had finally reached beneath her skin. She scowled in his direction and thought about whether she should try to demonstrate some kind of kitchen endeavour, but weighing up the advantage of staying to monitor the possibility of any admissions of a prison stay against getting her hands wet, she came up with a swift plan. 'I need to check my email. Give me a shout if you need any help.' Before climbing the stairs, she called back to her mum from the hall. 'Jean, go in and keep an eye on those two, would you?'

She started up the computer and logged into her email. Her heart hastened as Rachael Carter's name arrived in the inbox. She would answer that email second. She knew it would require more time. The first was from her friend, Mark, and it was entitled, '18th Birthday drinks.' She opened the message and realised it was in reference to that night. 'Meeting at the Apartment at eight. See you all there!' Hannah thought for a moment. Would it be devastating for her father if she went out in the city centre on his first night back? She opted for pleading forgiveness over seeking permission and responded, 'See you there.' She then carefully read Rachael's email.

Hi Hannah,

I hope you are enjoying your French exchange. I'd love to be there to meet Etienne! You need to believe me that I did not share your secret. Someone else must know about your dad. You will have to trust me because I'm not going anywhere.

The holiday is going great, but my mum has had a personality transplant. She sunbathes and drinks cocktails and only phones work in the morning for a minute to check in. I've never seen her like this. I assumed she had met someone, but she seems to be happy on her own.

The crazy thing is that she did not have an affair with Terence Craig! I have been punishing her for four years for the wrong thing.

She has been spending time with Terence though. You will be amazed when I tell you why. I can barely take it all in and I can't wait to tell you when I get home.

Enjoy your time in France. See you at the end of August!

I remain your best friend.

Love,
Rachael.

***

Jean's voice cut through the subdued atmosphere of the house like a serrated knife. Shelley heard Hannah's familiar footsteps on the stairs in response to Jean and knew that her sister was in a rage. 'Mum, for goodness sake,' Hannah seethed in raw whispers. 'Etienne's still here. Could you keep it down?'

'Ach, take the poker out of your arse,' came Jean's reply. 'Come on. Your dinner's ready.'

Shelley followed Hannah to the table, amused by her sister's embarrassment. Harry looked up at Jean as she entered the room and said confidently, 'You could hear you at Killarney!' They all laughed, with the exception of Jean, who folded her arms and delivered an affected glare, 'Excuse me Mister Foghorn. Since when did you get so quiet? Did your tongue do time too in pris...prison?'

The last word lingered in the air. Hannah's eyes bored a hole in Jean's. Etienne's looked to Hannah for answers. Shelley covered hers with her hand and Harry's dropped into the creamy sauce surrounding the mussels.

Mrs McAdam did nothing with her eyes and instead feigned deafness, 'Etienne, son, this is lovely. Did you know that Jean is also French?'

Shelley burst out laughing, Harry looked slightly less nervous and Jean had the appearance of a child who had escaped a scolding.

Etienne spoke. 'Fook me, Jean, you did not tell me this secret.' He evaded the prison comment, either unaware of the truth, or endowed with an abundance of intelligence and kindness. Shelley suspected the latter to be the case.

She listened closely as a conversation developed between her dad and Etienne. She could see that Etienne was trying to impress Harry, regardless of the unspoken revelation about his crime.

'What I don't understand here in Belfast is...well...the socialism,' said Etienne. 'Why did the working class Catholics and Protestants not fight together against the authorities for better conditions? Why did they turn against each other?'

Harry's face brightened as though he'd just that second been given his freedom.

'That's it Etienne. That's exactly it. The middle class used the working class. The Catholics who campaigned for better jobs in the civil service were as turned off by working class people collecting money outside churches for IRA prisoners' families as they were by Protestant Orangemen walking up and down their streets. The middle class

56

Protestants made an even bigger mess. They turned a blind eye to defenders in their communities, afraid of speaking out against their activities, yet the minute the Troubles were over, they disowned them and called them scum. Politicians got people all worked up about the evils of Catholicism and then sat back in their comfortable homes watching areas like the Shankill go up in flames. The politicians say they have no blood on their hands, but knowledge is like dynamite to the educated man, and many educated men used their knowledge and their words to incite bitter hatred.'

Etienne's eyes did not leave Harry's face. Shelley's eyes did not leave Etienne's. She was aware of her dad's thick Belfast accent, but Etienne seemed to be completely fixated.

'The loyalists are always told that they are animals,' he continued, 'and so they raise their backs up.'

Shelley stayed at the table as Mrs McAdam moved into the living room. Hannah departed rolling her eyes, while Jean quietly shifted around the kitchen. Shelley knew she was listening too.

Harry became more animated, 'You know what to do if you see a bull, son?'

Etienne shook his head.

'You move away and you do not take your eyes off that bull until you are safe. If you turn and run, you'll invite the chase.'

Etienne nodded.

Jean dropped her tea cloth and made a comical face at Shelley. Shelley realised that this speech was rehearsed in the head of a man who had time to connect with the part of his mind that remained dormant among people who were busy living, people who had stopped thinking.

'The middle classes turned and ran with their eyes on their own safety. The problem is that no one is looking the bull in the eye. And so, the bull lowers its head, arches its back and flicks its forefeet. It is ready for the fight.'

Shelley refilled her glass at the sink. Jean nudged her and whispered in her ear, 'Would ye listen to thon? He's talking bull now.'

Shelley smiled and put her finger up to her lips. She tuned in again as her father continued.

'The Shankill has become mono-social with nothing but the people who have been trampled on and left behind.'

Shelley stopped what she was doing when Etienne asked, 'And the IRA?'

Her dad leaned forward and rubbed his chin. 'The IRA, they were Marxists in the beginning. Their revolution was supposed to be for the working man, but they made a mistake. They attacked the Protestant working class and then blood flowed. People became animals on both sides. They all forgot about the Marxist revolution.'

THE FLOWER THAT LOOKS AFTER SLEEP

Shelley hadn't left her bed since Etienne had left Ireland. She heard Jean on the landing, 'Harry, what's wrong with her? Do you think we might need to phone a doctor?' Hannah came next, 'Mum, she's probably been drinking in the park with those wee girls from Woodvale. She's got a hangover.' And then a surprising voice, a new voice in their home. 'She'll be okay. I think her trouble has passed.'

What did he mean? Had he seen something? Shelley became alert for the first time in three days. The voices disappeared then and she drifted, holding her duvet against her cheek, trying hard to hear him and feel his touch.

Shelley retraced the evening before he left. She would have been happy to tell Etienne the truth about prison, but she was mortified at the thoughts of Etienne uncovering she had been complicit in all the lies. That was it, she decided. She was no longer going to lie for her sister. If she wasn't covering up for Hannah, she was making up a whole world for her to live in that suited a notion of who Hannah believed her friends wanted her to be. Her sister would have to start telling the truth.

Etienne had declined Hannah's offer of a night in the city centre and asked Shelley instead for one last walk around Belfast. They had frequently drifted around the city when Hannah had been at work, and so the request hadn't come as a surprise. Shelley had trembled at the possibility of a walk on his last evening.

They had travelled less than block when Etienne turned to the door of the old fish shop and pointed at the plaque. 'Your mum showed me this.

58

The red poppies will always remind me of you.'

Shelley was surprised. Etienne hadn't acknowledged her foot at all and had never spoken of the Shankill bomb. She wasn't sure if she should be pleased by the poppy reference or saddened. A symbol of the First World War and bloodshed on the fields of France, the poppy had been adopted on the Shankill Road as the memorial for every atrocity to shake the community during the Troubles.

'Do you remember?' Etienne asked.

'Yes' she replied after a moment.

The truth was that Shelley hadn't thought about the Shankill bomb for a long time. The day that they took her daddy away was the day that she remembered: she could lay a wreath at that one moment in time. Shelley looked around and tried to recapture what she knew. The ground on the Shankill did shake when the dust came tumbling down, but she had passed out and only memories that were placed in her head by other people now remained. The recollection of learning that her daddy wasn't coming home was all hers and it was soaked in pain. She could still squeeze out the last drops of it because it lasted right up until the day he came back. She breathed deeply. Dreams of him dying in prison, thoughts of him being alone and unhappy, and the torment of watching her mum struggle alone were gone.

Shelley willed her mind to dream of Etienne again. She pushed back the sleep that was calling her and remembered him there beside the poppies. She had smiled to disguise the pain, but she didn't speak. She had continued walking, aware that Etienne wanted more of a response than the one she had given.

'I was playing with Hannah and I ran away.' She pointed back. 'I ran out onto the road and there was no reason for running onto the road.' She turned again and walked. Etienne listened to the silence. Shelley looked at him, knowing he could hear something. 'We did this story in school called *Chicken Licken*. Do you know it?'

'No,' Etienne replied.

Shelley explained, 'A chicken thinks the sky has fallen down and he tells all the other animals. They are all eventually led to a trap by a fox. The line about the sky falling down must have reminded me of something. The teacher asked me a question in class one day about the story...I think it might have been a couple of years after the bomb...anyway, I told her that I knew what it looked like when the sky fell down because the sky had fallen down on the day of the Shankill bomb.' Etienne was walking slowly, paying no attention to the road ahead. 'Next thing you know, I had to see a counsellor. I didn't want to go to counselling. It was just my way of describing the bomb. A great big cloud of grey sky fell on me. And then I blacked out. That's it. I was lucky.'

'Lucky?' Etienne's voice revealed surprise.

'A seven year old girl died.'

Shelley saw Etienne retreat and look towards the falling sun on the Black Mountain. He didn't speak.

Shelley closed her eyes again and buried her face in the covers of the bed, the heat radiating around her like the warm breath of Etienne on her skin. Her mind slowed as she went through each detail again. They approached the gate of the Shankill graveyard and looked inside. It was more like a park with ancient trees and tombstones, and it had a surreal quality as the red sky tinted the grass in contrasting shades of velvety green. Etienne pointed to the middle, 'This Virgin is very big.'

Shelley laughed as she looked at a white statue under a red bricked arch at the centre of the graveyard. 'That's Queen Victoria. She's the Queen's great granny.'

Etienne smiled, 'What is she doing here with the dead?'

Shelley looked up to the sky for an answer, 'Who knows? The people around here really like royal stuff. And Protestants don't make such a big deal about statues of Mary.' Shelley's eyes filled with the fire of the sky as she recaptured something. 'Last year we went on a school trip to County Cork. It was this cross-community thing. Anyway, there were statues of the Blessed Virgin everywhere. Some of them were lit up and quite a few of them had really red lips painted on them.' Shelley looked around the park and said to Etienne, 'Keep an eye on that gate.'

Etienne looked back towards the road. Shelley opened her jacket pocket and pulled out a lipstick. By the time Etienne turned around, Shelley was apprehensively standing under the first property she had ever defaced. She bit both lips and looked at Etienne. He smiled. A gate by the road creaked open and Shelley pulled Etienne behind the statue of the Blessed Queen Victoria.

The emotion of thinking over the past, the thrill of her rashness, and the slight chill that now breezed through her open jacket, awoke her senses and enlivened a fearlessness within her. She reached out and kissed Etienne on the lips. Her foothold on the uneven grass was tenuous, and with only her lips holding her in place, her hands fell around him. The last time she had kissed someone had been the previous summer on a dark coach on the long road back from Cork. A boy called Paul, who attended a Catholic school on the same side of town, had kissed her for approximately two hours without surfacing for breath. It had all been in preparation for this, she realised, as Etienne's lips moved softly over hers.

His hand gradually made its way up her back and under the jacket and blouse that were no longer the subject of the breeze. Shelley felt weak from the touch of his hands on her naked back, and once the brush of his beard had passed without evidence of the amusement it had initially caused, she was completely immersed in his long, sensuous kiss. She looked up and thought she might stumble again when she saw how deeply his eyes penetrated her own. She responded to what was now becoming a precarious situation with his hands with words that came with no oxygen passing to the brain. 'I wish you didn't have to go.'

Etienne stopped and then kissed her again, this time pulling her tightly towards him so that Shelley found herself in immeasurably close contact with him. His hands were moving up her back again and a deft flick swiftly removed her bra strap. Her eyes were wide open now and she knew that Etienne was waiting for her approval before his hand moved around. Her entire body was shaking uncontrollably as she buoyed him on through a deeper and more abundant kiss. Replete with warmth and deprived of oxygen, she needed an excuse to sit down as her strong leg weakened and her weak leg gave way, and the excuse came with a loud clang of a gate. Etienne peered around the virgin Queen and Shelley fixed her clothes, smoothed down her jacket, rounded the corner of the statue and looked up at the Queen with a whole new level of benediction. Etienne looked concerned, 'You want to go now?' he said. Shelley, unable to speak, took his hand and they moved back towards the main road in complete silence.

As they approached the site of the Shankill bomb, Etienne looked at Shelley with eyes so unyielding that every muscle and tendon holding her together seemed to give in to him. He placed his arm around her shoulder and stopped by the poppies again. 'La fleur qui garde le sommeil,' he said. Shelley did not understand, but the words were so musically aired that they contained a whole world of language in their song. She looked at him and he responded to her unasked question, 'The flower that looks after sleep. *Les Pavots*. Poppies. It's a poem from France. These people will sleep in peace. I am thankful that you were lucky.'

They continued to walk arm in arm. Before they approached Snugville Street, Etienne stopped. 'One more kiss. It's the last opportunity.' The kiss was soft and sad, and checked tears glistened in Shelley's eyes. She realised that this was the last chance to take a walk with Etienne under a Shankill sky, and that three weeks had passed without him knowing that she had wanted to kiss him all along. They held hands and looked back to the spot where a bomb had once turned people to dust. Shelley closed her eyes and imagined a bed of poppies and a little girl. She squeezed Etienne's hand and asked him to say it again. 'La fleur qui garde le sommeil.' She repeated the words over in her head and promised she wouldn't forget them. 'She is sleeping now on a pillow of poppies.'

Shelley could hear her mum and dad on the landing again, debating her welfare, but she was content to sleep and dream of Etienne and of saying goodbye. She held a folded note in her hand with a poem called *Les pavots*, crafted by the hand of a wild French boy with his soul in his eyes. He had touched her skin, he had touched her heart and he had given her the gift of knowing that the people she had passed by were wrapped in soft petals.

She had been given a new daytime after ten people in a fish shop had come together in the evening of their lives.

***

The silence was stifling. Harry sat in the living room with Jean, both of them staring at the TV, neither of them watching it. Nine and a half years of wishing for the commotion of his home had passed by and yet he was still behind bars. Hannah stopped playing the dutiful daughter once Etienne had left, and Shelley was asleep all the time. Jean seemed keen to talk, but she would take a deep breath and then nothing would come from her lips.

Harry was in the way. His legs were longer than the living space, and the order he was accustomed to in prison was completely erased. He had learned to become afraid of the furniture as the invisible electric fence circuiting each item set off a nervous tick in Jean's eye, and his pride had drained at the realisation that these bricks belonged to Jean. They had talked of buying the house from the council when he was in prison and when Jean's business had started to flourish, but it had been a surreal notion, like the stories of the new neighbours he had never met.

His only sanctuary was the small kitchen. Jean, surprisingly, hadn't resisted him cooking after the first night. She had watched in amazement and even sat down once or twice to read a magazine, her endless energy perhaps quietened by the removal of an infinite chore.

Harry was free from prison walls and the artificial life he had lived: working yet not contributing to the economy, talking to people he didn't want to talk to, watering plants that didn't need watered and watching people starved of morality come and go. They had been his family and he had known each detail of their lives intimately. He understood the patterns of their sleep. He knew when they were in trouble and always tried to have a solution. They turned to him as a child turns to a father. His freedom was this family of strangers inside four walls that didn't belong to him. His freedom was that of a father whose son was gone.

Just as the thoughts of Robert crushed his chest, Shelley appeared at the door like a draught. Her eyes were streaming tears, her face red and blotchy and her breathing uncontrolled. Jean's body changed from tense to soft in response to the apparent distress of her daughter. Shelley sobbed as they tried to ask her what was wrong. Hannah came then like the wind itself, heralding a handwritten note in the air.

'What's going on?' Jean looked bewildered.

Hannah was different too. Harry knew his daughter was tough on the outside, but he was always conscious of a soft pain ebbing on the inside that was hidden behind the metal. Now, her pain seemed to cut through her skin, and it was delivered by a sharp tongue as she wailed in an completely unnecessary high-pitch, 'She has been seeing Etienne.' She held the note out, but as Harry reached to look at it, Shelley's hand moved towards Hannah's face. Shelley grabbed at the paper, but Hannah swiftly moved her arm down and a silent rip tore up the peace to which they had all been assigned.

'What have you done?' Shelley cried. She held one part of the letter in her hand. Hannah dropped the other on the floor. Shelley reached for it frantically and pieced the two parts back together in the air. Harry had never seen Shelley lose her temper in his life. He had never had a complaint from Jean about Shelley while he had been in prison, but he watched a rage swell in his daughter's face and recognised the unrestrained tempest that moved through her body and that was now declaring itself in shrill words.

'You bitch! Look what you've done! You bitch!'

Hannah stood back too, demonstrating no recognition at all of the intense acrimony in her sister's eyes.

Shelley launched her body on Hannah's and yelled, 'You've ruined it! You've ruined it. You bitch! Etienne gave me that.'

Harry reached down and pulled Shelley back as her legs continued to kick and her red face continued to burn.

Hannah's hands were in the air and her voice was lost in the swirling blizzard of rage in the room, 'Okay, okay, Shelley. Calm down.' Hannah was shaking.

'It's a poem from Etienne,' said Shelley, her shoulders heaving.

'I know that.' Hannah looked to her mum for help. 'I want to know why he was sending you poetry. Mum, speak to her. Tell her. If he was doing anything with you, then...'

Harry felt Shelley's body vibrate again as his arm remained across the top of her chest. She broke free.

'Shelley, love, what's going on?' It was Jean's voice, soft and tearful.

'She ripped the poem he gave me! She ripped it!'

'Yes, I know, but why did he give you a poem? Did you like Etienne? Were you...seeing him?'

Harry's mind turned back to the graveyard where he had seen his youngest daughter pull Etienne by the hand. He had walked for twelve minutes. He had checked his watch. It was enough time to walk to the park and back. It had been an effort to make the graveyard gate bang so hard. Harry stood back and watched them then, walking hand in hand down the street. They had stopped at the door of the old fish shop before moving on and kissing. It had looked innocent, but Harry had remained awake all night listening. He had checked at three in the morning and Shelley was asleep downstairs on the sofa bed with her sister. She slept so deeply that she missed the run to the airport in the morning. She awoke eventually, went upstairs, got into Etienne's bed and slept again. Harry said nothing.

'If he went near you, I'll kill him.' It was Hannah again. Harry understood now. She was trying to protect her sister, but she was saying entirely the wrong thing.

Shelley's voice broke. 'It's none of your business! You didn't even like him or go near him the whole time he was here. Etienne was my friend!'

Hannah was incensed. 'What do you mean? That's rubbish. I took him everywhere with me.'

'Only when it suited you. You didn't like him being around your snobby Methody friends.' said Shelley.

'They're not snobby, and that's not true. And I did like him. I just didn't have a crush on him like you.'

Shelley lost control again and catapulted towards her sister. She grabbed her by the hair and pulled her to the ground. Harry held her back again as she screamed. 'You don't know anything. You and all your lies and your stupid friends. You're a stuck up cow and I'm not lying for you anymore. I'm going to email Etienne and tell him the truth.'

Hannah, aware possibly of her physical disadvantage, seemed to engage her head at the same time as eyeing the note. She pulled it from Shelley and ripped it in half again, dropping the four parts to the ground. 'You do that, Shelley, you tell the whole fucking world that your dad has been in prison for murder. Go head. See how many friends you have then.'

Hannah raced from the room and slammed the door behind her back. The house shook as her slight body thudded the stairs with its wrath.

Shelley sat on the floor and Jean placed her arms around her. Shelley was sobbing again. Harry perched on the end of the sofa and listened to his daughter as she coughed out barely decipherable words. 'It was a poem about poppies. He gave it to me because he said that the poppy was the flower that looks after sleep. He made me think about the people who had died again, and I had forgotten them. I pass the poppies all the time and never think.' Her voice was low now and cracking under the strain of tears. 'He translated it on this side, but now it's completely ruined.' Shelley wiped the tears from her eyes and stood up. 'I'm going for a walk. Sorry for ruining your first week home, dad.'

Harry reached out and kissed his daughter on the head, 'You didn't ruin it, love.'

Alone again with Jean, Harry pulled her towards the sofa. He placed his arm around her and sat back looking up at a family portrait of his three children. Silent minutes purged the anguish from the room and restored its peace. 'Robert would have enjoyed that.' Harry spoke softly. His wife looked up at him and smiled at him sincerely for the first time since he came home.

'Yes, he would. Robert always enjoyed a good fight. I can't believe it, though. Those two girls haven't said a cross word to each other in years.'

'And is that normal?' asked Harry.

'What?'

'Two sisters not fighting?'

'I don't know...I thought...I suppose not, no,' said Jean.

'I think Shelley has been holding a lot of stuff in.'

'Hannah is the one who hides,' added Jean.

'I think Shelley has been hiding too,' said Harry.

'Maybe.'

Harry could feel Jean's shoulders relax.

'Jean.'

'What?'

'I've missed you.'

Jean shot up and regained her adrenaline. 'Sorry, I need to get the polishing done. I'd better get to it.'

She walked away. Harry looked at his hands and breathed deeply. He counted. He then stood up and walked to the door. Closing it gently behind him, he stared at the sky and watched the tapestry of clouds as he had done for so many years from a cell. He then walked freely down his own street and felt his pride return through his stride. He saw the Black Mountain ahead and knew he had to go there.

***

Catriona stood outside Norma and Terence Craig's detached home three doors down from her own. Norma Craig was dying and she wanted to talk to Catriona. Terence opened the door and greeted Catriona with grey-blue eyes awash with sadness and peace. He paused and looked at her, silently gesturing his hand to invite her in. She became aware of a familiar acknowledgement, which moved through her spine with the sensibility of a forty-five year-old woman, and beamed off her cheeks like the glow of a twenty year-old girl. Terence was grey now, grey not only in his hair, but in the pallor of his face, yet Catriona could still see the spirit of the life he had been leading until death had made its passage towards his home.

Catriona was tanned and refreshed following her holiday. She had caught herself in the mirror before leaving her house and saw the rejuvenation reflecting back. Her light brown hair had flowed over her shoulders with highlights from the yellow streamers of sun that shone through her front porch each morning. It felt wrong to be so revived and full of life when she was entering the home of a woman who was dying.

She looked again at the familiar tinge of hopeful melancholy in Terence's eyes. When she had moved into Windsor Park and seen Terence by his car, she couldn't stop looking at the beautiful sadness in his eyes, the eyes that were part of her body and inherent in her shame.

She walked through the hallway and the light flickered around her in particles of silver dust, the sun shaded by the dark stained glass windows of the front door. It was an old home filled with old things, the old things that wealthy people liked to retain. Catriona knew about wealth. She had done well for herself, but she didn't live with the sense of past that was found in the dust of the Persian carpets that ran through the ground floor of Norma and Terence's home. Catriona had already been there when Norma was absent. She had crossed the carpets in silence, noting the antique cabinets and fine, faded heirlooms. The journalist who had taken an extraordinary interest in their lives, had followed her from the window and recorded all the details. Terence then had to tell Norma the truth. She had already been diagnosed with cancer of the womb and an unspoken agreement made lies impossible, the anathema of death. Their daughter, Helena, also knew. Catriona regretted not explaining everything to Rachael, but she had seemed too young at the time. It wasn't right to burden her with more turmoil than the divorce had already incurred.

Norma was seated upright in the shaded conservatory with her legs stretched across a sofa, her frail body wrapped in blankets and her strong eyes welcoming Rachael like an open fire. She was overlooking a forest of thick green trees in an overgrown, but densely pretty garden. Catriona had been humbled by Norma, whose mortality had brought her a spiritual clarity that Catriona knew she herself did not possess. In the unconventional triangle that had become their friendship, Catriona never once doubted the sincerity of this woman who was becoming a friend. After the local Sunday tabloid had made its attempt to rip their morality to shreds, there were no further meetings alone between Terence and Catriona. Norma was always present.

'I told Rachael.' They were Catriona's first words and they were greeted with still faces from both Terence and Norma.

'How did she take it?' Norma asked. Conversation tended to assume an isosceles shape, with two strong female sides.

'Well. She's excited. That's what I feared in some ways. It could lead to disappointment.'

'I have a feeling it will lead to healing.' It was Norma. Her eyes were on a spot somewhere in her mind, beyond the immediate proximity of the room.

'Norma, I...I wish we could all meet him.' Catriona's voice shook as she said the words.

Norma smiled, 'Thank you. That means a lot to me.'

Terence was in the kitchen now pouring water into the kettle. 'Catriona, I want to tell you this. I want Terence to be happy. Whatever it takes.' She stopped speaking and looked at her hands. 'I want him to be happy.'

Catriona listened but didn't understand what she meant, or perhaps her unconscious mind refused to interpret what Norma had said. She paused to acknowledge that she had heard the words and then swiftly changed the subject. 'We can't get hold of anyone by phone. Ever since that movie, *The Magdalene Sisters*, journalists have taken an interest in uncovering the truth about those places. All communication has to be in writing. The nuns are taking a lot of blame right now. Everyone wants to know what it was like.'

Catriona watched as curiosity rose in Norma's cheeks. Impending death could not disguise the prying heart of a woman. Catriona released a hesitant smile. 'Do you want to know too?'

'Not if it's too horrible,' said Norma.

Catriona had never spoken of her time in the mother and baby home, but any words shared now with Norma were safe and likely to depart the world within weeks of being spoken. It was a sad thought, that the keeper of her story had such a finite amount of time to digest the images she was about to consume.

Catriona barely knew where to begin. Nothing about that summer had been okay, but she had never been good with spoken words and her initial thoughts slid across the icy plane of a memory that had yet to thaw. 'It was okay' she said.

Terence arrived back in the room, but this conversation was between two women. Terence was an observer in the tight circumference of female sharing, despite his own pain.

Catriona continued, resolving to be honest, conscious that her words might seem cold. 'I was so removed from reality that if a nun had stuck pins in me at night, I wouldn't have noticed, but the truth is that the nuns were good. They were my salvation. I needed them. I needed their help.' Catriona checked her mind again, like a thermometer of emotions. There was no response from Terence or Norma. They were waiting. She continued. 'My biggest fear was that my parents would walk in. That terrified me. The shame of being caught was stronger than the shame of giving up a child.'

The words poured out too fast and Catriona noted the change in Norma's complexion as her curiosity faded. Catriona reprimanded herself for sounding cold again. She never had fathomed how to demonstrate the warmth and depth that she often felt. She had read books where other lost mothers from a generation of 'fallen women' had used words like 'achingly painful' to solicit the heart of their readers, but Catriona had an ordered mind, too systematic perhaps. She was always aware of a scale of tragedy and could prioritise some emotions more than others. The death of a baby troubled her more than anything. There had been one stillbirth in the mother and baby home the night that her son was born, and it haunted her more than her own plight. She had been completely consumed by the mother and tears had flowed as though borrowed from the young girl's distress.

Catriona thought carefully about what she should say next. Her story was accurate. She knew it was stronger than other memories. A story locked in the stillness of the time retains its purity, she realised. 'I know that what I've just said sounds...cruel, probably. But you know...things were different. I had to fight with my mother and father to allow me to go to university. They wanted me to stay and help on the farm. I caused so much trouble. Can you imagine what would have happened if I'd come home and said that I was pregnant, that I'd gone off to Dublin and brought back so much shame on them? No, they couldn't have handled it. I wouldn't have had a home. And then what? I'd have ended up in one of those places anyway and I'd have stayed there, and then I really would have a story to tell you.'

Terence looked her in the eye. The look told her to stop, but now that her lips were moving and the memories re-visited, she needed to expel them. It had become a mechanical thing that her mind no longer controlled. She spoke again. 'The end was always going to be the same. Etienne was always going to be taken away. The only choice I had was a life of toil or...' She breathed deeply and looked up, away from the judgement of the people around her. 'The only choice was an education and chance to escape.' Catriona looked into Norma's eyes and swallowed back an emotion that started to rise in her throat. She felt her neck redden.

The women both now stared into a prism of time and swirling, glittery dust. Terence broke the strain. 'The adoption agency has the registered adopted names of children born in the home in June 1978. We've exhausted all information through the church. The agency is helping. The birth certificates in the home were destroyed, but the adoption certificate is more important. It will have the adopted name on it instead of Etienne. There can't have been that many babies born on that particular day. I think we'll find him.'

Catriona looked at Terence and saw a young man of twenty years old. As he had risen through the ranks of politics, she had seen him on TV, but he could never age for her. The beautifully naive look of loss in his eyes could not be overshadowed by years, no matter how folded his eyelids became with time. Catriona would only ever see the young man who had cried when she had said she was giving up their baby. He had offered to marry her, to raise the child together, but he was a romantic. She knew the career he had ahead, the same career as his own father, and she had been sure that he could not have coped with a baby at the age of twenty. Marrying a Catholic girl who was pregnant could have jeopardised his career. He needed to finish his studies. He never admitted it, but Catriona suspected he understood it was best.

It had been tempting to marry him and make life easy for herself, but Catriona could not allow someone to marry her who was forced to do so due to circumstance. She couldn't suffer the idea of being with the wrong person, a fact in her considerations that had been endowed with so much irony over time. In 1978, marriage was a life decision.

Terence had then suggested that his sister adopt the baby. No one would know. His sister could be trusted. Catriona knew that, but it had to be all or nothing. She couldn't accept that she would know the whereabouts of her child. Her life would have stopped. She would have become obsessed. She had visions of standing in front of his sister's front door watching a small boy come and go and haunting dreams of taking him away and hiding him. The dreams would always end at the point when he was in her arms.

The dreams would always end because she wouldn't have known where to go or what to do with her child.

She turned to Terence. 'I did a terrible thing to you, but you would have had an awful wife, one who never finished her studies and who lived in your shadow. I would have resented you. Instead, you found your equal in Norma. You know that now.'

The silent response in the room was piercing, but Catriona needed to say all of it. 'Norma, I was selfish when I was twenty years old. I thought that I was owed an education and I grabbed it. I believed that I couldn't give to a child unconditionally. I had to make a decision at the age of twenty that would dictate the rest of my life. The risk was the lottery of parents. The reward was my sanity.'

Norma spoke. 'But what about the baby?'

The soft pulse of the clock in the hall was the only sound. Catriona bowed her head as her spirits fell into the morbid shadows of the grey light against the even pattern of sound. Norma's voice echoed and Catriona held her hands over her face. Twenty five years of grief flowed through her fingers because of the words of Norma Craig. She cried without restraint and felt arms around her that had once meant so little to her, but that now contained a great weight. Catriona had survived up until that moment, but now she needed her son's father.

The rushed decisions of her youth were now achingly painful, and emotions flowed relentlessly from the depths of her womb, where a baby had once grown contentedly and where hard limbs had kicked against her skin. She had not ignored the child's call. She spent eight months, from the moment she knew, soothing her stomach with her hands. She spent eight months talking and sharing things with the person inside her. Those precious months when she had carried Etienne, the baby whose adopted name she did not know, and later when she had carried Rachael, had been the least lonely months of her life. She had loved her son and had held him for the first eight weeks. She had covered him in all the love she could give in the time she had to give it. The love had then seeped from her when he was gone, and milk burst through her darkened nipples onto cotton. She had cried through the raw misery of hard, inflamed breasts that could not contain the dripping love when a bottle was held to her

69

child's lips by a kind nun.

The mother and baby home had been okay, and the nuns had been good to her, but the mother and baby home had been her own personal and psychological hell in the choice she had had to make. Marrying Terence would not have been a choice. It would have been an acceptance of the life she had dreaded. And now, when the fear of her youth had long passed, the grief for what she had done had come to life like the burning residue of overflowing breasts.

As Catriona's body folded into Terence's arms in the presence of his dying wife, she felt closer to him than to any man who had ever held her. Terence was Etienne and Etienne was Terence. She couldn't separate the two and his grip on her felt like the closest she had been to her son since the day she said goodbye twenty five years ago. She had paid for her freedom by giving part of herself away.

***

31 July 2003

Dear Jean

Please take your time reading this email. Stay a while longer in the study beside Robert's bed and when you are tired, lie down and sleep deeply.

I'm not surprised by the fight between Hannah and Shelley. In some ways, they are liberated. Imagine the burden they have been carrying for so long. They have seen a window of opportunity to be children again and they've taken it. They know that Harry will look after them.

You said you have a stranger in your home, but it's not the case. You know a younger version of Harry and that's important. You are one of the only people who knows that part of him. This will sound odd, as everything in our world does, but when I was in your company, I wanted you to know who I used to be. I wanted you to see the person I was before I lost my leg in the bomb. The only person who shares those memories with me is Annie, and she has another life now with someone else. I would love to have a conversation with that young man who was filled with the promise of life. You know that version of Harry and if you search hard, you will remember how he made you laugh and smile.

I'm going to tell you something about my marriage. Annie and I separated for a brief period before we finally ended the relationship. It was before the Shankill bomb. When the Shankill bomb happened, Annie was really upset. I know she blamed herself for Shelley and Hannah running around the corner when she was having tea with you. One night, she sat at the table and wrote a letter. She said she was writing to Shaun in America. It made sense to me because I was aware that Shaun had been Robert's host dad on the summer program in Washington D.C. and I knew you were in no fit state to write letters to anyone. I saw her hand move across the page swiftly from the corner of my eye, and I swear she changed. I knew there was something there. It was like the presence of a third person. Life moved on and it was never mentioned. When Annie called me years later to tell me about moving to America with Shaun, it took me about a week to realise that I had witnessed a small part of the connection she had with him when I watched her write that letter. It hurt like nothing I have ever experienced, despite the years that had passed. We worked harder to save our marriage than anyone I know, but neither of us stood a chance when the missing piece of Annie's life lay elsewhere.

You will wonder why I've written all of this and it is this: I know how unfair it is to lack the knowledge of a missing piece, and I will not step on another man's toes when he is trying to save his marriage. For reasons we will never understand, we needed to be with each other from the time of Robert's death until today, and I will never regret it despite how wrong it was. The only way I can respect you now is by respecting your husband. You don't like me wearing my heart on my sleeve, but I want you to know that you are beautiful and loving, and even when you are cursing the life out of the English language, I love listening to you and sharing time with you. You make me laugh and you make me cry even if you don't see the tears in my eyes.

So, where does that leave me? The problem is that I love a woman and respect her at the same time. Respect has to come before love this time. You need to work things out with Harry. I can't distract you from that. I won't say, 'If one day...' because that makes it a dilemma for you, and it gives you a way out during the bleak days.

I know that Harry will want to go to Holland to see the place where his son died, and if we meet, I will look your husband in the eye and know that I have put you before me by respecting his marriage.

Goodbye Jean. I will see you again some day and I will be your friend. Please sleep now and find some peace.

With love and respect,

Roy.

***

Hannah's weighty silence dragged at Jean's heels. Jean placed Hannah's suitcase on the scales at check-in, but felt no lighter after depositing it. She walked to Departures with her daughter and was glad that Harry had had his appointment at the Job Centre at the same time. His presence would have solicited unwanted conversation. Jean's mind was a padded cell of words, and, as she watched her daughter, she realised that she too could not engage in discussion with a busy mind.

Jean understood what burden Hannah was carrying. It was fear, a childish fear of being away from home, that walked in front of her, trying to trip her up, forcing her to slow down. Hannah had fussed over every tiny detail, ensuring that all parts of her outfits were assembled on the bed before packing them. Jean had tried to talk her into removing some of the shoes from the case. The only thing that she knew about Etienne's family was that they lived in the countryside. Hannah was a city girl and the contents of her suitcase, including six pairs of four inch heels, made Jean nervous. When Hannah wasn't looking, Jean squeezed an extra pair of jeans, a rolled up mac and walking shoes into the case. She had seen how Etienne dressed and suspected his appearance might be more than individualism. Such an effort to look unique suggested he was following a trend. Her daughter had a simple view of the world, and followed high street fashions in a vain attempt to be tall. Jean worried that Hannah might stand out from the crowd.

She was happy to have found something light with which to fill her mind. She would focus on Hannah and think of Roy on the way home. But the corridor was long and she was walking slowly behind Hannah and her mind drifted away from shoes to the email.

She had expected the email. Subconsciously, she had wanted it.

And when it came, it brought a charged release and a deep sadness: she felt free, yet filled with loss. The first line had been a blow; her stomach muscles buckling in the knowledge of what was to come. Then, there was the promise of happiness and with it the relief. There followed the story about Annie, and Jean started to understand.

Jean had read the letter twice, unable to concentrate on the individual words, but knowing the sense of it. She had sent a swift reply, a disordered gut response, thanking Roy for all that he had done. She didn't admit that she also loved him: something always held her back from saying it or writing it down, despite discernible feelings. What were unspoken words? she wondered. Did they mean anything if they remained imprisoned in her mind?

Words seemed so vacant suddenly, yet she knew that telling Roy that she loved him would have been a betrayal to Harry. The simple utterance of something she felt deeply changed its value, perhaps. Fine tears had escaped slowly from her eyes when she clicked send for the last time.

She didn't abide by Roy's instructions and wallow in sorrow. Roy had been her guide every day for a year and a half, and she knew that she couldn't follow his advice anymore. It was time to find courage and to live again. And so, Jean didn't lie down. Instead, she walked, retracing the route she had taken with Etienne: up the Shankill Road, across Woodvale Road, down the Crumlin Road and back along Snugville Street. By the time she got home, it was eleven o'clock. She went to bed tired and shrouded in a sorrowful peace.

The morning came like nausea. She had gone to the computer to check for a reply. There could be no reply to a final message. She then saw his name, Roy Steen, on each line in her inbox. She shifted down through the emails and caught snippets of his stories about Robert and about their time together, and a searing, throbbing pain dredged up from the pit of her stomach and gathered in her throat like a pill that had not been washed away. She deleted each one, and, as her mouse clicked the tiny boxes, saline swam through her teeth, filling her mouth with the salt of grief. Written words. Were they any less important than spoken words? Were they more powerful than no words at all? What did they mean? It mattered little because they were gone. The time they had both invested in creating them was spent. She was cleaving reality with an axe in order to find some honour in a life that lacked truth.

Jean knew that Roy was her missing piece, but Roy affirmed the values that she didn't realise she had. If the restoration of Roy's values had grown from a recollection of the battle for his marriage, then Jean's stemmed from that same source. Her present was suddenly implicated in the secrets of Annie's past. Roy said he had taken away her dilemma, but the choice was still there. She could tell Harry it was over. It was unclear to Jean why she held onto Harry. It wasn't a choice, but an acceptance of unspoken values, the strength of words that had not been formed.

It was time to say goodbye. Hannah was still quiet. Three weeks was the longest period she had ever been away from her daughter, but she knew that Hannah was strong and that she would fight the fear. Jean looked into her daughter's eyes and saw something new. She didn't capture it because Hannah fell right into her arms. Jean was not prepared for the fall, and her hands were still by her side. She slowly placed her hands on her daughter's back and held her while she wept. Jean looked at her again and kissed her on the cheek. Hannah walked away, her body still quivering in the convulsion of emotion that had just poured from it. Jean turned and walked back to the car. She moved swiftly.

Then, alone in the car, she released everything. She released the pain of a farewell to the man who had become her conscience. She drove home with tears flowing down her cheeks, a weight in her head and a conscience like a feather.

LA PAIMPOLAISE

'J'aime Paimpol et sa falaise, son église et son grand Pardon.' The words swept through the cottage like a hearty gust of wind. Etienne's father, Mathieu, sang the soulful ballad in its entirety after dinner. He had been serious up until that point, the patriarch seated at the end of the bulky oak table, but when his voice broke into song, a smile travelled across his face that mirrored the pride of Etienne when he played his cornemuse. The song, *La Paimpolaise*, was a folk song about Paimpol, the town in Brittany where Hannah was to spend the next three weeks of her life. Etienne helped her translate the chorus. 'I love Paimpol and its cliff, its church and Festival of atonement. I particularly love the Paimpol girl, who awaits me in Brittany.' It didn't have much rhythm or indeed meaning in English, but Etienne assured her that it was a special song for his father.

Hannah learned that Mathieu was from Lyon originally and had fallen in love with Elen on a holiday in Brittany. She was his own Paimpolaise. Much like the story of the song, Mathieu would also spend months on end at sea. He worked on an oil rig in the Middle East, where he was due to return before the end of the week. He had been welcoming, but Hannah struggled to decipher his baritone French words and strong accent.

Hannah observed Etienne closely. The confident young man who had cast a spell on Jean and everyone else in Snugville Street with his unconventional dress code and unerring maturity, faded into the background when his father demonstrated his might as the convener of family affairs. Etienne, who was the eldest of the three children, shrank to the size of a sibling, and an orderly hierarchy took shape. Hannah had never been in the presence of such a strong patriarchal figure, and it filled her with fear and admiration in equal measures. She could picture Harry at the dinner table as a child, but she certainly couldn't remember him instilling silence in his children. It was a strange mix of authoritarianism and liberalism as the alternative family dress code of the three children sat parallel to the conventional tradition of their father; a man who was dressed in corduroy trousers and a navy blue shirt, and who demonstrated no taste for African ear adornments. Hannah was sure that his neat grey beard had been sculpted with care.

Etienne's sister was called Kristen. She was fourteen with short spiked hair purposefully bordered with a long purple head scarf. Her ankle length skirt was tie-dyed in a mix of green and purple and her wide brimmed boots were attached with a precariously short lace. The overall look was that of unconventional beauty. Kristen was identical to her father in terms of her wide features and pale face, but she had the grace of her mother's piercing brown eyes. Erwan was eight and Hannah was already convinced she was in love with him. He watched her with adoring brown eyes all the way through dinner. Elen was quiet, but if a smile could have demonstrated the heart of a woman, then Hannah was relieved to be in her presence. She had bobbed dark brown hair, diminutive features and dark skin like Etienne. The bond between Etienne and his mother was tangible. She looked at him with the expression that only a woman with a son possesses. Hannah remembered that same dreamy gaze from her own mother, as though, knowing that her son would one day leave her, she emitted and stored all the love she could there and then.

The children all stood up suddenly and started clearing away the plates. Hannah jumped to attention, recognising her place, and followed Etienne into a small utility room. She looked around and realised that the house didn't have a kitchen. The only evidence that dinner was prepared there was a pot on an old fashioned stove beside the dinner table. The utility room was essentially a larder with a dishwasher and a sink. Hannah took in the full length of the cottage. Etienne had explained that it was three cottages knocked into one. The floor was covered in white tiles, and dotted around the room, were heavy pieces of sombre dark oak furniture. Hannah ran her hand across the intricate detailed wooden carving of a dresser. Elen followed her with her eyes and said, 'It's traditional Breton furniture. It was a big mistake. I hate it now.' It was an invitation into Elen's world, the world of a woman who was eager to discuss something feminine. It was also a welcome change of pace from the deep political questions proffered by her husband at dinner. Mathieu had wanted to know everything about the peace process. Hannah provided him with as much information as she was able to give, but the only summary in her head was that the politicians elected to the Assembly after the Good Friday peace agreement were not easy bedfellows, and that ancient feelings of mistrust did not disappear overnight. The administration of the new devolved assembly had been delayed. That was about as much as Hannah cared to impart. Anything deeper would have taken her into a world that was not hers.

Hannah followed Elen into the living area, and again had a feeling that something was missing in the sparsely decorated and extraordinarily clean and tidy space. She knew that this would be a kind of paradise for Jean, with the exception that there were no soft furnishings. The small square windows set into walls that were at least a foot deep, were unadorned. Hannah continued to look around the room, searching for a centre of focus, but her eyes fell on another small oak table with four chairs. Two more chairs were pulled out from the table and pointed towards a TV. It would have been easy to walk by it and not notice it was there. Hannah realised, then, that what was missing was a sofa, and she marvelled at how the family moved from one set of hard chairs to another.

The end of the room that housed the TV also had a large bookcase and adjoining desk. Breaking from the austere simplicity of the ground floor, the bookcase was a mess of papers, pens and slanted books, books that had the unusual frayed appearance of having been read. Etienne switched on the TV and pulled out a wooden chair. Hannah thought about Shelley, slouched across their tiny sofa on Snugville Street with her gigantuan limbs, and wondered how she would exist in Etienne's oak-surfaced world. Connecting the two names in her head reminded her of the confrontation she had planned to have with Etienne about the poem for her sister, but the circumstances of the world she was now in dictated that any such encounter with Etienne would be impolite and completely unnecessary. Here, in his own home, under the custody of his father, Etienne was the same age as Shelley, and therefore no longer breached the code of conduct that had given Hannah such cause for concern when the adult version of Etienne had slept under the same roof as her sister. He hadn't even had a glass of wine with dinner. Hannah noted that neither she nor Etienne were offered one. Mathieu was the only person drinking.

Etienne turned towards Hannah and spoke in French, as he had done since her arrival at the train station in Rennes that afternoon. It was unusual to hear him speak in his own language and it transformed his personality from a deep philosopher to an ordinary boy, 'Hannah, I know you are tired, but tonight there is a fest noz,' he said. Switching to English, he added, 'How do you say it? Festival of the night?' Etienne explained that it was a traditional Breton festival. Hannah felt energised despite the long day of travelling, and was keen to go. Mathieu warned that the car park would be busy and that they should leave soon, and so it was agreed that fifteen minutes would suffice for Hannah to settle in and get ready.

Fifteen minutes was not achievable by any sense of the imagination. Hannah could transform herself speedily for a night out in Belfast, but this was out of the question. She went to her room and measured up what sacrifices would have to be made. Firstly, her fake tan would not work out under so much pressure. It was best applied in advance, so she would wear her new jeans. Secondly, she had no time for a shower. Slightly troubled by the idea of leaving the house without her usual fastidious attention to smooth legs and underarms, she resolved to keep her arms down for the remainder of the evening and selected a shimmery top and matching diamante sandals. She then pulled out her hair straighteners and make-up and set to work. She emerged on time at the top of the stairs to find the entire Ollivier family staring up at her. 'Oh shit' was the only thing she could think of when she realised her error. They all remained in the same clothes as before, and the tilt of their heads told her that the fest noz was not perhaps an occasion for so much sparkle.

The first challenge was getting from the front door into Mathieu's car. It had been raining and the dirt path they had crossed en route to the house that afternoon was now soggy. This was not a good terrain to cross in silver four-inch heels with fine diamante studded straps. Hannah could feel the muck slide through her toes and the heat slice her neck. Etienne had seen her dressed like this many times. Why did he not tell her? Her heart was beating fast and a rising state of mortification was tempered by the kindness of Kristen. 'I love your shoes. They are amazing!' Her words seemed genuine and at odds with her boots, boots the likes of which Hannah had not seen since her dad worked in the shipyards. Etienne then turned and smiled, 'You look nice. I think my friends will like you.' Hannah felt her head twitch like her mother and completely rejected this compliment under the part of her brain that assigned Etienne to brotherly love. Her words bounded from that same part of her brain in English, 'Flip me, Etienne, is there a full moon?' Etienne provided a translation and Elen, who was seated in the front, laughed. Erwan, who could not resist joining the tail end of every conversation, spoke next. 'Je pense qu'Ana est très belle.' Hannah turned to the little boy in the back set of the people carrier and promised that she would marry him one day. This elicited a smile from Mathieu and a stream of laughter from Elen.

The fest noz destination was inconsistent with the vision in Hannah's mind. She was expecting a pub in the town centre and she had been keen to see the town. Instead, they seemed to be moving deeper into the countryside. Etienne explained, 'It's in Plouha.' They arrived at an old stone building and again Hannah struggled through the muck. Inside, the hall was brightly lit and packed with people. Hannah had never been to a party that comprised so many generations. The first person she noted was an elderly lady, who was dressed in a long black dress that belonged in photographs she had seen of the Shankill in the early 1900s. She looked to be about ninety-nine. Then there were children milling around the dance floor, all similarly dressed in dark jeans and t-shirts, and almost completely impossible to identify by gender due to the length of their hair. One girl stood out from the crowd owing to her pink tiara. Hannah felt relief and a sudden affinity with the girl. She smiled when she realised it was a boy.

Etienne kissed everyone in sight and talked animately to his friends. Clearly he had not seen them since his visit to Ireland and they were eager to find out details of his Lira crusade. Hannah was then assailed by kisses. After greeting four friends of Etienne and concurrently imparting and receiving sixteen kisses, Hannah felt exhausted.

An elongated note from the stage signalled the start of something, and children and adults moved onto the floor, forming a circle. This, according to Etienne, who was smiling and keen to share his culture, was the *An Dro*. The musical introduction gave Hannah time to digest the kaleidoscope of tie-dye skirts and floating scarves on the girls, and she feared, suddenly, that she was about to be thrown into a situation that might jeopardise her health and safety in her high heels. Her hands were raised by Etienne to her right and an unknown man, or possibly boy with long hair and beard, to the left. They each linked Hannah's little fingers with their own. She felt exposed by the lack of grip and wondered how on earth they would stay together with such an inconsequential join. Her arms were suddenly being circled up and then back down in the opposing direction. The movement of the feet was simple and it didn't take long to catch the slow rhythm. A wooden instrument, similar to a recorder, emitted a soft tune that bobbed up and down as the circle moved to the left like a restrained cogwheel. A clamour of horns and pipes then followed, as the music built up and the pace quickened. Memories of her dancing years flooded Hannah's body with nostalgia, and she joined the spirit of Etienne and an entire hall full of strangers in dance.

The lights were dimmed and condensation started to appear at the windows as heat infused the room. The ninety-nine year old woman, who assumed the role of dancing elder, had a most serious face. Hannah felt she needed to keep in tune with the music for this woman alone.

Etienne explained that the next dance was the *Gavotte*. It was a slow circular dance and Hannah slotted into its rhythm with ease. She was incredulous that her social life had moved so seamlessly from Belfast's new revived city centre, to what felt like an ancient pagan ritual, as women and men linked arms in tight circles and stepped from left to right in chugging movements. The rhythm accelerated for the next dance and Hannah spun around the dance floor with Etienne in teacups. The natural faces around her were radiant in sweat. Her concerns about raising her arms were soon allayed when she recognised that wild shrubs sprouted in a rather unassuming way from many of the girls around her. Etienne was smiling, and as he pulled her around the dance floor, she could see that he did not expect her stamina and footwork. Irish dancing steps had been so much more intricate, and it was difficult not to fall into a pattern of Irish dance as the music rose to the tempo of a jig. She smiled at the thoughts that an

Irish ceilidh might ever permeate the social lives of Belfast's teenagers. Her friends would be busy downing shots and dancing in tune to deafening music in one of Belfast's shiny new nightclubs, all dolled up to the nines in short skirts and high heels.

Hannah saw around her an ethereal happiness in dance and music, and experienced a discernible internal peace that came with dancing freely in such a large commune of joined hands. When the music stopped, she watched and wondered if the people of Brittany had always been this united.

***

'You want to what?' Jean turned from the sink and assessed her husband.

'It's only an uphill walk.'

'You want to go hiking up the Black Mountain?'

'Yes.'

'You and me?'

'Yes, Jean, you and me.' Harry was smiling.

Jean had her left hand on her left hip and her head tilted to the same side. 'What for?' she asked.

'It'll be good for the soul!'

'Good for the what?'

'*The soul,*' Harry repeated.

'I'll tell you what it'll be... It'll be wet!' Jean exclaimed.

'Trust me, you'll enjoy it.'

'Jesus, Harry, if you're not cooking fancy Italian meals, you're wanting to travel up mountains. Next, you'll be taking me to Paris.'

Harry laughed. 'That would be lovely, but...'

'But we can't afford it.' Jean said.

'We will soon,' Harry responded. 'First we need to go to Holland.'

Jean felt the blood pump in her cheeks.

Harry continued, 'I want to see where Robert lived, where he spent his last days.'

Jean recomposed herself. 'Oh. Of course you do...of course.'

'We'll see how this job works out.' His eyes flicked away from Jean.

Jean sensed his unease at the prospect of working in the factory. It was a temporary contract with an agency, and although she knew that he was grateful to have found any kind of work, something was irking him about the job. Jean suspected it was the idea of being on a production line after the wide open spaces of the shipyards. 'You were lucky, you know. You shouldn't complain. You'll be working again by the end of the summer.'

Harry scrunched his hands. 'Yes, I know. I don't like the idea of these agencies. They can lay you off at any time. My grandfather would turn in his grave.'

'What's your grandfather got to do with it?' Jean asked.

'He was one of the men who led shipyard workers in the Docker's strike in 1907.'

'The what?'

'I read about it in prison. I knew he was involved, but I didn't know what he'd done. You know, everyone was involved in that strike. Everyone. Catholics and Protestants. The police even mutinied against the British army. If the Troubles hadn't...'

'Harry, love, don't talk about the Troubles. Nobody wants to go over all that again.'

'I'm just saying that there was a fight that working class people could have had together, but instead they turned against each other.'

'I know, but sure it all worked out. That lovely generator factory will be a sight cleaner than the shipyards used to be. You'll be working less hours too. The unions got their way in the end.'

'But these temporary contracts. It's not right. You work day to day. You don't have any security. I know I don't deserve any, but what about the young men who are leaving school. They have no rights.'

'You served your sentence. If there's one thing that I know, it's that you served your sentence! So yes, you do have rights. Don't ever forget that! Anyway, enough of all this nonsense. There's a mountain calling out for a pair of auld hillbillies. I'll get my walking shoes on.'

Harry had been home for two weeks, yet Jean noted that he had already taken over the driving seat. It was a strange, but reassuring division of labour. They hadn't had a car for long before Harry's arrest, so Jean had rarely experienced the feeling of security that now came with being in the passenger seat beside Harry. In the short period of time they had spent together, some habits reformed automatically. Others retained a chilling strain.

Going to bed had been the first struggle. The presence of Etienne had removed any debate. Harry walked straight into their room, but through the night he got up and down and moved around the house like a thief. The intimacy of being in the same bed, albeit at opposite sides, had been too much of a leap. After Etienne had gone, Jean stayed up late each night and slept in Robert's bed. The unexpected consequence of Harry's presence was that Jean did not collapse in a ball of internal pain at night. She went to bed and slept.

Jean watched Harry's hands move around the steering wheel. She had yet to touch them, but they looked less coarse than when he had worked at the shipyards. His entire body seemed more trim and less bulky, but he retained his strength and breadth and was visibly cramped in the 105. They drove up the Divis Road in silence.

The August weather was unpredictable, but there wasn't a cloud in the sky at the foothills. The wind uprooted Jean's short hair in the carpark when she got out of the car. She raised her pink hoodie to cover her hair and looked around at a telecommunications mast and a barren landscape, not feeling immediately instilled with anything soulful, but avoiding any commentary on the fact. She pulled a raincoat free from its pocket-sized cover and looked at her husband. It was the first time she had looked at him properly since his return. She had always found a way of averting her gaze from him. The wind cut across his thinning hair, revealing a slightly receding hairline, but his long features and blue eyes were striking. He looked well. She could see the outline of a muscular torso when his t-shirt clung to his chest in the wind. 'You're not looking too bad for an auld fella of fifty.'

Harry's chest bulged and shoulders expanded. 'You're looking well yourself, young thing.' He was smiling.

Harry took Jean's hand and an army of emotions marched over her mind in time to their footsteps. Holding Harry's hand was like quashing the missing piece, yet she was also reminded of the guilt she had sometimes felt when she had held Roy's hand. She silenced the thoughts and walked on.

They started to rise up towards Divis mountain. Jean stopped and took in a view that she hadn't seen since she was a child. To the right was Belfast, laid open like the centre page of a book. It was a beautiful book with raw edges and torn pages. Set against a turquoise sea, it was a story of industry, from the twin yellow cranes of the old shipyards to the growing sprawl of mammoth aluminium sheds. It was a book covered in markings and scribbles, with characters that bounded off the page and walked into your sleep. Jean's eyes crossed the city centre and back to West Belfast, where the Shankill lay nestled beyond the foothills. She sighed as she considered that it was a book that the people of Belfast had forgotten to read from beginning to end, as they pored over the last few chapters and erased the parts that made them feel uncomfortable. Politicians and romantics on every corner of the city had tried to re-write it to suit their own cloudy memories of the past, but here on Divis, Jean could see the truth etched in the soil and the sludge reclaimed from the sea. This was Jean's home and the sense of belonging caught her in the neck like the wind that was now cutting across the long grass. This was a people's Belfast, with no demarcations of Irish and British, no coloured kerbstones to mark out Protestant or Catholic and no symbols of violence and politics. It was an open book and an invitation to read.

To the left, the housing estates of Greater Belfast sprawled out underneath the hills like paint spilling from a tin into the sea. Her eyes travelled back up the hill to boggy fields that were yellow with toughened grass and gorse. She looked at Harry and spoke, 'We used to take our

Sunday school trips up here. It never felt that spectacular back then, but I remember the yellow cranes and the sea.'

'It's the first time I've been,' said Harry. 'I spent forty years knowing it was there and the minute I was on the inside I started dreaming of this. I wanted to see this.'

'Did you not go with Sunday school?' Jean asked.

'No, we went to Bangor for ice-cream on the train and I only remember going once.'

'That was probably better fun for a child, but I'm glad you brought me here today,' Jean said.

'We're only half way up Divis. Get your ass in gear Suzi.'

Jean laughed at the Suzi reference. It had been many years since she'd heard it. She'd had a Suzi Quatro mullet and tight leather jacket when she met Harry in 1975. Harry always referred to her as Suzi when they first started going to the clubs together. At the age of twenty, her slight body and skinny legs were always covered in leather. Jean smiled thinking about Hannah and her high shoes. She too had tried hard to compensate for her vertical dimensions with platform shoes that were of an industrial scale in being noticed.

Jean realised that this day out with Harry was the nearest thing to a date that they'd had since the Suzi Quatro days. It was easier to talk to Harry while walking, and in the seventies, they had always been walking. In the house, she had found it impossible to connect with him. She wondered now if that had always been the case.

They reached the top of Divis and walked around the marker at the summit. Jean squinted into the sun and was consumed by the ferocious beauty around her. 'Put your hood up again Suzi! said Harry as they walked back down the hill. 'The Black Mountain won't be so kind.'

'How do you know?' asked Jean. This version of Harry was at once a curiosity and a nuisance. He knew something about everything, and Jean felt her level of expertise in life diminish in his presence, even though she had been living freely for nine and a half years, while he had been dreaming of the world outside.

'Have you ever looked up at the Black Mountain and not seen a cloud?' asked Harry.

'Sure there isn't a cloud in the sky!'

'Don't say I didn't warn you!'

They walked for about a mile before commencing the gentle climb up the slopes of the Black Mountain. Despite the hard terrain elsewhere in the heat of summer, the bogland on the Black Mountain was soft and sludgy. The wind started to tug Jean's hood against her neck and her feet began to sink. The higher they climbed, the less easy it was to speak. A soft drizzle settled about them and Jean inhaled its moist dew. Harry was ahead of her now. Jean watched his long agile limbs and thought of Roy.

Why was she thinking of Roy again?

He revealed himself to her as the mist fell around her, yet he had been hidden to her in the bright sunshine. She tried hard to push him out of her mind. Roy had lost a leg in a bomb as a young man and his walk was similar to Shelley's. Harry walked with ease, as though his body had been preparing for this trek all of his life.

They reached the summit and an impenetrable cloud wrapped around them as the sky darkened. It was as sudden as that. Decisions made in the sky by swift clouds seemed contrary to the flow of nature and of time. Jean looked back towards Divis. It was still set in a sweep of yellow sun, yet there was no Belfast below the Black Mountain. They walked on in relative darkness to a peak marked out by a stone well. The wind puffed up into a fury; the rain seeped through her trousers; and Jean looked up to find that the sky now mirrored their terrain with its own mountain range of brooding clouds. Giant hexagonal shafts of light bounded towards her face and then disappeared. Jean held out her hand and tried to touch one. It was gone before her hand was raised. She wondered if ancient people had seen this same mysterious shift in nature, a pagan people who marked out life in light.

'I'm sorry.' It was Harry. Jean turned to him and saw tears disguised as rain on his face.

Jean nodded. She knew he was sorry. She had always known. She turned away.

'Jean, I am sorry for what I did...'

'You served your time.'

'I wasn't talking about the...about the murder. I'm sorry for it too, but I meant...'

'I wasn't talking about the murder either,' Jean replied, still facing the rain.

Jean's mind was stone again as the idea of it lingered in the air, the idea of Harry being in love, the idea that they had never discussed it. The hurt that had been stowed away in an unearthed memory was now travelling through Jean like the black clouds that passed through the Black Mountain with such haste. It was there beside them both now, the unspoken shame of Harry's past, only this time she could touch it. It was no longer locked up in a prison. It was there, sitting in the mist. Harry had loved Linda and it had hurt.

Jean had seen her in the bank. She had walked right up to her and watched. She didn't tell Linda who she was, but she looked at her for a while. She listened to her voice as the other clients stopped with her. She watched her body move across the room and something that had never mattered, suddenly did, something inconsequential when she thought of Roy. Jean had often wondered in her younger days if nature had been working against her relationship with Harry on account of the vast difference in their height. When she saw this tall, blonde woman, she could picture them together. She could picture Harry and Linda walking, two equal bodies holding hands and kissing.

Jean's eyes started to fill as the hurt evaporated through the pores of her wet skin. There was silence and they both allowed the wind to consume them. Harry was still facing the black curtain of Belfast. He placed his arm around Jean's shoulder and pulled her close. She stepped to the side. She froze, but she warmed again with the movement of the shards of piercing light in the sky, diamond shapes now appearing and instantly diffusing.

'I'm sorry too.' She didn't face him.

'You don't have anything to be sor...'

'I do. I...do,' said Jean.

The noise of the wind was a distraction from a conversation Jean was now having using only her voice. Her dark thoughts about Harry, once locked away, were now free and dispersing into a spray of vapor. She could speak now.

'I met someone else.'

Harry didn't move. He didn't speak or look in Jean's direction. Jean could see from the corner of her eye that he too was immersed in the sky.

'When?' he asked.

'It doesn't matter.'

'Who then? Who?'

'You don't know him.'

'Did you...' Harry's voice had started to break.

Jean could hear the strain and it sounded like a man whose hope was drowning. She stared at a bright white light.

'Did I sleep with him?' Jean turned to Harry and found him with his head lowered. 'You don't get to ask me that,' she said. 'I never spoke about....'

'No...did you love him?' Harry asked.

Harry was crying. Jean had seen him cry before. She reached for his hand again and held onto it. They remained unmoving for a protracted time. She gave Harry time. She could see him crying by her side as his mother was laid to rest. Two years later, he had held her and cried into her hair as he helplessly watched his baby girl fight for survival after the bomb. And she could see him heave in pain in a prison when she looked into his eyes and told him that his son had died. Now, she could count four times when her husband had cried like blood.

The light was moving down the hill. The mist cleared swiftly as tears dried and Belfast emerged.

Harry took a deep breath. 'It does that. I heard it does that.'

'What?'

'The mist. I heard it clears just as quick as...'

'Oh.' Jean was relieved. The conversation was over. She hoped that it was over. She looked behind Harry and saw the fine line of a rainbow form a wisp of an arc. Its rays rose from the stone well on the ridge. They both walked towards it. Harry's hand was warmer now, his grip strong.

'It's beautiful.' Jean wasn't sure if she had said it aloud, but she knew that Harry had heard it. He nodded. The colours of the rainbow deepened, forming a wide arc from the stone well over the North of the city. Harry's eyes were fixed on the same spot as Jean's. They sat on the well together, Harry with his arm around his wife. The wind eased and they could hear the still rain again. 'Let's go,' Jean said as she stood up and reached for Harry's hand. They walked hand-in-hand over the rough terrain. Jean spoke, without turning to Harry. 'I missed you too.' Harry pulled Jean back. He held her tight against his body.

Jean still did not know how she felt about Harry, but she knew that his arms were strong and she needed him to hold her. He reached down to kiss her. She thought of being at home again, where a few miles turned into time and distance all at once. She thought of Snugville Street and of Harry in the living room as she turned away from the kiss. She slowly released herself from Harry's grip and moved back down the hill.

***

Hannah walked behind Etienne. They crossed country roads with wild flowers sprouting from hedgerows, and passed fields undulating with neat rows of cauliflower bursting with unkempt green leaves. It was a change from the dense verdant landscape to which Hannah was accustomed. The countryside felt lighter; less shaded than home. They passed the Rue de Pen an Run, with its dogs running free and gardens bustling with pink and purple hydrangea, before descending into the town, making their way through the increasingly narrow streets of Paimpol.

'There are more people around today,' observed Hannah.

'It's the Festival du Chant de Marin. It's busy. Like the Twelfth.'

'Like the Twelfth. You didn't enjoy it, did you?' asked Hannah.

'It was interesting. I told you. It was an education.'

They were shoulder to shoulder on the narrow cobbled Rue de l'Église when Etienne asked, 'How is Shelley?'

Hannah smiled. 'You must know better than me!'

'Why so?'

'Oh Etienne. Don't be shy! I know.'

Etienne slowed his pace. 'What do you know?'

'I know that you sent her poetry!'

'Ah!'

'Yes, ah...Why?' asked Hannah.

'It was a special poem for Shelley. About poppies.'

'Poppies?' Hannah thought for a moment and then closed her eyes as her mind rested on a door marked with a wreath. She swallowed. She hadn't recognised the word 'les pavots' and hadn't had the sense to look it up in the dictionary before she launched a tirade of abuse at her sister.

'Did you see the poem?' Etienne asked.

'Yes, I did.' She hesitated, 'Actually, there was a bit of an accident.'

Etienne raised his eyes in admonition. 'You say accident. Shelley said you did it on purpose!'

'She told you?' Hannah exclaimed, and lost the reserve she had practiced so well in the Ollivier household.

Etienne laughed. 'Yes, she said you are crazy. I think you are too.'

'Thanks for that!' said Hannah.

'Shelley, I like.'

'No way. Really?' Hannah was smiling now too.

'I detect sarcasm. I would like to return to Belfast to see her.' Etienne said.

'Jean would welcome you with open arms.'

'Jean is beautiful,' smiled Etienne.

'*Oh la vache!*' said Hannah. Erwan had taught her the phrase on her first night in France. It meant, 'Oh cow' and Hannah assumed it to be a polite alternative to an expletive. It amused the Ollivier family when she said it, owing to her enthusiastic tone. They had told her that everything she said in French sounded like a song. Hannah continued, 'Is it only me you don't like?'

'I like your father. He's an intelligent man.'

'Intelligent!' Hannah blared.

Etienne looked surprised, unaware perhaps that Hannah was not always the respectful daughter she had been in Mathieu's presence.

'You, my friend. You, are more difficult,' Etienne said plainly.

'Thank you, my friend.' Hannah switched to English. 'You have a way with words.'

Etienne was enjoying the exchange too much. Hannah could sense his feet almost lifting from the paving stones as they reached the harbour. 'Hannah, you are too Bourgeoise.'

'What the hell!' Hannah burst into English again.

Etienne smiled and explained. 'You try to dress like this...' He pointed to her black linen strappy summer dress and two inch wedges.

Hannah liked her dress. It was a day dress for wearing to the beach and completely inoffensive given that they had planned to walk to a beach. It was not bourgeois and she was not following any trends. Heat was now rising through her cheeks. 'You think I'm too middle class? Did you not just spend three weeks on the Shankill Road?' she said.

'But why do you try to be different from your people?' Etienne asked, again disguising any emotion.

'My people? Etienne, can I ask, who do you think my people are?'

'Your neighbours? You are not like them.'

'Would you prefer me in a Nike tracksuit or wrapped up in a union jack flag? The people on Snugville Street are not all the same and they're not caricatures.' Hannah looked into Etienne's eyes sternly as she spoke.

Etienne laughed this time and replied in the most French Belfast accent Hannah had ever heard. 'I'm winding you up, love.' It was a phrase that Jean had taught him.

Hannah punched him lightly on the arm. 'What's the plan for tonight then? More boring Fest Noz?'

'Do you not like them?' Etienne's eyes were pained.

'I do,' Hannah smiled. 'I'm winding you up.' She added 'so I am' with a wink in reference to another one of Jean's English lessons.

They reached the harbour and the tide of people continued to grow. Mathieu had already shown Hannah the quiet port of Paimpol with its oily fishing boats moored on the water. He had narrated ancient stories of men lost at sea, real stories that didn't concern a cliff or a church. Hannah remembered the song, *La Paimpolaise*. The cliff, it transpired, mirrored the soul of art, and existed on the outskirts of Paimpol and on the perimeter of truth. It was a convenient cliff, chosen by a songwriter searching for a word to rhyme with 'falaise.'

The port was filled the scent of petrol and salt. Coloured bunting was hooked from one boat to the next and music poured from speakers. Hannah stopped and listened to one of the bands. She realised then that *La Paimpolaise* was Mathieu's song, and not Paimpol's. It was not the song of this celtic people. The hearty tunes spilling from boats of the Festival du Chant de Marin were from men who raised their glasses as their voices soared like waves. Hannah couldn't understand a word, but she could sense the swell of a perilous sea through tempestuous baritone notes and elongated vowels as men sang in harmony on the decks of Paimpol.

***

Shelley was reading at the table and enjoying the new culinary fragrances that filtered through the kitchen. The kitchen now smelled less like a farmhouse and more like a continental market. She looked up to her dad, 'Remember Mrs McAdam said our family is French, well she said it was our great granny Sally who told her.'

'Is that so?' said Harry, tasting a scoop of the risotto he had prepared.

'Apparently they'd had money and had to move here.'

'Money indeed,' smiled Harry. 'I don't think your mum's side ever had money.'

'Mrs McAdam said they lost everything. She said she heard Sally and her mum discuss it one day.' Shelley explained.

'I wonder if she's maybe doting,' said Harry.

'Mrs McAdam's memory is as clear as a whistle if it happened before 1940. She said Granny Sally was poor, but educated. That's all she knows.

'Well, there were French people in Ireland, but it was a long time ago. Anyway, your mum has never said anything.'

'I don't think Granny Anna ever told her. What were French people doing here? Shelley asked.

Her dad stopped what he was doing and turned around, 'They were called Huguenots. They were Protestants. They left France in the seventeenth century. More than two hundred thousand of them fled after they lost their religious liberty. Quite a few came here. Some of them set up linen mills. I know they were in Lisburn, but I'm not sure if there were any in Belfast.'

'How do you know all this stuff?' Shelley asked.

'I had a lot of time to read, Shelley, love. I read everything there was to read about Irish history.'

Shelley looked at her hands. She hadn't asked her dad anything about prison since he'd come home.

'Dad, do you miss it?'

Shelley saw Harry's cheeks redden. He pulled up a seat and sat beside her. 'Do I miss prison?'

'Yes.' Shelley confirmed.

Her dad seemed unable to reply. Shelley wanted to speak and change the subject back to the Huguenots again, but she waited and watched.

'Shelley, only you could think of asking me that. You're a thoughtful girl, do you know that? I hated being there away from you all, but yet...in a way, I do miss it. Maybe it was the routine of it, but I'm sure I'll find a new routine eventually. I spent the entire time praying to get out and I dreamed of all the things I would do. I imagined life would be a certain way, I suppose.'

'And is it how you imagined?'

Harry stood up and walked to the cooker. He turned off the risotto and returned to Shelley. 'I imagined this. I imagined people talking to me about what it was like.'

Shelley looked into her dad's eyes. He had fine wrinkles around pale eyelids. If his watery blue eyes could speak, Shelley assumed they would do so quietly. His voice was strong, but his eyes were tranquil.

'I thought someone might want to know what it was like. No one wants to talk about it. No one talks about anything anymore, Shelley. People don't talk about the past or the Troubles. I've noticed that since I got out.'

'But why would you want anyone to talk about the Troubles? It's over.'

'It's not over, love. Look around you. Look at the state of the Shankill.

It might be over if you managed to escape this, but we're here aren't we? And people need to talk about what happened.'

'Did you talk about it...in prison?'

'Yes, I did. I helped...' He coughed and cleared his throat. 'After Robert died, I mentored some young boys who were in trouble. I talked about what I did and I told them the truth. I've never talked about it with you Shelley, and I want you to know that I'm sorry for what I did to that man and his family. I'm sorry for what I did to our own family. I'm sorry about Robert and about you. You were just a little girl and I left you...I left all of you.'

'I used to have bad dreams that you'd...Never mind, it's silly. Tell me more about the French people.'

'No, what were the dreams about? Did you dream about the bomb?' her dad asked.

'No. I kept dreaming that you were dead.'

Shelley felt her dad's strong arm around her. He kissed her head. 'I'm home now, Shelley. It's going to be okay.'

'Will those men not try to get you back for what you did? They know where you live.'

'I don't think so. All those people who got out of jail early as part of the peace deal are walking the streets,' he said.

'People are still getting shot though.'

'Shelley, I feel bad enough that I took away so much of your childhood. Don't worry about me now. It's time to enjoy yourself. You're at that age now...you'll be meeting boys and...' Harry's voice faded.

Shelley felt her cheeks burn with embarrassment in place of the sadness that had filled them only moments before. She sat back in her chair, and lifted her dad's arm from her shoulder. 'You don't want to talk about that,' she smiled.

'No, I don't. You're right. Shelley, if you meet someone, don't be scared to bring him home. Don't be ashamed.'

'Why would I be asham...Dad, I'm not ashamed. I remember the blood, you know. At least, I remember it now. I had forgotten to think about it until Etienne talked to me, and then I saw bits of it and I saw blood. You were my dad and I was bleeding. I know why you did what you did. It was wrong, but I understand.' She breathed deeply and looked at her dad's eyes, 'I still have the shoe, from my good foot. Mum kept it. I'll show it to you. I looked at it to make myself remember. I don't want to forget now.'

'You shouldn't live in the past, Shelley, but it's good to remember. It's nice to stop by the memorial and pay your respects. I'll come with you next time.'

Shelley watched her dad return to his cooking. She had thought about the seven year-old girl who died in the bomb frequently since Etienne had left. She'd only ever seen one picture of her and she recalled her smile and long brown hair tied up in a white bow. Etienne had left her with a kiss and an image of a little girl at peace in a bed of red flowers. He had revived a memory that had started to drift into the place where childhood memories disappear. Shelley knew that it was easier to push the memories away, but they didn't perish and they didn't sleep. They stayed in the back of the mind like guilt. Shelley realised that her dad was right: no one talked about the Troubles anymore. It made people feel uncomfortable. Memories were suppressed because of the guilt and the shame.

***

Mathieu had been gone a full week and the Ollivier home had lost its balance. The children were now in charge and laughter lapsed into anarchy. Upturned books lay on the floor; siblings slouched on blankets and cushions on cold tiles; and clothes and coats were strewn across seats. They were no longer penned in.

'Why don't you drink when your dad's here?' Hannah asked, enlivened by the anticipation of another debate with Etienne.

Etienne blushed. It was the first time Hannah had seen him embarrassed since the day that Jean had unravelled his ear fashions.

'I think you know why,' Etienne replied flatly.

'You're not allowed to drink, are you?'

'Not entirely.'

'Etienne! Jean will go mad! She allowed you to drink wine because she thought that's what French people do.'

'You don't need to tell her. Let her believe it,' said Etienne with a shrug.

'But you could've got her into trouble. Imagine something had happened! You could've ended up in hospital getting your stomach pumped.'

'Hannah, Hannah, always so serious. Relax. Mum lets us drink when dad's away. Actually, she says no too, but she doesn't complain when we come home from the fest noz drunk. Enjoy yourself. You're on holiday.'

Hannah felt nervous in the freedom that had resulted from Mathieu's departure. Jean had set few boundaries and little discipline, and it had resulted in a self-imposed confinement for Hannah. She'd built up her own concrete walls over the years and established her own rules. Hannah had made every decision by herself since the age of eleven. She realised that Etienne had experienced a different type of liberty. His was the freedom to think. Hannah rarely had time for that. Thinking deeply about the state of the world was something that happened when parents took care of all your material and emotional needs. Etienne was a thinker because he didn't need to worry about paying for anything.

'I miss your dad,' said Hannah, surprised by her own words.

'He's good...in small doses. We miss him too.'

'You're lucky, you...' Hannah stopped, realising what she was about to reveal.

'You can tell me...'

Hannah, unnerved suddenly, cut across Etienne. 'What has Shelley said?'

'Shelley said that it's up to you to tell me about your dad. Look, my English isn't as bad as it might seem. I did hear the word prison. Sometimes your mum talks fast, but I heard that word. I know an Irish guy here in Brittany whose father was in prison too, so it isn't a big deal. Your country was at war for thirty years. It's understandable.'

Understandable. Nothing could have been further from the truth. Nothing was understandable in the country in which Hannah had been raised. She hated all of it, all the politics, all the nonsense. It never seemed to end. Even in so-called peace, the horrors of Northern Ireland's past seemed to live on. Why couldn't people stop talking about it? Was the violence the only thing that people abroad knew about her country?

'Etienne, Shelley can talk to you about it if she wants. I'm tired of the whole thing. I find it hard. My dad did an awful thing. He was in jail for a long time and I'm sorry that the timing of the exchange...I didn't think he'd be home until Christmas and I...'

'Hey, don't apologise. I'm glad he came home when he did. It's a shame I didn't get to spend more time with him, like you did with my dad. You enjoyed his stories, didn't you?'

'Yes, I did.' Hannah smiled. Mathieu had made her feel special. He had driven her around the sites of Paimpol in the company of a quiet Etienne, who gazed out the window in the back of the car and listened, forming his own unshackled world in the silence. Mathieu had showed her the Côte de Granit Rose, a terracotta-pink hued stone coastline. She had marvelled at rocks that were shaped like impressionistic lumps of humans gathered together in lines and in circles, bodies both upright and flat, rocks entwined like lovers and smoothed by the savage elements and wild sea, but it was Mathieu's voice that had enthralled her. Mathieu had explained the history of the place with a passion that belied his origins. 'The Bretons are a Celtic people, just like you. They came here from the big Britain over the sea, La Grande Bretagne,' he had said.

His voice had become animated when he retold a mythical story of Welsh settlers slicing the tongues of native wives to preserve the language they had brought to the land. The preservation of language was all about the place, Hannah realised. Mathieu had checked to see who was listening and whispered to Hannah, 'The Breton language was pushed out by Brittany's own ruling elite before the French got their hands on it. Latin was the language of scholars, not Breton.' He had smiled and looked over

91

at Elen as he spoke. Elen was a primary school teacher in a Breton language school and her involvement in the Breton revival seemed to amuse Mathieu as much as it impressed him. Mathieu's whisper made Hannah think about identity and how it was created as much as it evolved: it was a shoring up of borrowed memories, false memories, emotional memories and memories that change like the sea.

'I should say that I also like your mum and dad...and your siblings. You are the difficult one,' Hannah said with a smile.

Etienne, who was lounging on the floor, lifted a cushion from below his head and propelled it at Hannah.

***

Harry was told to start sweeping. There was nothing to sweep. The concrete factory floor was gleaming like cool ice. He locked eyes with the young foreman, silently seeking an explanation.

'We stick to the schedule,' said the foreman.

He had been purposefully welding a generator box for most of the day, and half an hour before the end of his shift, he had been handed the brush and told to down tools. Every task in the factory was timed to the last second and Harry hadn't understood the pace.

The last half hour dragged and Harry realised he was tired. He was tired, not from any physical strain, but from the repetition. This was an endless routine for the men who worked alongside him, the men who had been there for nine and a half years. They moved in the still world of their headphones, drowning out their own thoughts, their minds fixed on the continual join of metal.

The box that Harry was building was similar in its dimensions to his cell. It was more constrained, in some ways, with the noise of cut metal and the endless health and safety regulations. He had only been welding for one day, but he knew what time looked like from this angle.

Harry was in prison again; yet he was free.

He was free because he was contributing to his family, to the economy, to his country. His aching arms that had practised so hard in the gym in the artificial confines of habit, were now creating something: a machine that would power the creation of glass monuments in the opaque skies of China; a machine that would power hospital machinery in disaster zones; a machine that would power his mind into believing that he could once again leave his mark on the world.

Harry thought about the shipyard where he had worked for twenty-five years. The job had been dirty, and the camaraderie had been fierce and had tested him as a young apprentice. Harry knew that there had been nothing romantic about the weightlessness of limbs that had been stretched and scorched and consumed in showers of fire. There had been nothing

92

utopian about coughing up a chest full of metal dust. The prize in the shipyard was knowing that he had made a small part of something that was colossal in its utility and its worth. Watching a finished ship roll away from a dry dock was inspiring, but didn't happen often enough to keep the mind alive each day. Achievement in the shipyard had come in small tokens and Harry knew that men needed small tokens of achievement to survive.

He held the brush and moved it back and forth. Sweeping the clean concrete served as a reminder of the futility of his life for nine and a half years.

Harry resolved to not slow down his work the following day. He would continue at the same pace. And then he would sweep until the end of his shift. He would sweep needlessly and remind himself of the beauty and the worth of the showers of fire as two swathes of metal became one. He would sweep and remind himself that this was his freedom.

***

Another Fest Noz, this time in a nearby fishing village. Hannah was surrounded by the Ollivier family and a table of drinks.

'C'est mieux!' said Etienne as he sat down beside her at the table, eyeing her hair.

Hannah was now careful to ensure that she appeared natural and understated, but she had continued to wear her hair straight until this, her last night. She fluffed her natural curls with her hands and said, 'I'm glad you like it. I copied you.'

Elen laughed, 'She's right, you know. You have the same hair now.'

They were joined by Gildas, a fisherman and friend of Mathieu, who had shown Hannah how to cook lobster. She had closed her eyes as the clawing lobster was immersed in the boiling pot. The entire experience had put her off eating it until Elen pointed out that the sweet white fleshy sea-food she had enjoyed in a restaurant with Mathieu, had, indeed, been lobster. Hannah had never seen a man cook before that summer, and suddenly there was Etienne and his mussels, Harry and his Italian cuisine, and Gildas and his lobster. Hannah's first journey into adulthood was accompanied by a steady ascension of food; boiled spuds steaming out of her life like a distant memory. Gildas didn't speak a word of English and his French was even more incomprehensible than Mathieu's. Hannah had tried hard to converse with him, but settled in the end for smiles and nods as plate after plate of food was laid before her.

'You came', smiled Hannah.

'Yes, I did. I'll stay for an hour. I wanted to say goodbye before you left.' said Gildas.

He explained that traditional dance was not his cup of tea and Hannah wondered for a moment why he had come to say goodbye. She then blushed. Gildas had looked so much older when she had first seen him that she had not considered him to be attractive. Now, as her cheeks burned, it was all she could see.

She relaxed and followed the first few dances from her seat. Elen stayed for a short time with Erwan and Kristen before taking them home, leaving Hannah alone with Gildas. There was nothing in Gildas' appearance that suggested he was a fisherman. Hannah had never met a fisherman, but his face looked too refined to have worked against a wild Breton tide: his tan was the result of an even dust of sun rather than a slap of wind. Etienne's word *'bourgeois'* came to mind as Hannah looked at his smart jeans and navy designer polo shirt. Hannah knew that she could only get away with smiling for so long before he noticed that she didn't understand. It seemed more polite to leave him and to dance.

On the dance floor, Hannah continually found herself beside another man who appeared less conventionally alternative than the others. She was at ease in the heat and sweat radiating from his body as his strong arms led her around the room. She didn't have to reach up as she had when dancing with Etienne. During a lull in the music, she saw him standing at the bar and realised what was different. He was clean-cut, shaved, with short brown hair and his arms were muscular, his walking boots belonging to a hiker and not a Breton man celebrating his individualism. He looked as out of place as Hannah. Dancing resumed and Hannah's dance partner moved in her direction again. She was unsure of his age, guessing that he might be in his early twenties. His face was taut and almost muscular. She bowed her head, realising she had been caught staring. She lost him then.

Hannah waved up at Etienne who was in a trance with his pipes. He smiled and walked to the guitarist at the centre of the band. The dips and ridges of a familiar landscape of music echoed memories of Hannah's past. She danced faster and soon realised she was dancing to the sound of a reel. Her legs lengthened and she raised herself as high onto her toes as was possible in her footwear. She felt her calves tighten and saw Etienne clapping on stage. Everyone moved back. Hannah was dancing solo and a feeling of pleasure buoyed her on to dance the last reel that she had learned at her old dance school. She kicked off her shoes and danced swiftly and accurately and whirled around with complete freedom. Her feet were no longer her own: they had been borrowed by the dance. She stopped when she couldn't remember anymore and bowed. The applause was both embarrassing and intoxicating. Etienne was smiling broadly and clapping with pride, as were all the band members. A memory claimed her confidence and she felt her body and legs weaken. She was dancing on a stage with Shelley after the Shankill bomb. She was holding her sister's hand and supporting her as her new foot trailed behind the other, and a new emotion now entered the foray: she missed home. She missed her sister and she missed Jean.

She moved back to find the fisherman, but he had gone. He hadn't seen her dance. Why did it bother her that he hadn't seen her dance?

Hannah felt exposed and alone after the commune of hands, but she became aware of movement to her left. She looked to the side and saw her dance partner make his way to her table.

'That was great! Would you like a drink?'

He spoke in English, a distinct form of English that, mixed up with the emotions already surfacing through euphoria and drink, made her feel like crying.

'I'm okay for a drink. You should have joined me!'

'No. Two left feet.' He smiled his Belfast smile and sat down. 'Are you the girl with the Ollivier family?'

'I sure am.' Hannah smiled, bemused, yet pleased that he'd heard of her. 'How did you know?'

'Small town. I heard there was an Irish girl coming. What do you think of Brittany?

'I think Brittany is just about the most Irish place I've ever been,' said Hannah.

'Ha! You're not wrong. I worked in a local school when I was at college. The kids used to bring me Irish CDs in all the time. I bloody hate traditional music.'

'You dance well to it for someone who doesn't like it,' smiled Hannah.

'You can't avoid these things.'

'How long have you been here?'

'Too long. I spent a lot of time here as a kid. Then I studied in Rennes and forgot to go home.'

Etienne appeared. His hand was held out to Hannah, 'Come on. Let's dance. Last chance before you go home.'

Hannah took Etienne's hand and followed him, a pang of regret flowing through her as she looked back over her shoulder at her Belfast friend.

'I'll miss you, you know,' Etienne said as he led Hannah around the dancefloor.

'Don't be saying things like that! I'll go home thinking you like me.'

'I don't like you. I can tolerate you, though,' he smiled.

'I can tolerate you too!' Hannah replied.

'Do you like France?' he asked.

'Tonight, I feel like I love France.'

'Tonight, you have too much attention from men,' Etienne said, his smile protective and warm.

'Will you come back here?' he asked.

'I will. I'll bring Shelley next time!'

'You can send Shelley next time and you can stay at home!'

'Not a chance! You will not be alone with my sister until she's eighteen.'

Etienne laughed and moved swiftly around the dancefloor. Hannah's arms were strained. She missed the ease of dancing in the arms of the Belfast man. She looked around for him. Like the fisherman, he was gone.

Hannah felt the darkness stir about the hallway in the Ollivier household, and recalled the French translation for darkness; *les ténèbres*. The word was plural, as though the darkness was more than just a singular black colour, as though it contained life and movement. She walked into the dining area of the open plan space. The movement now combined with heat and low murmurs. Life was in les ténèbres. The sound of a switch clicked behind her. She turned to see Etienne in the illuminated hallway. He was smiling. Hannah turned back and the outline of faces at the far side of the living room became visible.

'Surprise!' There was a chorus of voices and then a flash of light.

Erwan and Kirsten stood at the front of a small party of Etienne and Elen's friends. Hannah held her hands up to her face and looked at Elen, who placed her arms around Hannah and said, 'You didn't think you'd leave without a party for your eighteenth birthday?' Hannah's heels now began to work with gravity as her legs trembled. She wanted to call Jean straight away and tell her about the party, the party that hadn't even happened yet. Hannah knew it was already a success due to the fact that someone had thought of it in the first place. She also knew that it was a success when she realised that seated at Mathieu's place at the table, was the quiet fisherman who had disappeared from the Fest Noz.

By one in the morning, only four of the party remained: Etienne, Gildas, Martin from the band and Nicolas, a friend of Etienne's. It was the first time Hannah had met Nicolas. He was a spectacle of yellow from his hair to his toenails with peroxide hair, a tongue piercing like a dagger, two stretched ears, a cropped white T-shirt, yellow three-quarter-length trousers and yellowing feet that looked as though they had walked from Africa in the sandals that were joined to them. He was singularly the most expressive and feminine male that Hannah had ever met. He looked at Hannah with adoring eyes and spoke to her in English for most of the night. It was difficult to concentrate on his words due to the movement of the tongue piercing which ran into terrible conflict with any word beginning with 'th.' Nicolas was an English student and completely in charge of the party from the point of Elen's departure.

Hannah knew that she shouldn't have been shocked when Nicolas produced cigarette papers and a small bag of twisted green material, but some puritan part of her was indeed astonished. She had never actually seen marijuana, but she knew that she was not looking at the herbs of provence. The smell was overpowering, like freshly ground coffee mixed with furniture polish. Nicolas explained with pride that his grow room in

Rennes had been a triumph and that it was now paying for itself in rent.

Only Gildas seemed as bemused as Hannah. Hannah wondered again how old he was. He had a quiet confidence in his dark eyes and looked out of place once Elen left the room. Nicolas, Etienne and Martin went outside with their joints and Hannah was alone with Gildas by the oak chairs near the TV.

'Your dance was beautiful.'

Hannah looked up. Gilda's soft voice was sincere, and, for the first time, Hannah clearly understood every syllable of his French.

'Thank you. I didn't think you'd...I thought you'd left.'

'I had to collect the food for the party.' Gildas tipped his head slightly and smiled, 'You noticed I was gone?'

'Yes,' smiled Hannah. 'I thought you'd have said goodbye.'

'I'm sorry you're leaving tomorrow. I wish I'd had the chance to take you out on the boat. Maybe next time. Will you come back here?'

'Yes, I think so. Nicolas told me about English courses they run at the lycée during the summer. He said I should apply for next year. I might.'

'I'll give you my email address. Contact me if you're here again,' he said.

'Can I ask you something?'

'Yes,' he said.

Hannah lost her confidence and bowed her head before looking up again, 'I wondered how old you are. That's all.'

Gildas' face was tinged with red. 'I'm afraid I'm a little bit older than the people here tonight. My days of partying past one are long gone.'

The smokers returned and Nicolas' voice was first to be heard, his spindly body still charged with something extraordinarily energetic despite the drugs he had taken. Hannah realised the the voice of Nicolas and the mix of young people was not easy company for Gildas. She wished she could be alone with him again.

'I have to go now,' said Gildas.

Hannah walked him to the door. Taking her right hand in both of his, he said, 'I hope you can make it to France again.' He kissed her cheeks four times. Hannah wanted to reach up and kiss him on the lips, but she did nothing. She stood still and watched him leave.

Returning to the living room, Hannah felt drawn to sleep. She listened to Nicolas for a while before creeping silently away to her room. She imagined a small living room with soft chairs and the scent of potpourri. She could taste the crunch of lightly boiled cabbage and hear the crooning of a distant hoover. Her mind drifted to the soulful eyes of a quiet fisherman and the strong arms of a Belfast dancer. She dreamed of a kiss from Gildas, she dreamed of the dancer's arms moving over her body, and she looked at the sky through the window as particles of sleep dropped onto her eyelids. She drifted, knowing that she needed to visit France again. For now, echoes of home filtered out the noise of a party; a party that marked the farewell of a beautiful, yet sorrow-filled childhood, and the daunting promise of a freedom that Hannah was impatient to explore.

CHIMES OF YOUTH

Catriona passed through the bell tower of Trinity College and listened out for the faint chimes of her youth. She surveyed the lawn: the bicycles hooked up to the railings seemed to belong to another era, as though they had been planted there with their silver bells and rattling chains to increase the resonant sound of the past. The pathways were filled with tourists as the summer holidays continued on into the start of autumn.

The grey stone hadn't evoked so much poetry for Catriona when she had walked through the college gates for the first time at the age of eighteen. Her overriding memory of Dublin from that time was that of a tired city. It felt old and dusty in her young eyes. Now, whilst the new Dublin was fettered in mirrors reflecting the boom of the Celtic Tiger and the rushed architecture of success, Trinity College with its smooth grey brick, its white pillars and its symmetrical facades, felt suffused with a quiet simplicity.

Catriona walked to Parliament Square and sat down on the illuminated white steps leading up to the chapel. She looked across to the theatre which was bathed in shadows and her body was transported in tune with the chapel bells. She placed her hand on her stomach. It was there on the chapel steps that she had told Terence about the baby. Had it been a conscious decision to meet him there again? The text had been sent quickly, 'Meet me at the chapel steps at twelve.' She had always met Terence on the chapel steps, she realised. Everything that day acquired meaning beyond its proportions.

Terence had been to Dublin with work. It was a risk to meet him in such a public place, but the press had long forgotten them. He approached from the other side of the square, dressed in a tailored grey suit, blending seamlessly with the architecture of the college. Catriona, who was wearing a bright green blouse and A-line patterned skirt, felt immediately in contrast to him. His strained face, as he emerged from the shadows of the theatre, was visible. Catriona waved. Terence continued to contain any expression until he was right in front of her. He smiled and sat down.

'You look like a ray of sunshine,' he said.

Catriona searched for a response, but she was unprepared for Terence's words.

'Thank you,' she smiled.

'That maybe sounded a bit odd,' he added.

'It did, yes, and completely unexpected.'

'You have a glow about you.'

'Thank you. You're full of charm today. Is politics so inspiring?'

'God no. Sometimes I wonder why I ever got involved.'

'It's in your genes, that's why.'

'You know, the memories came flooding back to me the minute I walked through those gates. I remember you on your bike.'

'So do I! My bell bottoms used to get stuck in the pedals,' laughed Catriona. 'Anyway, do you not want to hear how I got on at the adoption agency?'

'Do you have something new?' Terence's face hinted at colour.

'Look at this.' Catriona held out a page with a note carefully written in her own handwriting.

Terence read aloud, 'Name of adopters: James and Anne Rogers.' He looked up at Catriona, his eyes seeking affirmation.

'Yes, Terence, there were only two children born in the mother and baby home that night. The other baby died.' Catriona reflected quietly for a moment on the stillborn child with the young mother before allowing her lips to broaden into a smile. 'We have the surname.'

Terence was staring at the piece of paper. He looked at Catriona with glistening eyes.

'There's more,' Catriona said as she took Terence's hand. 'He's been looking for us. His name is Aidan.'

'Aidan...' Terence's voice was barely audible. His hand was shaking. He placed his arm around Catriona's shoulder. 'We're going to find him now. I really believe it. We're going to find our son,' he said.

'I hope so. We have a name. That's the main thing. I was worried he'd be one of the kids sent to America, and that we'd never see him again. They're going to contact Aidan. We'll have to wait. Catriona stood up. 'Come on. Let's go for a walk. I can't sit still.'

'I have to get back. I've got work to...'

'Terence, come here.' Catriona removed Terence's tie, rolled it up and slipped it into his jacket pocket. 'That's better. Now take your jacket off. We're going for a trip.'

'Where to?'

'You'll see. Follow me.' Catriona had a skip in her step. She moved lightly through the cobble stones with Terence by her side.

'Don't panic. I'm not going to lead you into my dorm and undress you.' Catriona said, as they left the college. She watched a smile emerge from his eyes before criss-crossing through the bustling traffic on College Green.

They walked along the busy footpath among the tourists. It was an unfamiliar crowd. Catriona had visited Dublin many times over the years, but she had yet to walk through it with reminiscent eyes. She thought of Dublin as it was then. She could picture the old ladies, still in their silk headscarves despite the fashions of the times, trailing their canvas shopping trolleys behind them. Now the streets were filled with eager shoppers with blinkered eyes, and the odd plastic bag discarded and floating through the streets. She could see old men in caps and baggy blazers selling newspapers as her eyes adjusted to the the bright raincoats and gore tex satchels of the German and Italian tourists. Were the people walking faster too? Was there less gossiping on corners, perhaps? In the Dublin of today, would anyone even notice if a twenty year-old girl had a baby out of wedlock? Would it pass as gossip in the coffee shops where women now consummated their whispers?

'Imagine how different things would be today,' said Catriona. 'I was made to feel so ashamed of that pregnancy.'

Catriona awaited a reaction as they turned onto Trinity Street. Terence was still mute. Acknowledging their destination with a smile, he started to lead the way towards Dame Street. Opening the door to the Stag's Head, he finally spoke, 'There's no shame in the birth of a child. Ever.'

The foggy haze of smoke and sweat of back-to-back drinking of their student days was gone; in its place clarity and light shone on the oak panelled walls and ceilings, the golden light from the gilt-edged stained glass windows casting autumnal hues on the sparse floor. They ordered their drinks in silence. Catriona knew that Terence's mind was enlivened by the same information she'd had in her grasp since ten that morning.

Terence looked at Catriona once they were seated. 'What if we find him?'

'I thought the same thing. I never allowed myself to imagine beyond today, beyond knowing that there might be some record of him and that he is alive, even.' said Catriona.

'I've only ever thought of him alive,' said Terence. 'I knew from the moment you appeared on my street that he was alive.'

Catriona looked at Terence's face, golden in the glow from the window. She could see the young Terence again.

She spoke gently. 'We had a nice time didn't we...before...'

'Yes, I did, anyway. I wasn't sure if you...'

'What? That I didn't enjoy this?' Catriona looked around. 'I did. I was having a ball. I loved everything: the books, the atmosphere, the escape from the bombs in the North. It was like a different world down here. It's hard to imagine that we were only a hundred miles from Belfast. And I did enjoy this...the thing that we had. It was good.'

'I thought were searching for something better,' said Terence.

'No, not better. That wasn't it. I didn't want more. I wanted less. I couldn't handle moving to the next stage, getting married, all of that. You couldn't have coped either. I saw the shock on your face. You were terrified.'

'I was terrified of what my father would have said, that's for sure. It makes me angry now to think that we were here, and that we were adults, yet we were still just kids, afraid of authority, afraid of churches, afraid of parents.'

'Afraid of society. I didn't tell anyone. I knew if I told one person that it would be real.'

'It was real. What you said about...about being ashamed of the pregnancy, that was wrong. It was of its time. They shouldn't have made you feel like that. If your daughter walked through the door tomorrow and told you she was pregnant, what would you say?'

Catriona felt a jolt in her body. She looked down and reflected for a moment. 'I've never considered it before, but when you said that, I instinctively said to myself, "god forbid." I really did. After everything I've learned, my instinct was to be horrified. I don't know if its nature or I've been brainwashed, but I'm not sure I could have hidden that emotion. I'd have been disappointed. Why is that? She's almost eighteen.'

'We're conditioned to think like that,' said Terence.

'I still don't want her to get pregnant, but if she does, then I promise I'll hug her first and then cry when I'm alone,' Catriona smiled.

'Why do people get so upset?' asked Terence.

'They get upset because they've been parents themselves and they know how hard it is. They want their children to get an education first so that they can have a break before being thrown in at the deep end. Maybe...I don't know. That's what I would think anyway.'

'It's different for a man. If it had been Helena, I'd have wanted to kill the bastard who did that to her.'

'Terence! You, of all people, can't say that!' Catriona exclaimed.

'I know. I can't, but that's my instinct and you told me yours was negative too. It would annoy me that some little toe rag had got his hands on my daughter and then left her to deal with the rest...with the fact that she'd have to go through life as the girl who gave away her baby, the girl who got rid of her baby, or the girl who got pregnant at university.'

'So reputation would be important to you?'

'No, it wouldn't. You know, I had visions of your dad's face when you told me you were pregnant. I was ashamed. He invited me into his home once, and look what I did to his daughter. I listened to your story...the one you told Norma about how the nuns had been kind and how other things are harder in life than giving up a baby. I believed every word you said, but the scale you were working from was a tough one. You're a strong person.'

'It was selfish.'

'There's a scale of selfishness too. There were other options. You could have married me and had the lifestyle your father would have wanted. In some ways, that would have been selfish too,' said Terence.

'Marry a Protestant?'

Terence smiled, 'Yes, marry a Protestant. He would have got over that eventually!'

'Eventually!' Catriona laughed.

'Catriona, I need you to know something. I know that my wife is dying and I know that it might seem like an inappropriate thing to say, but that young man, our son... his father loved his mother. Sitting here now in this bar, I remember it more than ever. I may have been young, but I loved you. I didn't know if you felt the same way.'

Catriona leaned over the table, 'I did love you Terence. I had the world in my hands and didn't know it. I can see things more clearly now. I don't want you to ever believe that I didn't love you. Our son was conceived by two people who loved each other. Maybe that means something. And Terence...Norma wants us to find him too. She wants you to be happy no matter what it takes. She told me so. We'll find him for you, for me and for Norma. When you go home tonight and tell her, she'll have a little peace knowing that Aidan is out there looking for us.'

***

Jean nervously pushed the newspaper towards Hannah.

Hannah took one look at the picture. 'Oh my god!' She stopped and looked up. 'Oh Mum, poor Rachael. Poor Catriona.'

'Poor Terence!' added Jean. His wife has just died and he has his photo plastered all over the Sunday tabloid.

'I can't believe it. That journalist has always had it in for them. At least his wife died before this was published.

Jean looked over Hannah's shoulder at the photographs of two lovers on the steps of Trinity College. There was Catriona, her tanned limbs decorated in a green and white patterned skirt and her matching slingbacks propped to the side like a movie star. Her caramel hair was glimmering in the sunshine and the side of her face exposed, as she held Terence's hand. Terence's head was lowered to a piece of paper. They looked either deeply sad or deeply happy. It was difficult to tell. Jean thought of Roy for the first time since the end of July. 'They look restful,' she said eventually.

'What do you mean?' asked Hannah.

'They look at peace in each other's company.'

Jean's eyes moved to the headline. 'Trip down memory lane for unionist and his lover.'

'They aren't lovers, Mum.'

'How do you know?'

'Rachael told me.'

'What did she tell you?'

'I'm not supposed to say. Rachael doesn't want anyone else to know in case it gets leaked to the papers.'

'I won't tell a soul.'

'Well, the article is right about one thing. They were lovers. At least, they were girlfriend and boyfriend, but it was a long time ago, when they were at university in Dublin.'

'And?'

'And they had a baby.'

Jean stared at the paper. She lifted it and looked more closely at the faces of the two people in what could have passed for a postcard. 'A baby.' Jean repeated, reassessing the emotions on the faces.

'He...the baby...is twenty-five and he's been trying to find them. The adoption agency has written to him to let him know they've found his parents. There were some problems because the birth certificate was destroyed in a fire.'

'Oh my goodness. And what about Terence's wife. Did she know?'

'Yes, Rachael met her several times. That's why Catriona was hanging about at their house.'

'And what does Rachael think?'

'She's excited. She wants to meet her brother. And here's the funny thing...Catriona called him Etienne before he was adopted. His name is Aidan now.'

Jean thought about Catriona as her eyes scanned the paper. She hadn't seen her son grow. Was it worse to see your son grow and then to lose him than to never know him at all? She recalled Roy's words. The story of one so young is worth telling. Jean had shared her son's story. Memories were starting to disappear from her mind, but she had a sense of something stronger. She couldn't locate the exact details of Robert's first day at school. She could search in her mind and pull out fragments, but the overall picture was too difficult to decipher. The only thing she could really remember was that she was there. That mattered now somehow. Why hadn't it mattered before?

'That poor woman. She must have been going through hell. Imagine, all these years of not knowing anything. It must have been terrible.'

'Maybe she's a fighter,' said Hannah.

'A fighter, indeed...I suppose we all need to be strong. And that goes for you too.'

'Me?'

'Yes, you. I see how you are with your dad. You're pretending. It's not nice. It's not nice to be in the same room as the pair of you. When are you going to forgive him?'

'He doesn't need my forgiveness. If he wants forgiveness, he can ask God for that. If he wants understanding then I don't understand. I look at him and I feel ashamed that he's my father.'

Jean felt weightless. The echo of her daughter's words was oppressive. She controlled her voice and spoke clearly, 'I'm ashamed to have a daughter who thinks like that.'

She walked away from the table and started preparing dinner. Hannah remained where she was, motionless. Jean watched her from the back and saw Hannah's shoulders start to move up and down before she left the kitchen in silence.

***

Was it worth trying again? Harry wondered. He had started to avoid any conversation with Hannah. Her voice was unresponsive; her glare cold.

'What are you studying?'

'English.' she replied.

'What's the book?'

'It's Shakespeare. Othello.'

'I haven't read it. What's it about?' asked Harry.

Hannah didn't raise her head. 'It's too complicated to explain.'

Hannah's clipped answers were like lacerations. Harry had been home for three months and Hannah was still spitting knives in his face.

'I was thinking. Now that I'm working, you should cut back your hours at the shop. I can help you get through your A levels.'

'Thanks.'

'Thanks, yes, or thanks, no?'

'Thanks, I don't know.'

'Hannah, we can't go on like this.'

Hannah didn't respond. She breathed deeply and shrugged.

'For god's sake, would you look at me?'

Her voice increased from a mumble, 'I'm trying to study. I've got my mocks before Christmas. I need to study.'

Harry sat down. He lifted Hannah's book and turned it over. 'I'm going to talk to you for five minutes and then I'm going to leave you to study. Now, are you going to talk to me?'

Harry watched his daughter's cheeks redden. Her mouth was drawn downwards, her eyebrows creased.

'Are you going to talk to me?' Harry repeated.

'Yes...I don't know. What do you want me to say?' Hannah asked, her voice shaking.

'I want to get to the bottom of this. You need to tell me what is going on. Have I done something?'

Hannah threw a look in Harry's face that felt like seething hatred. He breathed in and counted to five. He looked back. 'What is it?'

Hannah sat up straight. She started packing her books away with trembling hands. Harry reached out and clasped her hands in his.

'Don't touch me!' she said, yanking her hands back from him. Her voice became stronger. 'You want to know what you've done? You murdered a man and I don't get it. I don't get any of it. And I don't like you being here. I don't like you being in the house because I know that it's not over. Someone else is going to get hurt. They'll come after you eventually and when they do, it'll happen all over again. I have exams and I can't concentrate and I can't cope with all of this.' Her voice broke into sobs. 'I can't do it. It's not fair. I want to do well and this is too hard. It's too hard living here with you. Why couldn't you have been a normal dad? Why did I have to have you?'

Hannah was shaking uncontrollably as she spat out the words. Harry watched his daughter gasp for air; her neck red; her eyes spilling over bleak tears. He reached out to steady her as she continued to tremble. 'Okay, Hannah, sit down, please. Sit.'

Hannah's body collapsed onto the seat, her head falling into her hands. She wept. He watched her with a feeling of fear before walking out of the room and calling upstairs for Jean. He checked Hannah again and she was still sitting at the table heaving tears into her hands.

Jean crossed the living room and moved towards the kitchen, 'What's up?' she asked.

'It's Hannah. Wait. Wait, don't go in there' Harry whispered.

'What about Hannah?'

'She's just broken down on me. She completely lost it.'

'What for?' asked Jean in a hushed tone as she tried to push past Harry into the kitchen. 'What have you said to her?'

'Wait.' Harry pulled at Jean's arm. 'Wait, Jean. Please. She needs a minute. Has Hannah ever been stressed before about exams?'

'Yes. She's always stressed.'

'How stressed?' Harry asked.

'She moans about failing and tells us she can't do the housework.'

'Does she tremble?'

'No.'

'Does she cry?'

'No. Why? Is Hannah crying? Hannah doesn't cry. Ever. Well, she did in the airport two days after you came...'

'It's me. I knew it. I think me being here is too much for her. She can't handle it right now with the exams.'

'No, love. She's working too hard. She always did, between the shop and the babysitting and the school work,' Jean explained. 'It's not you,

Harry. It's the work.'

'Jean, Hannah needs to rest, but she also needs to talk to someone about the things she is thinking. She can't get over the murder. She can't get her head around it.'

'Oh.'

'Yes, look, is there anyone she can speak to?'

'I don't know...Rachael, her friend?'

'No, is there an adult?'

'I can't think...maybe we could speak to a teacher...Wait, she's fond of Catriona, Rachael's mum, but she's going through a lot right now.'

'Could you try speaking to her? To Catriona?'

'Okay. You never know. It might take her mind off the newspaper stuff. I'll find an excuse and give her a ring.'

***

Jean looked around Catriona's house with wide eyes. The closest that she had been to such simplistic beauty was the dentist's waiting room, where she would flick through the magazines and enjoy consuming the art of living. Jean had read about *feng shui* in one of those magazines and wondered if it had infused Catriona's living room with the harmony that had lightened Jean's step as she walked across the tiled floor. Everything was perfectly proportioned; two box shaped sofas facing each other like a stage for compulsory human interaction. Jean's eyes focused on a glass bowl on the coffee table where small pink petals swirled in the water.

Catriona's living room was set up for talking, yet the cool baby blue suede of the sofa on which Jean was seated, didn't look like anyone had ever been placed there to talk about anything. Jean ran her hand across a yellow velvet cushion, automatically checking the stitching: it was perfect with concealed zips and hidden seams tucked away neatly. The windows were adorned with simple white blinds and an orange light filled the room like sunset, a trick of light on a November morning. Catriona arrived and moved the designer books aside and placed the coffee mugs on the glass coffee table between them.

'This is amazing,' said Jean as her eyes moved around the room.

'Thank you. I was a bit obsessed after the divorce and went through a long decorating phase. Rachael tells me you're home is gorgeous.'

Jean turned to Catriona and blinked. 'My house?' Her eyes moved to the ceiling rose and she released a smile, 'Rachael has excellent manners.'

'Sometimes she does. Sometimes she behaves like a right little brat. Do you never wish you could give them a good clip round the ear?'

Jean laughed, 'It would speed things up a bit, wouldn't it? Nowadays, it's all endless bloody talking.'

'I know. It's tiring. Try dealing with a teenager, a divorce and an affair plastered all over the papers.'

'Ha! Try dealing with two teenagers, a husband due to come home from prison, and a naked French boy.'

'Naked!' Catriona exclaimed.

'Oh aye, did you not hear? The first morning he arrived, we walked past the room and found him lying there with everything on show. He'd left the door open.'

'Oh goodness,' said Catriona.

'Oh goodness, indeed. And there wasn't much boy about him, let me tell you. He was a seventeen year-old man!'

Catriona laughed and Jean felt a release as her shoulders relaxed. Catriona was not at all how Jean had imagined.

'It was good of you to do the exchange. I gave Hannah the leaflet because I knew that Rachael wasn't interested. I had no idea...'

'It was you?' Jean blared, 'You put her up to it? Well thanks a lot.' Jean was smiling.

'Oops. Sorry,' said Catriona. 'It worked out okay though, didn't it?'

'Honestly, it was the best thing that happened in our house in a long time. Ever since Robert...well, we'd been getting on with things, but it was like seeing the world around us in a whole new way. He wrote to me the other day and asked me to go to France.'

'You should go!'

'We'll see. There are a lot of places I'd like to go to,' said Jean.

'But you'll never see them properly unless you see them with a local. You should go and stay with his family while the offer is there. I was meant to live in France one summer. I didn't go in the end...I...' Catriona lowered her eyes.

'It's okay, love. I know about the baby. Rachael said it was all right for me to know.'

'Yes, she explained. I know that it would clear up that other business if the papers knew the truth, but if Aidan learned about his identity by seeing his story in a newspaper, I'm not sure it would bring him home.'

'I think you're right. The other thing will pass and the papers will move onto someone else soon enough. How's Terence?' Jean asked. It felt like a strange question that she had no right to ask. She wasn't part of their world, yet suddenly, her world and Catriona's seemed to collide in the quiet ambience of the bright room.

Catriona's eyes were strained, 'Terence is okay. I think. He and Helena need time, so I'm giving them space. I don't want to get in their way. Jean, it's not how it looked in the paper.'

Jean raised her hand, 'Catriona, love, you don't need to explain yourself to me. I'm not here to judge anyone.'

'But I want you to know. I need to tell someone who doesn't, well, who doesn't know me well. People who are too close sometimes think they know everything about me. I can't explain it to my sisters or my brothers. They know Terence from when we were together and they presume there's something going on because of how we were back then. We were together for a couple of years, you see. I ended it afterwards. Anyway, we'd just heard that Aidan was looking for us, so I took Terence's hand. It felt like the right thing to do.'

Jean had known there would be an explanation. She'd already pieced together part of the story due to the looks shared by the couple in the postcard image. Jean wanted to ask something. She knew she shouldn't, but the conversation would move on and she'd lose her opportunity, 'Why did you end it?'

Catriona looked Jean in the eye. 'End what?'

'Sorry. I've only met you a couple of times, and I don't know you at all. It's the first time we've ever had a proper conversation and here I am being nosey. I shouldn't have asked. Ignore me.'

'It's okay. What did you mean?'

'I wondered why you had ended the relationship when you were both at college?'

'We'd given a baby away. We couldn't stay together.'

'Why not?'

'It would have been wrong.'

'Did you love each other?' asked Jean naturally, yet still aware that she was having a conversation with a relative stranger.

'Yes, we did. We had a lovely time together until life got so complicated.'.

In that moment, Jean recognised a feeling that she hadn't had for a long time. She was having an adult conversation that was as pure and devoid from emotional clutter as the space they occupied. It was rare for Jean to find someone who spoke as plainly as Catriona. Jean couldn't understand why Catriona and Terence had split up. It didn't seem necessary in her categorical mind where the baby issue was sad, but separate. 'I know I shouldn't say this', Jean explained, 'but when I saw that photograph, you didn't look like two people who were once in love. The reason that the papers got it wrong is because you looked together...really together.'

Catriona blushed and played with her hands. Jean realised she may have gone too far. 'You two look like friends,' Jean said.

'We have to be friends. We have a journey ahead. I've read stories and sometimes the child never connects with the parents.'

'Oh don't I know about that! That's why I'm here.'

'Of course, Jean. I'm sorry for talking about me. We're here to talk about Hannah. I love Hannah. She's a lovely girl, so well brought up. You did a great job.'

'Are we talking about the same Hannah?'

Catriona laughed.

'What do you think we should do?' asked Jean.

'Well, from what you've told me, it was completely out of character. I can't imagine Hannah being like that either. It might not be Harry at all. It might be the stress of exams. She's very driven.'

'I know. She thinks the world will end if she doesn't get through this year,' said Jean.

'There was something else... Jean. This is difficult, but my friend teaches English at the school. She said that something happened in school at the end of last term. Some of the students in her class had been making fun of Hannah for having a father in...a father in prison.'

Jean's body faltered. She stared into the distance. When she tried to speak, her throat was hard and dry.

'I'm sorry. I shouldn't know any of this, but Hannah stopped speaking to Rachael too. She thought Rachael was behind the rumour. They sorted it out in the end. They're friends, but...'

'I didn't know any of this. What else did the teacher say?' asked Jean as she used all her energy to push back tears that were forming in her eyes.

'That was it. She couldn't discuss a pupil and she just mentioned that one thing. She would get in trouble if she knew I'd...'

'Don't worry. I won't be complaining to the school, but I think I understand now,' said Jean.

'I know this might make things worse, but for the sake of getting her through her mocks, it would be no problem for her to stay with us. She'd have space and she could study and then come home.'

Jean held her hand to her chest. 'No, no, I couldn't let her go...not Hannah. It would be like she was moving out. I couldn't.'

'It's just an offer. I wouldn't want Rachael to go anywhere either and believe me, she has threatened to move in with you many times. It's there on the table anyway and it would be a pleasure. All we're doing right now is waiting. Hannah would cheer the place up a bit. Think about it.'

***

'My mother taught me not to hate, so I learned to hate all by myself.' Hannah read the first page in her diary. She'd never kept a diary before. It was a stupid idea and she knew she would burn it later, but Catriona had bought it for her. Here she was in the middle of Catriona's life taking up space in her home and in her heart when Catriona had problems of her own. Hannah lay back on the bed. She couldn't have asked for a more beautiful room, better food or better company. She had peace when she needed to study and she was a short walk away from Methodist College. Life was easier now. But she missed home.

She missed Jean.

Each day for four weeks, she'd returned home from school to an empty house. Catriona was at work and Rachael had signed up to every extra-curricular club available to escape the boredom of being at home alone. Jean had always been there after school: she would be there peeling potatoes and talking, endlessly talking. Hannah's mobile phone rang. It was Jean.

'Mum?'

'Yes, love. How are you?'

'Okay.'

'How did the last mock exam go?'

'Failed it.' they said in tandem.

Hannah laughed.

'Funny how failure always has an A in front of it with you.'

'I won't get any As this time, trust me.'

'We'll see,' said Jean.

There was silence.

'Hannah, love, I...'

'Want me to come home?'

'Yes.'

'I know.' Hannah said.

'Please.' Jean's voice was somber.

'What's the point, mum? I'd only fight with him.'

'You could call him dad. Don't say him.'

'I'd only fight with dad.'

'I didn't expect you to stay so long. I want you here. Your dad wants you here. Hannah, none of us can change what's in the past. Your dad did something bad. Now he wants to make amends.'

'I know. But this year is important. Catriona said it would be okay to stay...that's if it's okay with you.'

'No, it's not okay. It's like you've moved out and it's too early for that. This is your last year with us, your last months and then you'll go off to university and...'

'Okay, look, I'll come home at the start of the Christmas holidays. We'll take it from there.'

'Come home on Friday and I'll make you cabbage and spuds. Bring Catriona and Rachael too.'

Hannah smiled. She thought of the day she had come home from France, the first time she had ever actively requested Jean's home cooking. Jean had smiled all the way through dinner, with a steadfast look of satisfaction that told the world that her work as a mother was done.

'Okay, see you on Friday for tea. Bye, Mum.'

'Bye, love.'

Hannah returned to her diary and continued to read. 'I learned to hate him when I was seventeen. I don't know why it was okay before then.

Perhaps it was because he wasn't coming home.' Hannah placed the pen between her teeth and stared at the page. She swiftly ripped the page from the book and tore it into tiny shreds.

She didn't want to hate her father. She wanted to love him like she used to. She knew that she had loved him once.

Why did he have to do what he did? She could have loved him if he'd stolen something or if he'd had an affair. She could have loved him if he'd hit her.

Harry wasn't capable of hurting one of his children with a slap on the hand or a tap of a wooden spoon. Harry had simply destroyed lives. He had killed a man. He had killed someone's son, and left his own children behind.

Why did he have to be a murderer?

THE WHITE CHAIR

'Who the hell is Nathan?' asked Jean as she and Harry stood by the front door with fairy lights flickering around them.

'Keep your voice down. He'll be here any minute!' Harry exclaimed in whispers.

'You can't ask random people to come around at Christmas,' Jean said, reducing the volume of her voice to a chastising wheeze.

'He's a friend and he has nowhere else to go.' Harry replied.

'Where's his family?' Jean asked, her arms firmly locked across her chest.

'He lives alone and his family don't talk to him.'

'Why not?'

'They disowned him.'

'Why?'

'He got in trouble.'

'What kind of trouble?' Jean puffed.

'He was in prison.'

Jean's hands moved up to her head, 'In the name of God, Harry. Who the hell are you bringing into our home on Christmas day of all days? Hannah is home. Is he a paramilitary?'

Harry paused. He knew the answer well. Nathan had been part of an underground world that would make his family feel uncomfortable. If Hannah couldn't forgive her own father, there was little chance of her relating to Nathan. 'I know it looks bad, but wait and see. The boy needs help. He's still in a bit of bother. If he goes home he'll get...here he is...open the door Jean.'

'No, you open the bloody door!' Jean whispered. She brushed past Harry and darted through the house like an electric charge.

Harry walked to the door and welcomed Nathan in a cheerful tone,

'Merry Christmas, come on in, son.'

Nathan reached out and shook Harry's hand, 'Thanks for this, mate. It's good of you.'

Jean was back, an alternating current of compassion. Harry knew she would come around, but he couldn't have reckoned on her changing her mind so swiftly. She reached out her hand, 'Merry Christmas. I'm Jean. Call me the sous-chef,' she smiled and bowed like a jester towards Harry.

'Take a seat,' said Harry, in wonder at the ability of his diminutive wife to puff like a light wind and bellow like a raging fire inside a split second.

Nathan started to settle into the white chair by the window. Jean's face glowed as her arms gyrated. 'No wait, Nathan', she said. 'Come on over here by the fire. Get some heat into you.'

Jean was now moving around the small space like a blizzard. Harry rolled his eyes. Her precious white chair. A guest had come into their home on Christmas day and all Jean could think about was protecting her chair.

Hannah joined them. Harry hadn't told anyone about Nathan's arrival. He thought he could minimise the tension by revealing the news on the day rather than getting everyone worked up beforehand. Begging forgiveness was to be his lot in life. Seeking permission was not within his grasp among the three strong women in his home. He introduced Hannah. She stayed for long enough to be polite and moved off to help Jean when Shelley came along.

'Oh, right, and are you staying for dinner?' Shelley asked, clumsily looking from Harry to Nathan.

Harry breathed a sigh of relief when they left the room. Nathan's outward appearance didn't reflect the internal workings of a mind that Harry had come to know, but it did give something away about his place in the world. Clad in a Nike tracksuit and Nike trainers, he was all bones and pimples and had the spindly look of a teenager. Harry looked at his eyes and sighed. They were sunk into his head like dark craters. Harry wished for just one moment that Nathan had worn a pair of jeans and a shirt for this occasion. It might have made a difference to Jean and to his daughters. Minimising tension was Harry's new crusade since Hannah had returned from Catriona's.

Nathan served as a distraction at dinner. Hannah's silences were less piercing than before. She seemed as bemused by the presence of Nathan as everyone else did. Harry observed it all from his position by the cooker where he was preparing dinner. Mrs McAdam, as always, kept the wheels of conversation turning.

'Funny, the last time we were all sitting here eating a meal, there was a big French man in the seat you're in.' said Mrs McAdam. 'Oh you should have seen thon boy,' she went on. 'He'd hair down his back like a fairy and this great big hole in his ear!'

Nathan smiled.

'I'm not sure fairy is the right way to describe Etienne,' said Hannah. 'I mean he was dressed in black the entire time he was here.'

'How do you know Harry?' asked Mrs McAdam, the only person at the table not to have assumed the obvious.

'Nathan did the same course as me...horticulture. He was good at it,' said Harry.

'Are you looking for work then?' asked Jean.

'Yes, I've applied for a couple of jobs,' Nathan replied.

Nathan's voice was soft and Harry realised that Jean was hearing its familiar tone for the first time. Nathan continued to speak, his voice deflecting the sound of cutlery and amplifying the curiosity surrounding his presence.

'It's hard with a record, but I've got people helping me. Harry's been helping me.'

His head moved in Harry's direction to acknowledge him. Harry looked at his wife and his daughters. He could see that they could hear it too.

Mrs McAdam didn't seem to notice. 'It must be hard, all the same. You keep at it son,' she said.

The others remained quiet, standing up in turn to deliver their plates to the sink. Mrs McAdam's trifle was the last dish to be served. Harry had managed to make fresh broth for starters and turkey and ham for main course, but he acknowledged his limitations in the kitchen when it came to dessert.

Nathan looked increasingly uncomfortable after the last spoonful of trifle. He had been there for less than an hour and yet, Harry suspected that his friend was ready to be alone again. It was something that he too had experienced after being released. The well practised ability to thrive alone was the gift that prison had given him. Once Harry had learned to listen to the tempo of his inner voice, he was able to master the feelings of hopelessness that had plagued him for his first two years in prison. Having learned to function alone, he often found it chaotic engaging with so many people at one time.

Nathan was silent for a while. He then spoke quietly and sincerely, 'Thanks. That was really nice. And thanks for... you know...letting me come on Christmas day. It must have been weird having a stranger here and that. Thanks anyway.' He stepped towards Harry and shook his hand again, 'Harry, mate, thanks for dinner.' He turned to the others, 'Listen, I'll leave you guys in peace. I'll head on.'

'You don't have to.' Hannah was standing up. Harry's eyes widened. 'We wouldn't want you to be alone. Stay a while longer.'

'No, it's okay. I'm happy watching TV for the rest of the afternoon, thanks. This was nice. It was good,' Nathan said.

'I'll drive you home then. Where do you live?' Hannah asked.

Harry looked at his daughter. He was at once relieved and warmed by her kindness and the care in her voice.

'No, honestly. I'm all right. I'm only down the road. I'll be home in twenty minutes. Everyone, see you all again.'

Hannah, Shelley and Mrs McAdam followed Nathan to the door. Harry heard the TV blare and the sound of chatter from the living room.

Jean stood up from the table and walked towards him. She spoke quietly with words that cleaved the peace they'd had throughout dinner, 'What the hell was that all about?'

Harry retained his cool. 'It's Christmas, Jean.'

'You know what I mean. That boy, that man... he's like...' Jean's voice started to shake. 'What the hell are you trying to do? Recreate the past? Bring back your son?'

'Oh don't be silly. He's not like Robert at all.'

'I'm not talking about what he looks like. I'm talking about the voice. I'm talking about his place at the table. Harry, what the hell are you playing at? He's not Robert.'

'I know well that he's not Robert, and what a ridiculous thing to say! I helped the boy in prison, that's all. I met him the other day and he said his family weren't speaking to him.'

'He's old enough to look after himself! What age is he?'

'Twenty-five.'

'And what was he in prison for?'

'He was carrying a gun. He served five years.'

'A gun for who?'

'You can guess,' Harry replied. 'Look, I know he wasn't good enough for you and your house, but...'

'What did you say?'

'I said he wasn't good enough.'

'How dare you!' Jean said, enraged but retaining her hushed tone.

'Oh come on, Jean! You wouldn't even let him sit on your precious white chair. You took one look at him and he wasn't good enough for you and your bloody clinical house with all it's fucking white stuff.'

'You bastard.' Jean's voice was louder now. She shoved Harry hard on the chest and walked out into the back yard. Harry followed. Jean continued, her hands surrendering in the cool air, 'You have no idea, have you? You are so stupid that you can't see why none of us sit on that chair by the window!' Jean's eyes were inflamed, 'We don't sit on that chair because we are waiting for the day that someone will come along and shoot a spray of bullets through the front window. Did you think the vase on the window sill was a decoration? No! It was put there by me to protect my daughters. So you can fuck off with your theories about me and my house. I am not the person you just described.'

Harry looked down. 'Sorry Jean. Sorry. I didn't know.'

Jean was shivering in the cold. 'Harry, this is hard. Why did you go and make it harder by bringing Nathan here on Christmas day? I mean, any other day would have been...'

'No, today was the right day. Any other day wouldn't have mattered. He has no one and he knew Robert.'

Jean stopped moving. She looked up.

'He said Robert was in a youth gang.'

Jean bowed her head again.

'You knew? Jean, did you know?'

'Yes' Jean said.

'Why didn't you tell me?'

'Because you were a mess. I didn't want to make it worse.'

'Is that why he went to Holland?' asked Harry

'Yes. Annie arranged it...with...with Roy.'

Harry heard it. The word reverberated off the brick walls of the backyard. Roy. He heard the hesitation and explanation. He looked at Jean. 'Roy,' he repeated in a quiet tone. 'Was it Roy?'

Jean was shaking. 'I'm cold. Let's go in. I don't want to talk any more. This is getting silly. Come on.'

'No, wait. You went on those trips to Holland and you became distant. You came to see me in prison and you were different. It was Roy, wasn't it?'

'What difference does it make? It's over. It's in the past. I don't want to talk about it.'

Harry tried to calm his breathing and engage again with the part of him that he had taught to reflect calmly, but he couldn't find that person: he was Harry again, Jean's husband. His mind raged with incoherent thoughts. He did want to talk about it. He could picture Roy. He could see him in photographs that Robert had sent to him, photographs where Roy held Robert by the shoulder like a father holds a son. And now his wife. 'We have to talk about it. Is it Roy? Do you love Roy?'

'You don't get to do this on Christmas day. Mrs McAdam will be looking for her tea.'

'Is that why you won't let me touch you, why you turn away in bed at night?' asked Harry, knowing that he was now treading on thin ice.

'Oh don't be so daft. I'm going to put the kettle on.'

Harry clutched Jean's elbow and turned her towards him. He counted in his head to quell the frustration that was now tearing at him. He spoke calmly, 'I've served my time. I've fitted in around your life. And you continue to reject me. It makes me feel like...like shit. Why? Is it because of him?'

'No. I turn away because I don't feel all that attractive, if you must know. You were going to leave your family because I didn't measure up to the woman that you wanted to be with.'

Harry released Jean's arm. He could see the hurt in his wife's eyes. 'Yes, Harry, I went to the bank. I saw her and I can see why you chose her. She was perfect for you. And look at me.' Jean's face was contorted as her eyes moved up and down her own body. 'Why the hell would you want this?'

'Jean, no, stop, you're beautiful and I...'

'I know that you loved her. I thought I loved Roy, but I would never have left my family for him. You...you were planning a new life. You were going to leave all of us.'

'Jean, please.'

'Let me speak. I'll tell you something about us...I am trying my best to love you. When I hold your hand, I mean it. When I kiss you, I mean it. None of this is fake. This is real. If you want me to start pretending that everything is perfect...well, I can't do that. I don't know you. I don't know the Harry who cooks and who brings strangers into the house on Christmas day. I need time to get to know you.'

Harry reached out and took Jean's hand. 'Come on. I'll make the tea. Go and sit down.'

'No, do something for me, Harry. Go to the Royal for a pint. Just go. Stop making so much effort and get yourself a Christmas drink. You'll find someone there you know.'

Harry kissed Jean softly on the cheek and opened the door. 'I have no desire to go near that place. It's not who I am. You want the Harry back that you knew so well. It's easier that way, isn't it?'

'Maybe...I don't know. I suppose so.'

'I won't be that man again. I'll never be that man.'

***

Mrs McAdam looked out of place in Robert's box room seated in front of a computer. The sight of her there in her dressing gown and curlers was as contradictory as the shiny plastic computer perched on top of an antique Singer sewing machine table. Shelley was reminded how many times she had logged on in any given week due to the number of bruises up her legs from impact with the decorative cast iron. She ran her hand along the faded oak and thought of two women who now intrigued her; her granny Anna, Jean's mother, and Anna's mother, Sally. Jean had said that the sewing machine belonged to her granny Sally. It was a family heirloom and was now the only tangible connection that Shelley had with her maternal past.

Shelley had asked Mrs McAdam around to help with the ancestry search on a new website she'd found. Despite her antipathy towards school history, she was now immersed in the past, the history of her own family proving decidedly more interesting than that of strangers. The

Adams side of the family had been easy to piece together, and Shelley had managed to trace a line of shipyard workers, dockers and millworkers as far back as 1840 on the paternal side, and a family of Scottish farmers dating back to the plantation in the 1700s on the maternal side. Harry had a strong insight into his own past and had been able to help. Jean, however, wasn't so well informed, and was aware of next to nothing about her ancestry. Mrs McAdam's acute memory of her formative years was proving critical to Shelley's search.

'Let's look at this census,' said Mrs McAdam. What's the fancy thing your dad bought called?'

'Broadband,' smiled Shelley

'Right, broadband, get to work,' directed Mrs McAdam.

'Look here,' said Shelley, 'This is the census from 1901. The family at this house is called Gordon.'

'But it's not the same house, love.'

'What do you mean?' asked Shelley.

'The street was redeveloped and the numbers changed.' Mrs McAdam placed her reading glasses on the end of her nose and looked at the screen. 'Look, here. White. Your great granny Sally was called White and she never married, so her mother must have been White too.'

'Brilliant.' Shelley clicked the name with adrenaline pulsating through her fingertips. She and Mrs McAdam leaned into the screen together. Shelley read aloud, 'Mary Ellen White, Age 38, Female, Head of Household, Church of Ireland; Sarah White...' She stopped and turned to Mrs McAdam, 'Sarah?'

'Sally is short for Sarah,' said Mrs McAdam.

'Okay. I don't really see the connection, but anyway it says Sarah, age 11, Daughter, Church of Ireland. So there you go. Both Church of Ireland. Both probably St. Matthews. And then there's Edward Chambers, Age 40, Male, Boarder, Presbyterian. Oh Mrs McAdam, what's going on here? A male boarder? And a Presbyterian of all things!'

'Yes, it wasn't so unusual to take in lodgers. Look at some of the other houses and you'll see.'

Shelley moved back and forward through each house on Snugville Street, enjoying the instantaneous new broadband connection as much as having a peek around the door of the residents of her street one hundred and three years ago. 'This is amazing,' she said. 'Baptist, Church of Ireland, Wesleyan Methodists, Protestant Episcopalians, Presbyterians. Mum said there were Catholics years ago. Let's see.' said Shelley, continuing to scroll. 'Ha! Brilliant! Look, the Fegans. *Roman Catholic.*'

Shelley reopened the record for the White household and considered the dynamics of the 1901 living arrangements. She thought about what might occur under a roof with two apparently single people of the opposite sex, with no husband on the scene. 'So, who was this lodger then?' asked Shelley.

'I've no idea, love. It's before my time. People had to do that in them days to get money. He was probably a relative if Mary's husband was dead.'

'If Mary's husband was dead, then we know that he must have died before 1901. Great granny Sally was only eleven in 1901. That's sad. She lost her dad at a young age.'

'There should be a marriage certificate for Mary if she was married,' said Mrs McAdam. 'We need to figure out her maiden name. I have an idea. Let's make a trip to the Shankill graveyard.'

Shelley sat upright. 'What for?' she beamed, a vision of Queen Victoria lit up like the Virgin appearing before her eyes. Shelley was convinced, despite the six months that had passed, that someone still might identify her as a vandal in the Shankill graveyard.

'We can check if Mary was buried there. It must have been around 1929 when she died. If we find her plot, we can see the names of the other people in the grave to see if she had a husband.'

'Great idea,' said Shelley. But you're forgetting I've got the world wide web and broadband in my hands. We can look up the burial records at Belfast City Council.'

'Thon machine is magic,' exclaimed Mrs McAdam.

Shelley laughed. 'It sure is!'

She typed Mary White and 1929 into search fields. Less than a second later, she had a record in front of her. 'Look at this. Mary White. Age 66, City Cemetery. We can click on the burial plot and see a list of names of the others buried there. I think you might be right, Mrs McAdam, this is magic!' Enthusiasm surged through Shelley's bones as a list of names was displayed. 'I had no idea that searching for dead people could be this exciting,' she said, running her eyes down the names. 'Both Sarah and Mary are here. The rest are all Dodds.'

'Dodds would be her maiden name then,' said Mrs McAdam.

'Is there any other reason why Mary wouldn't have been buried with her husband?'

'I've no idea. Not many poor people divorced in those days, but Sally did tell Anna that her parents had money, so maybe they were divorced.'

'What do we do next?'

'You've got the name Dodds,' said Mrs McAdam. 'If that's her maiden name, she would have had Dodds on her marriage certificate. Can the machine tell you that?' asked Mrs McAdam.

Shelley searched the Church of Ireland site for information on wedding certificates. 'I can't find anything here. I think we'll have to go back to the church. Mary would probably have got married in the 1880s if she was 66 when she died in 1929. It says here the records from that time were destroyed. I'll go back to the church and ask the rector what he has.'

Shelley thought about how this whim about French ancestors had developed into a search for her identity. Knowing who her great great grandfather was had taken on a significance that seemed out of proportion with the mark he'd left on her life.

'Let me know when you go to see the rector. He's gorgeous.' said Mrs McAdam.

'Mrs McAdam!' Shelley exclaimed. 'He's in his thirties and you're in your...well, you're getting on.'

'Ach, nonsense, I saw how he looked at my ankles.' laughed Mrs McAdam. 'I'd love a wee excuse to wear that new red dress your mammy bought for me too. It shows them off very nicely.'

Shelley recalled the story about the kiss as she watched Mrs McAdam's eyes shine mischievously.

'You know, Mrs McAdam. We could maybe find George, the man with the saxophone if you'd like to have a look online.'

'Oh, I know where his plot lies. I don't need a computer for that.'

Shelley was confused. 'Did George die?'

'Yes, sure you know he did.'

'I don't follow,' said Shelley and then, thinking for a moment, she looked back to Mrs McAdam, 'Was George...was he Mr McAdam?'

'Yes, love, of course he was. Who did you think he was?'

'But you said he was a...you said he was a Catholic.'

'He was a Catholic and then he married in St. Matthew's Church of Ireland.'

'What did people say about a Catholic coming to live in the Shankill?'

'We never let on,' said Mrs McAdam. 'We told people he was Anglican and we didn't lie. He converted when we married.'

'And he died in the war?' asked Shelley.

'He did.'

'That's awful.'

'Aye, it is. He died in the Belfast Blitz when I was in hospital. We'd moved down to Percy Street. I came back here to live with my mother after that.'

'What were you doing in hospital?' Shelley asked.

Mrs McAdam turned slowly to Shelley, 'I lost a wee baby. The only child of my own. She was stillborn in the early hours of the morning on Easter Tuesday 1941. She died under a full moon and the Germans liked to attack under the light of a full moon. What hope had a wee baby after hearing the bombs through the night? They returned again on the next full moon. I was lucky then too. God was looking after me.'

Shelley froze. She hadn't known. Mrs McAdam had told many stories about the Belfast Blitz. She had said there was a bomb every two minutes that Easter night, but hadn't mentioned where she was when she had heard their deathly whistles. Shelley recalled stories of dust floating in the air for two weeks across a city where people slept in houses with no roofs as the rain and constant ashes poured down on them through canvas sheets. Mrs McAdam had said that the morgues were so packed that church halls, swimming baths and markets were filled with dead bodies, and nearly one thousand people had died in one night, but Shelley had not known about George, his wife and his baby and their tragic moonlight serenade.

'It was a wee girl,' Mrs McAdam continued. 'I was going to call her Hannah.'

Shelley couldn't respond. Her throat was filled to aching. Mrs McAdam must have only been nineteen, she realised.

'Don't look so sad, Shelley. I survived. If it hadn't been for little Hannah, I'd have been at home with George on Percy Street, and I would have died too. I got my family in the end. I couldn't have asked for a better family either. I have the two best granddaughters any woman could wish for.'

Shelley was now numbed by love and sadness for the small woman with soft, wrinkled skin by her side.

'Shelley, love. You know I won't live forever,' said Mrs McAdam.

Shelley quickly found her voice, 'Ach, don't talk about that. You'll be waiting for your card from the Queen. You've years to go.'

'I don't need another eighteen years. I've had a good life. Anyway, if the Lord is kind enough to take me, would you make sure that my windows are clean, and that my hair is sitting nice. You know for when the people come round to see me lying. I keep having this dream that my curlers will still be in.'

Shelley smiled, 'Of course. But you'll not be going anywhere for a long time.'

***

'*Tragic end for victim of Irish linen decline.*'

Jean stared at the page. The article, printed in 1890, was small and inconsequential: it was neither an obituary nor a full story and its details were as chilling as the spring wind that retained winter in its grasp outside. Herbert White, Jean's great grandfather, had taken his own life as a result of 'temporary insanity.' Shelley had explained that if Herbert White had lived and died only decades before 1890, the words would have been much more harsh. Herbert White would have been carried off in the night for the crime of self-murder and buried in an unmarked grave. It gave Jean a morsel of comfort that attitudes towards suicide had evolved a little by the time of his death. Shelley, who should have been studying for her exams, had looked into the laws on suicide with more application than it seemed she would ever give one of her GCSEs.

They were seated at the kitchen table: Shelley, Hannah and Harry; all waiting with their heads lowered for Jean to speak, but Jean didn't know what to say.

She thought of her own mother. There was nothing temporary about her state of mind. It was as enduring and unpredictable as the rain on the streets of Belfast. One day, she would be swinging Jean's hand like a child, laughing and dancing through the park where serious mothers kept their children in line; the next she would tell Jean that she wished she had never had children. Jean chose to believe her when she was healthy and ignore her when she was sick. She wondered now if Herbert had the same enduring affliction. 'Temporary insanity' was a term for a coroner's report; a reprieve for a middle class man who had committed something that would otherwise be deemed criminal.

Herbert White had a family: a daughter, Sally who was only three months old, and a wife called Mary. Shelley had been diligent in her research. She had located the marriage certificate for Mary and Herbert at St. Matthew's church, and she had found the burial plot at the municipal cemetery. He would not have been permitted a burial on consecrated ground, and instead was buried in a plot reserved for suicides, a plot that his wife would not share when her time came. Herbert bid his own life a harrowing farewell at the age of thirty-one, when Belfast was still known as *Linenopolis*, the linen manufacturing capital of the British Empire. The mass production of cheap cotton gradually killed the linen industry in Belfast and Herbert White had fallen victim to its steady decline.

Mary White, it seemed, was left with nothing but the riches of her education and her upbringing, and some material possessions that Jean's grandmother had retained. She would have been an educated woman, a middle class woman. At twenty-seven, she would have lost her income and gained a harsh independence. Jean wondered if Mary would have been cast aside by her middle class friends when she moved to the newly built houses on the Shankill, modest homes designed for millworkers.

Jean looked down at the 1901 census. A flicker of hope left her wondering who Edward Chambers had been. Jean closed her eyes and prayed for something that had already passed; she prayed that Mary had found some kind of fulfilment in the harsh circumstances she'd been given.

'Oh why am I crying over history?' said Jean, aware that her children and husband were still awaiting a reaction at the kitchen table.

'I cried too,' said Shelley.

'So did I,' said Hannah.

'It's sad,' said Harry.

'Why do some people have to suffer so much pain?' asked Hannah.

Everyone turned to her. Jean knew that it was Hannah's voice, but the words emerging from it seemed to belong to Shelley.

'Life has no meaning without suffering,' said Harry.

Jean looked at Harry, certain this time of the connection between the voice and the words. He often said things that didn't immediately make sense. It was part of the new person that she was slowly growing to know as her husband.

'What does that mean, exactly?' asked Jean, slowly and with care.

'You can't escape life, death or suffering. Suffering is part of human life,' said Harry.

'But why do some people suffer so much? Why do the people around here suffer so much?' asked Hannah.

'Because in war, there is a lot of death and suffering,' said Harry, his eyes now distant.

'There was no war when Herbert White died in 1890,' Hannah replied. All he lost was his money. He had a wife and a newborn baby. Why wouldn't he have wanted to live to see his little baby grow?'

'We don't know his circumstances,' said Harry. 'Maybe he lost his dignity.'

'Maybe it was in his DNA,' said Jean, looking down and rubbing her hands on her legs.

A tapestry of Jean's family was laid out on the table before her, and depression and suicide were threaded through it across five generations. Only Sally had lived a full life, despite the shadow into which she had been born.

'If it's in the DNA, why does it hit some and not others? And what about us?' asked Hannah.

'You'll be okay, Hannah. Both of you will,' said Jean firmly, looking to Harry for help.

'We can't know anything for sure,' said Harry. 'Life throws all sorts of challenges in our path. When Robert died, I spent months thinking that it wasn't fair, that it should have been me and not my little boy. The guilt made me think that way. I had to say to myself, "This is the situation I've been given. What good can I do with it?"'

Jean wondered how someone so thoughtful had grown from the broken man who'd handed himself into the police for the terrible crime he'd committed. She wondered if prison had been Harry's salvation, if all the suffering they had gone through had been for this. She turned to Shelley and Hannah. They were both deep in thought. Jean could see Hannah bite her lips in the way that she did when she was fighting tears.

Harry broke the silence. 'It helps to have someone who cares for you. In prison, I couldn't have survived without you all. And Nathan.'

'Nathan?' asked Jean a little too abruptly.

'Yes, in the last years of prison, helping Nathan helped me. He's not that different to us, you know. He had a good family and was well brought up, but he took drugs when he was thirteen and that one act dictated the rest of his teenage years. He owed the dealer money. To pay back the money, he had to deal, so he became trapped in a paramilitary gang. And then he was found with a gun in his hand. Going to prison was the best thing that could have happened to him.'

Jean reflected for a moment before realising that she needed to break the sombre mood. 'This is all a bit bloody depressing. So much for your theory that we're French,' she said, pursing her lips and looking in the direction of Shelley.

'You still might be,' said Harry.

'White isn't exactly a very French name, Dad.' Shelley observed.

'Le Blanc is, though' smiled Hannah.

'Le what?' said Shelley.

'*Le Blanc.*' Hannah repeated.

Shelley looked at Hannah again, awaiting a translation.

'You've got to be kidding me,' said Hannah, her voice filled with an unusual mix of patronisation and compassion. 'You're doing a GCSE in French next month and you don't know what blanc means?'

'You said leblanc,' protested Shelley.

'Yes, Shelley, the white. Herbert the White. *Herbert Le Blanc.* I think we need to sit down and practise a little before you walk into that exam room.'

'I've no interest,' said Shelley

'You've no interest in learning French?' asked Hannah.

'None at all.'

'But what about Etienne?' asked Jean.

'Etienne who?' replied Shelley.

Jean locked eyes with Hannah, whose mouth had dropped open. 'What's happened to lover boy?' Jean asked.

'He's got a girlfriend,' said Shelley flatly.

'What?' said Jean.

'She's older. She's a student. He said I was too young, but that he will always think of me with affection.

Jean couldn't contain a smile, 'With affection?'

'Yes, he's full of shit, isn't he?' smiled Shelley.

Hannah, to Jean's amazement, spoke softly to her sister, 'You're too good for him.'

Jean sat up straight and knew what she had to say, 'Shelley, take my advice and find yourself a fella with a full ear. I mean, imagine you're caressing his beautiful long locks and next thing your hand gets stuck in his ear. It wouldn't be pretty, love. It just wouldn't be pretty.'

Hannah bit her lip as a smirk escaped from the corner of her mouth, Harry smiled at Jean, Shelley surveyed the table with a look of dismay that turned gradually to a smile, and laughter flowed again in Jean's kitchen.

Jean watched the tears subside and realised that she'd had to search for

125

meaning in her life many years before Harry had gone to prison to reflect upon it. As a child, she learned quickly that thinking everything was 'unfair' was futile. She'd settled for living, and she'd done so through caring for her brother and then for her own family. She didn't waste time seeking happiness: the laughter seemed to flow of its own accord, despite the suffering.

NEW MOON

The end of almost seven years at Methody and fourteen years of school should have heralded a new beginning, but Hannah was conscious instead of a feeling of loss, of grieving the passing of three quarters of her life. Teachers said their goodbyes and made their best wishes for the exams, but come September, they would move onto another set of Upper Sixth pupils with their university applications and their need for encouragement. Hannah felt saddened that Miss Walker's beautiful face, her scarves and her stories wouldn't be part of her life again.

As they ate lunch together on a bench in Botanic Gardens, Hannah realised it would also be the last time she and Rachael would share stories about what had happened that morning in chemistry, or what Miss Walker had revealed about her time in France or India or indeed Brazil. There would no longer be a deal made about who was caught taking drugs or who had had their stomach pumped at the City hospital after a night at the Bot nightclub. Theirs would be conversations limited to how hard each exam had been, and then, finally, they would be part of a world where anything was allowed because everyone was an adult and no longer suspended in their childhood years.

Rachael had some news.

'We did it,' she whispered.

'It?' Hannah whispered in return, with that same pull of disillusionment that the end of school term had brought.

'Yes, it,' she smiled broadly.

Hannah blushed, unsure what the correct reaction should be. Rachael had always been a confident girl and never short of male attention or boyfriends. After her summer in Croatia, she had returned to Belfast more intrigued by sexual matters than ever. She was keen to get on with it and to find out what this big mystery was all about.

'And?' said Hannah, who had now placed her sandwich back in its box and firmly sealed the lid.

Rachael smiled in such a radiant way that Hannah understood the answer and also why Rachael attracted so many men.

'What was it like?' asked Hannah, remembering the question she was supposed to ask.

'It was amazing,' smiled Rachael.

Hannah followed Rachael's eyes to a distant place, the coast of Dubrovnik possibly, and journeyed swiftly back to the present when Rachael added, 'Not at first though. Oh, it was so rubbish at first. You wouldn't believe it.'

Hannah caught a look of aversion in her friend's eyes, that removed all imaginings of turquoise seas and sandy beaches and pulled her into the world of Belfast where the deed must surely have occurred.

'It was a bit of a non-event. I'll warn you so you know, that's unless you've already...'

'No,' Hannah cut across her friend firmly. 'No.

Rachael was now going out with a twenty-one year-old student, a burly scrum-half with requisite cauliflower ears and hair on the back of his hands. She'd spotted him on the sidelines of a rugby match between Methody and Queen's university. After seeing his furry, thick calves at close range she had decided that he was the one, despite not entirely getting a good look at his face. Hannah didn't think much of his face. He had a good mop of curly black hair that framed a wide forehead, but she found his broken nose off-putting. It had been broken so many times that it made him look almost criminal.

Rachael's plan for her future had fallen into place quite nicely. Having relieved herself of Hannah's dream of clinking glasses in continental Europe, Rachael had formed a world around her rugby player boyfriend that Hannah surmised was fixed. She felt saddened that Rachael had moved on so swiftly from the adolescent world they had created at Methody, but she was also happy for her friend. Not only had Rachael stopped complaining about her own mum, but she had embraced the entire rugby playing family, the brother, the sisters and the parents, and was content to spend her weekends at the rugby club being part of their world. Hannah envied her sense of belonging as much as she feared anything so settled.

The world was still there for Hannah and her mind was a compass that pulled her towards home and pushed her to leave and to explore. She had tried hard to bury any ill feelings towards her father and enjoy these last months of her childhood, her real childhood, the one in which she was sheltered by two parents. Having sex with any boy was the furthest thing from her mind. Hannah knew that she was old-fashioned, but she was in no rush to commit herself to one place, one group of people or one person, and she was not willing to share her body with anyone unless she experienced belonging, trust and love.

'What about your brother. Any news?' asked Hannah, keen to change the subject.

'Terence and mum have hired a private detective. The adoption agency has had no luck finding him. The contact details he had given are no longer valid.'

'If you put Shelley to work, she could find him faster than a detective. You should see what she's done on our family tree. She's so smart, although I just wish she'd get some school work done. She's lazy when it comes to revising.'

'I'd say she's fairly normal. You're comparing her with yourself and you're some kind of machine. I wonder sometimes if there's a robot packed away in that blazer of yours instead of the real Hannah Adams.'

'Very funny! Maybe that's why I don't get a lot of interest from men.'

Hannah smiled and her mind skipped forward to France. She would return there at the start of July, to the place where two men had inspired her to dance. She had danced at a distance from the quiet French fisherman as as an act of giving, and she had danced in an affray of sweat and skin and had taken all the physical pleasure she could derive from the Irishman.

Nicolas, who Hannah had met only once, but who had been prolific in his emails, had found her a job teaching English for four weeks at the local lycée in Paimpol. She was returning to Paimpol and as she looked around the park, she wondered if France would bring her the promise of a future that Belfast seemed to lack.

***

It was an unusually warm summer evening and Catriona wanted to make the most of it. The scent of the garden was profoundly Irish in its dense foliage and shrubbery, but the touch of the sun on Catriona's back as she walked across the paving stones in her summer dress, was that of the Mediterranean.

Catriona led Terence to the patio in the back corner of the garden, where an arc of light formed around an old wrought iron swing chair that she had painted white. She carried the bottle of wine and olives and Terence followed with two glasses and some breadsticks. She set the wine down on a patio table between them and stared up at the sky. It was cloudless and tinted red. Terence sat on the seat to the left of the swing chair, his face bathed in light and shade as Catriona swayed gently. They were silent for a while, quietly sipping their drinks and staring at the sun.

A neighbour's black cat scurried across the lawn. Catriona held its gaze. It was eyeing her with its objective green eyes. It looked to Terence and then slid furtively into the next garden.

'There'll be a new moon tonight.' said Terence.

'Why's that? asked Catriona.

'My grandmother once told me that a cat would look you in the eye on the night of a new moon.'

'That cat always looks me in the eye every time he or she sees me. I'll check the moon next time,' smiled Catriona.

Catriona's eyes moved to the back bedroom and she realised that the roman blind was crooked. In all the years they'd lived there, Rachael had never closed the blind.

'I think she's been sleeping with him.' said Catriona.

'Who?'

'I think Rachael is sleeping with that boy...that man, I mean Jonathan.'

'What makes you say that?' said Terence

'I can tell by the light in her eyes, the glow on her skin, and her sudden deafness. I have to repeat everything twice.'

'And how did you recognise such symptoms?'

'Oh I know them well,' smiled Catriona. 'Only I was twenty.'

Catriona had given Terence time to mourn for his wife. Months had passed with no contact, until one day in April, they both exited their cars at the same time and looked at each other, as they had that first day.

Since that time, Catriona couldn't shake the notion that Terence's attention towards her had changed. At one point, almost all conversation had centred around their son. Now, they had opened their voices to a whole new world of activity going on around them. Terence had been part of Catriona's life for the past couple of months, to the point where it was unimaginable to occupy a whole day without his presence. He had filled that part of her existence that had been missing for a long time. Their meetings were still covert, hidden mostly in Catriona's kitchen.

Catriona had also noted a life about her home that hadn't been there before. There was something resembling heat and it radiated through the moving floorboards and left its mark in a light film of dust that would previously have been swept up instantly. There was the upturned look of the place, crumbs across the kitchen benches and black footprints on the hall floor.

And there was a whole new presence of black curly hair.

Catriona would see Jonathan, the rugby player, scurry down the stairs in his socks, only to turn back when Catriona walked through the front door. He would smile at her and say, 'Just leaving now. I'll go and get Rachael.' Catriona would watch him run to her room and then there would be the whispers and the movement, stealthy scratching movements like that of the cat that had claimed her garden as its patch. Rachael would then appear at the top of the stairs and either be all words and voice and commotion or completely silent; either way, overcompensating for something.

'Yes, she's definitely sleeping with him.' Catriona repeated.

Terence, who seemed to have forgotten the original conversation, was engaged elsewhere. He shook off whatever had delayed his response and spoke quietly, 'She's eighteen, isn't she?'

'Yes, she is. She seems very taken with this Jonathan character. I'm beginning to wonder if he's been here every day since she finished school. He seems like a nice young man, but so much older looking than Rachael.'

'How old?'

'He's only twenty-one, but you should see him. He's what you might call mature.'

Terence smiled. 'I've seen him. I know his dad. He's in politics.'

Catriona's eyes alighted on Terence, 'You've seen him coming around here, haven't you?'

'Yes, every day since the end of the exams. I don't think he'd be used to that much liberty in his own home.'

'Why not?'

'His parents are evangelical christians. You can maybe hold onto the fact that he'd have been taught that sex before marriage is quite wrong.'

'I'm beginning to fall into the evangelical way of thinking,' replied Catriona. 'I don't want anyone near my daughter.'

'Don't forget the conversation we had in Dublin. Remember, you said if she gets pregnant, you'll smile first. Don't forget to smile!'

'Hey, now wait a minute, don't you be making light of this situation.' Catriona laughed.

She stopped and looked at Terence. There was something different about him. *Colour*. That was it. He was surrounded by a rich palette of nature and his skin soaked it up. He had lost the grey look that had clung to him since he had been her neighbour. Perhaps she was too used to seeing him in a suit. The suit made his personality a blank canvas, someone whom the commentators in his public life could not assume to know. Here he was in jeans and a white casual shirt with his silver hair and his grey-blue eyes, and Catriona realised something.

She realised that she was still attracted to Terence after all these years.

Catriona blushed at the thought. She had always known he was handsome, but she now found herself alone with him in her garden embroiled in the zealous temperature. She looked at the wine in her hand and blamed it. Red wine always heightened the colour in her cheeks. Just as she wished for his touch, Terence reached out his hand.

'Catriona, we need to talk about what Roderick has found so far. Take some more wine.'

'No, no, I shouldn't. It's a school night. I'll only end up drinking half the bottle.'

Terence seemed more serious. Catriona set down her glass.

'Don't worry,' he said. 'It's not bad news. It's confusing news.'

'Go on.'

'We have full details now of Anne and James Rodgers, the adopted parents. James was born in County Meath near Dublin, and, at the time of adoption, he was a lecturer of Maths in England. Anne was born here in Belfast and she was a primary school teacher. We think they lived in England after university, moved back to Dublin, where they adopted the baby and then returned to Belfast. I've tried to find out if James was a lecturer at Queen's. It would make sense but he is not listed among the members of staff. We've also searched for Anne through the school boards, but nothing. They moved to Belfast and disappeared.'

'How do we know for sure they moved to Belfast?'

'They spent about six months at Anne's mother's house just off the Falls Road. Some of the neighbours confirmed they'd been there for a short time, but that's all they know.'

'Anything else?'

'James and Anne met at Trinity College.'

'No way!'

'Yes!'

'But would they have been there at the same time as us?'

'No, ten years before us. They were there in the mid to late sixties. James studied maths and you'll never believe this...'

'What?'

'Anne studied French and Irish...like you.'

'French and Irish?'

'Yes' confirmed Terence.

'I know you've probably ruled this out, but have you checked if they are still alive. Jean said that they were able to find her ancestors on the city council burial websites.'

'That's all been covered. Neither name has come up.'

'What about prison?' Catriona said it in a whisper, not quite understanding why it had come to the mind at all. It must have been thinking of Jean that had made her say it.

'All checked already with no return. There aren't that many university Maths professors on these islands, and James doesn't seem to have a job at any of the colleges and universities we've looked at.'

'Maybe they live abroad.'

'There is a huge chance that they live abroad. Maths professors are in demand. We've even looked at universities in America and in France. Nothing.'

'You said she was an Irish speaker. There are Irish language organisations. She might belong to them. I'll give you some names.'

'We could go on that, but I think you might have to get involved.

Roderick is good, but he doesn't speak Gaelic.'

'He doesn't have to, but I'll phone around a few friends to ask if anyone has heard of Anne Rodgers.'

'There is no evidence of her in the public school system at all.'

'What about private?'

'There isn't really a private school system to work from. Most of the private schools are Protestant.'

'There were Irish language schools in Belfast, I'm sure. That's where all those IRA guys learned to speak Irish, isn't it?'

Terence smiled. 'I suppose there's that.'

'Are you not friends with any of the Sinn Fein leaders yet? You could ask around.'

'We sit at the same table, but we're not quite friends yet. Give us another few years before I say to them, "Remember those days when you carried around guns and caused destruction all over Belfast, well, was your Irish teacher called Anne? It's just that I think she might be our son's mother."'

'No need for sarcasm, Terence Craig.' said Catriona, her mind filled with avenues of thoughts that all had dead ends.

'Let's have a drink and a toast to knowing what we know,' suggested Terence.

Catriona held up her glass, 'To Aidan, James and Anne Rodgers. We hope that you're sitting under the same sky that is so beautiful in Belfast tonight. Here's to finding Aidan.'

'Cheers.' said Terence as the shadow of a tall, slim girl and a bulky male appeared against the light and walked towards them.

THE SPRING TIDE

The Île-de-Bréhat was a carnival of colour and fragrance, and it was filled with people searching out the wonders of the early July spring tide. Hannah inhaled the scent of eucalyptus, smiled at the sight of pink geraniums drooped over old stone walls, and tiptoed carefully over the craggy stones in rugged rock pools where she paddled among children and their nets. As puffins kissed on the pink rocks, Hannah relished the start of summer; she was almost nineteen, school was over and she was in France with Gildas.

Gildas, who'd been the first to contact Hannah upon her arrival in Paimpol, spent much of the time describing the tides to her. Hannah checked her pocket dictionary for a translation of *'la grande marée'*, such was its prominence in the discussion they were having. She'd never heard of a spring tide, but realised that it involved the sea parting from the land in an extended farewell.

They were kneeling and picking mussels when Hannah asked, 'What exactly is a spring tide?'

Gildas' eyes came to life and he explained carefully, 'When you have a tide, it is caused by the force of the moon and the force of the earth.' He formed planets with his fists.

Hannah's head moved up and down.

'The sea is pulled by the gravity of the moon...'

Hannah disguised her scientific deficiencies with a continual nod.

The rotational force of the earth, she heard. *The sea bulges*, she heard. The rest of his words fell through the gaps in her intelligence. Hannah flicked the small swirls of worm-shaped sand and tried not to look Gildas in the eye. One of the first sentences she'd ever learned in French came mechanically to mind. *Je ne comprends pas.*

Gildas laughed, as though attuned to her thoughts.

He placed three shells on his arm in a vertical line. 'Look, when we have the earth, the sun and the moon all in a line, we have spring tide. It happens when there is a new moon or a full moon. Today we have a new moon.'

'And I take it that means the tide is very low,' Hannah said, her eyes narrowing to a distant horizon of water.

'Or very high,' he added. 'When the moon is closest to the earth, you get the biggest tide of all.'

'I wonder why it's called spring tide,' Hannah said, her head cocked to the side. Jean was suddenly infiltrating her thoughts. *Listen to your man*, she was saying. *Is this the language of love?* Hannah smiled, straightened her neck, and removed the hand that had found itself resting involuntarily on her left hip. 'It doesn't just happen in spring,' she observed.

'No, twice a lunar month.'

'A lunar month,' she repeated. Why hadn't she thought to listen in geography? Or was it physics?

'Yes, you know...the moon.' Gildas was laughing. 'Sorry,' he said, 'This must be very boring. You measure your day in degrees celsius and I measure mine in the tidal coefficient. Your head is in the clouds and mine is in the moon,' he smiled.

'I don't know if that's reassuring for me or not! You're in charge of the boat home,' she said, overlooking the tidal coefficient for fear of an explanation.

Hannah turned to Gildas and spoke slowly, certain that there must be a seductrice kindling within her. She just needed a little help stirring the flame, 'What kind of things happen at spring tide when there is a new moon?' she asked, almost gasping.

'All types of mysteries of nature,' smiled Gildas.

Hannah's face reddened.

'It's a ripe time for planting seeds.'

Hannah wanted to kiss him.

'The body and the mind also change with the moon's orbit.'

Hannah stopped breathing. *Gildas' body.*

'Things feel different when there is a full moon or a new moon.'

Was he still talking about the moon?

'I know people have recorded the increase in violent crime...'

Crime? Hadn't he sensed her *femme fatale*?

'But it's not possible to record the beauty, the positive energy that occurs.'

Hannah laughed aloud. She was on unfamiliar ground. Gildas stopped what he was saying and smiled.

'We should walk back to the boat now,' he said, pulling Hannah to her feet.

She stood up. He was still holding her hand. She walked by his side, the faculty of speech and her sense of reality anchored in the sand.

'Did you enjoy the island? Gildas asked softly.

'Did. Yes. Thank you,' she said in English, her linguistic processes in disarray. There were words but there was nothing linking them together.

He helped her onto the boat and then kissed her gently as she stood on the step. *Eucalyptus, geraniums, puffins, rock pools.* He was kissing her. He stopped.

The boat started to drift from the shore and Hannah's French floated behind it in the rippling current. She could only summon one sentence. *Je ne comprends pas.* Over and over. *Je ne comprends pas.*

He kissed her again as they approached his coastal home. She tasted the salt from his lips and wanted to place her hands over his body, but Gildas moved away silently and steered the boat to the dock at the end of his garden.

'We are home.' he said.

The beauty of the French language had now parted company from Hannah in an extended farewell like an unscheduled spring tide.

'Let's get you back to your dorm.'

Gildas reached out for Hannah's hand in the car as they drove through the winding country roads. He kissed her goodbye at the dormitories.

She slept soundly, with the sea tangled in her hair, sand clinging to her arms and legs and the taste of salt on her lips.

The morning didn't begin where night ended, but stretched lazily into the afternoon. She stood up eventually, looked in the mirror in the ensuite bathroom and saw that the pale girl with blue skin who had left Ireland only two days before, was infused with soft pink. She touched her face and moved her head to the side, her eyes still concentrated on the mirror, blue eyes that were large and instilled with life.

Her body was as petite as it had always been, but it felt fuller. Her breasts seemed to bulge through her skin. The sea bulging. Or was it the moon? Which planet was rotating? She turned to the side and looked back over her shoulder at the slope of her back. She shivered as she became aware of a swell deep in her body.

Hannah wouldn't see Gildas again until Wednesday. She would have to enjoy the noise of Nicolas and the challenge of teaching English to teenage boys and girls for three long days.

Her legs weakened.

Subject, object, verb, came the echo of Miss Walker's voice. *Tu me manques.* You me miss. You are missed, Gildas.

Hannah stood up straight again.

Hannah, Hannah, always so serious.

She walked back to her bed again and surveyed the sparse room with its plate cooker set on top of the fridge. Her eyes closed on an island and the soft laughter of Gildas as she recollected the past, the present or the future tense, and fell in love with French all over again. *Je t'aime*. Subject, object, verb. *I you love*.

***

'Hannah is so grounded. She'll be fine.' said Jean, as they walked from Leiden train station to the hotel.

Harry had been worried about Hannah. He didn't feel that things had properly been resolved and here he was with Jean in Holland, one step closer by land, but further removed from Hannah than he'd ever been. He couldn't explain it to Jean. She didn't understand. Jean was thinking of Hannah's safety and security. Harry was thinking that Hannah was almost nineteen, and that she would never know memories of her childhood that would make her feel pride in her father.

She had been easier to live with since Christmas, and after her exams, she had even started to linger on in the kitchen to talk to him. Every question she had asked him about the world had made him melt. She cared for Nathan. She wouldn't say anything, but he could tell when she would say, 'Is Nathan coming for tea again?' It was an invitation from Hannah more than an assumption of his whereabouts.

As they approached the lobby of the Golden Tulip, Harry realised where his real tension lay. Jean had arranged for them both to meet Roy for lunch.

They had hoped to make it to Holland for Robert's anniversary, but it hadn't worked out. Harry had impressed his young foreman at work and had been told to delay taking time off in case he was offered a full-time position. He had worked for the agency until the last week in June, before finally being offered a permanent position as a welder.

Harry and Jean changed quickly and made their way to the pub where they were to meet Roy. They walked in complete silence all the way. Harry had noted Jean looking up from time to time to speak, but she too seemed to lack any sense of voice.

Roy arrived at the door and Harry walked to him first, focusing ahead, determined not to take in any body language or verbal communication between Roy and Jean. He needed to crush the thing that had torn him up inside. He firmly shook Roy's hand. Roy looked directly into Harry's eyes.

'Welcome to Leiden,' Roy said.

Harry remained silent. He then stood back when Roy reached down and kissed Jean on the cheek. He held his breath and counted. He followed Roy to the bar, his fists clenched in his jacket pocket.

Roy turned hesitantly toward them both. 'I'm sorry I didn't get time to tell you this,' he said, 'Majella is here.'

'Majella?' asked Harry.

'She was Robert's girlfriend,' Roy responded. 'She's from Cork. They spent some time together and I met her last summer again when she moved here. She and my son have become friends.'

Jean's face folded. Harry reached out his hand to steady her and tried hard not to notice that Roy was to reach out too.

'Sorry, it's okay, I'll compose myself before I see her. Oh goodness, I'm a mess.' Jean looked to a pillared mirror and flicked away the mascara that had run down her cheeks. 'It's...I didn't expect...'

'I should've let you know,' said Roy. 'Come this way. We're at the back.'

Harry followed Roy, relieved that there was to be another person present and surprised by Jean's emotional response. He wondered if Jean had heard of Majella before. Perhaps Roy had told her about the meeting last summer, but Harry had come home last summer. He shook the thoughts away. He needed to trust Jean.

Majella was beautiful. She had a mass of dark, curly hair and the widest blue eyes he'd ever seen. There was something of Hannah in her, but Hannah, whose face was more composed and refined, was a tamer version of the girl that was before him now. Majella's features were wild like a gypsy of some bygone world. She had pale skin and freckles and an expression of vitality. Harry was mesmerised by Majella and her connection with Robert. He understood Jean's tears and found himself awash with emotion, but clinging onto his cool in Roy's presence.

'I'm Harry, pleased to meet you.' Harry said, after Jean had shyly introduced herself. 'Roy tells us you knew Robert.'

'I did. It was only for one summer, but it was special. Robert was lovely. You had a really beautiful son.'

Her voice was like a song and Jean collapsed again into her hands. Harry placed his hand on her knee and spoke to Majella again. 'Thank you. It's good to hear that.'

'I have some photographs,' she said and placed an album on the table. 'I made this for you this morning. It was a bit last minute. I'm sorry I didn't get time to make a better job of it.'

Harry lifted the album and opened it in silence. He could feel the weight of Jean's body against his left side as she reached out and stroked the spine of the album. Harry turned the pages slowly, enjoying each moment, aware that with the turn of each page, he would come closer to the end.

'These are incredible,' he said.

'Majella is a photographer,' Roy interjected.

'Ah but sure, I wasn't back then. It was a good camera that my mum had given me...an old manual thing. It took good photographs though, didn't it?'

'I think you're underplaying your role,' said Harry. 'These are amazing.'

'You're very kind. I found a box of old films on my last visit back

138

home. I developed them and discovered these.'

Harry lamented the time he had lost with his son, but was grateful for this gift of a few precious weeks of his face smiling widely into the lens. Robert was glowing and healthy and so different to the young skinny boy with a troubled look in his eyes who had said goodbye before departing for Holland. Harry had seen his son on three more prison visits after that, and always that troubled look had remained. Now Harry could see that Robert had reason to smile in Holland.

Harry's eyes met Roy's again. He should have thanked Roy for the short lifeline he had given to his son. Instead, Harry lowered his head and continued to look through the photographs.

Majella had included the photographs that Robert had taken of her as well as some group ones. There was only one shot of Robert and Majella together. Majella had her head resting on Robert's shoulder as Robert looked down, smiling at her face. She wasn't smiling, but she looked radiant. Jean stopped, gazed at the image and cried again. Harry knew there was only one page left but he allowed Jean to learn the tranquility on her son's face. The last photo was of Robert standing at the door of a bedroom, with a feigned look of sadness.

'Oh that one was a silly one I took on my last night. I asked Robert to show me his sad face. I know it sounds daft, but he had this amazingly deep look that I could never capture on camera. He would sit in silence and look thoughtful, I suppose, but then he would be away before I could capture it.'

Jean raised her head. Harry watched as his wife's eyes met the giving eyes of Majella. Something had been revealed that only they knew.

'You'll be wondering why we didn't stay in touch,' said Majella, softly, still songful.

'No, no, I wasn't thinking about that,' Harry said.

'Yes, I did think of that.' Jean said. 'I know you were both young, but I wondered why you didn't take each other's email address or anything.'

'We did,' said Majella. 'At least, I did. I took Robert's email address, but I never emailed him. I...' She looked down and took a breath. 'Robert told me about the place where he came from and some of the things he'd done before he came to Holland. He said it had all started with smoking a joint at school and next thing, the paramilitaries were on his back. Anyway, I made the mistake of telling my cousin. And I told her about Robert's...I told her about Robert's dad.'

Harry's pulse accelerated and he felt sweat on his palms and on his back. Jean's hand was on his now, reassuring and protective.

'I'm sorry. I shouldn't have said that, but I'm from Cork and the family would have been quite republican in their day. My cousin was worried what they'd think. It's shameful. It's shameful that I would judge someone in that way. I didn't mean to. Honestly.'

'It's okay, love,' said Jean. 'It's okay.'

Majella looked at Jean with pleading eyes, as she continued. 'I wanted to stay in touch with him, but at that time I believed what I was told and my cousin advised me to stay away. I just need you to know that I really did like Robert. I came back again to see if I could find him and I didn't know what to think when I learned he'd died. He told me that he loved me. He said I was the first person he'd loved. I feel awful that I didn't say the same thing back to him.'

Jean reached out her hand to Majella, 'Don't feel bad. It was a complicated time in Northern Ireland. If I'd been from Cork, I'd have been intimidated too. Robert would've known that you loved him. He had a greater sense and understanding of the world than most of us.'

Harry's heart rate evened and the sweat lifted from his skin, but Jean's response could not compensate for the self-loathing he now felt. His prison sentence was an inferno that had spread into every crevice of his children's lives. Harry could live with the pain of having been locked away, but each time he learned what an impact it had on his children, his hope slipped away.

He retained a cordial tone for the next hour as they ate lunch and drank wine. He was thankful for Majella and her ability to converse, and withdrew from reality as his mind rested on torturous words that Majella had so innocently uttered, 'I told her about Robert's dad.'

Harry barely noticed Roy in the end: he was quiet and the women were enjoying the conversation as Majella relived each photograph for Jean. Harry regretted that he was missing this information about his son, but he knew that Jean would tell him later and that the stories would be revised over again for Hannah and Shelley.

Harry walked solemnly back to the hotel, a tiredness dragging at his feet and at his eyelids, all the energy he had stored in prison now spent. He didn't talk to Jean nor admit that he felt home-sick, and as detached from Holland as a person could be from a country. In forty-eight hours, he would be home, and he would be happy to remain in his hotel room and sleep until the time came to board the plane. Once, he had dreamed of seeing the world, and he'd read books and atlases and selected countries he wanted to explore, but he had not known then that he was content to see the world from the pages he was reading.

It was Jean who suggested a nap, and Harry was relieved. It was the first time he'd lain down during daylight hours since his release. He placed his arms around Jean, as he had done every night since Shelley had quite naturally, without any discussion, taken up residence in Robert's old room. Harry would hold Jean close for a long time until Jean would finally wriggle away on to her own comfortable spot at the edge of the bed.

Harry had no sense of time when he awoke, but the emptiness in his stomach told him that it must have been evening. He moved his hand across Jean's shoulder and down her arm. She didn't stir. His hand followed her collarbone and up her neck. Jean turned then onto her back. She moved Harry's hand onto her breast. He kissed her hand and kissed her breast. He explored Jean's body without inhibition and felt connected to her skin and to the beat of her heart. Their bodies had met many times in the past: they had both given and taken and relished each other's skin, but never before had they shared this distilled pain. Harry knew that Jean was collecting his silent tears. She was absorbing his hurt over what he had done to his family. They made love and became each other's suffering until the only thing that Harry understood was his love for Jean. She took away his guilt and allowed him to feel part of the physical world in which he was living.

A SHIFT IN NATURE

Nicolas was still wearing his sandals from the previous summer and his bleached head zig-zagged around the hall like lightning as he trailed Hannah with him. He was fast, strong and completely uncoordinated, and Hannah wondered how she would get through the night. The fest noz was at a bar in the city of Rennes, and it lacked the sense of community Hannah had enjoyed at the family events in Paimpol. She and Nicolas were in the company of a party of English teachers, all gathered in Rennes to celebrate the end of the four week English course.

Hannah was outside breathing away the fumes of sweat that had filled her lungs when she heard a familiar accent, and a voice that was as foreign as it was recognisable. 'Do I have to follow you outside to get a dance?'

Hannah looked up and found the same tanned face and green eyes she had met the previous year in Paimpol.

'It's a small world,' he said. He reached out his hand and led her back into the hall. 'You could tell me your name this time.' he added.

'I'm Hannah,' she replied.

'I'm Aidan. Pleased to finally meet you.'

Aidan's smile was warm like relief. He placed one hand on her back and took her left hand with the other and danced. His arms were strong, but Hannah was able to keep up with him and didn't have to stretch her limbs as she had earlier in the evening. The feeling of homesickness that she had experienced throughout the day started to subside. Aidan danced with her, bought her drinks and danced again.

The music ended and their hands remained linked as they walked outside. Hannah's pale blue strappy dress, that had clashed with any attempt at an under garment, was free and floating over her breasts. She felt the skin on her nipples glide against the loose cotton through the late night chill. The dress moved and a breeze was trapped between her skin and the cloth, creating a gap that Aidan must surely have seen. He smiled and she shifted her shoulders, trying to tame her dress back into place, but she was caught between modesty and the thrill of the wind as she imagined Aidan's hands moving through the gap.

Nicolas appeared with a note and her cardigan and whispered in English, 'Here's the address for a taxi. See you back at my flat.'

Aidan placed his arms around her and rubbed her skin, 'You're all goose bumps,' he said, wrapping her cardigan around her shoulders and buttoning it down to her chest. He moved his hands across the wool on her back and pulled her towards him. When the crowds had dispersed, he kissed her. His kiss was deep and reassuring and Hannah blocked the reality of Gildas, the constant backdrop to her summer, from her mind, and abandoned herself in the moment.

Aidan took her hand and they walked. 'I live around the corner,' he said. 'I can call you a cab from there.' Hannah followed, but emboldened by the music and the warmth of Aidan's kiss, she stopped and kissed him again on the street.

'I wanted to kiss you last summer,' he said by his front door.

Hannah's cheeks radiated as she recalled the dance they had shared that night in Paimpol, and how close Aidan's body had been against her own.

'We're alone,' said Aidan inside the studio flat. He unbuttoned the cardigan he had so carefully secured and kissed her shoulders. Hannah shivered as he removed her straps, her dress floating thoughtlessly to the ground: it was a dress that had presumed a mind and a personality as Hannah stood still and watched Aidan remove his own clothes. In a room lit by streetlights, they both stood naked and Hannah knew that her mind was merely a flicker of darkness in a room where multiple darknesses now danced with the dim light. Her body was all light and life and a burgeoning flow of blood washed through her. Aidan's hands moved across her and her mind was lost. She wanted everything and she was enveloped in the semi-darkness and in the intense heat. Aidan hesitated, 'Wait, is this okay?' She didn't respond. There was no mind to engage, and as time passed through the breaks in the darkness, their seamless bodies controlled the night.

Hannah awoke with Aidan stuck to the skin on her back and the heat of his breath on her neck. She felt thirsty and her ears rang with the protracted sound of pipes and horns as memories of dancing with Aidan came to her again. She felt his groin stir behind her and she turned to find him smiling.

'Hannah. You did say your name was Hannah, didn't you?'

'Yes,' she laughed. 'I'm glad you remembered.'

His kissed her again in the intense way that he'd kissed her through the night. He got up and she felt a breeze on her skin and a slight pain. She blushed in recognition of the pain as an understanding of what she had done dawned in the dusty light.

Aidan prepared breakfast. Hannah's body solidified from the mass of blood and skin and moisture and she started to feel cold. She became self-conscious for the first time that she was still naked as she searched by the bed for her idle dress. She pulled on her cardigan and wrapped it tightly around her, regretting the morning and wishing to be warm again in the heat of Aidan's skin.

'Take a seat,' Aidan said.

Hannah noted the same set up as she had in her own dorm in Paimpol. Aidan was cooking from a double plated electric stove that sat on top of the fridge in a kitchenette in the same room as the double bed. He was in boxer shorts. His body was short, but muscular, tanned and strong. Hannah felt flushed as she realised that she was staring at his naked torso and dreaming again of the night she'd had. She turned away smiling and saw a letter on the table that was addressed to 'Aodhán Mac Ruaidhrí.'

'I believe I've been misspelling your name in my head,' said Hannah.

Aodhán pulled on a white t-shirt, 'You wouldn't be the first,' he smiled, and laid a plate of omelette and toast on the table. *Bon appetit.*'

He ate in silence.

'I enjoyed dancing with you,' he said finally.

'Thank you. It was good. It was a relief, to be honest. Nicolas has the arms of an angry octopus.'

'I also enjoyed the dance through the night,' he smiled, his green eyes flashing with mischief.

'I did too,' she laughed, increasingly self-aware that it was a conversation that crossed the boundaries of her experience. 'Actually, it was...' She looked up before finishing, 'Aodhán, it was my first time.'

Aodhán's fork bounced off the plate. He searched under the table and resurfaced flustered and red. 'Hannah,' he choked, 'I wish you'd told me. I'd never have... I'm sorry.'

'It's okay. I think it would have spoiled the moment if I'd told you. Your face is like beetroot. I kind of thought that it was a special enough thing that you should know too.'

'Of course, of course, I'm glad that I know now, but I feel that I've done something I shouldn't have done. I mean, is it okay? Are you okay?'

'I'm okay.' Hannah's confidence was slipping away as Aidan's protective tone settled around the room, clothing the passion of the night.

'Hannah, listen to me. I know that you're safe here....you can be assured of that. I'm hoping that it's because we met before or because we are both from the same town, but you need to be careful around here. Anywhere really. There are people who are...'

'Hey, stop it. You're killing the night for me. It's kind of you to look out for me, but I'm sensible enough. My mum said that when I die, they'll etch, "Here lies Hannah, the sensible one" on the grave.'

'Sorry. You just seem like a nice girl and you don't know me at all. I wish that you'd known me a little at least.'

'I kind of felt that I did know you. I don't know why. It was natural to me.'

'It was. Yes, it was. Can I drive you back to Paimpol?' he offered.

'You don't have to do that. It's an hour and a half each way. It'll take up your day. I can go with Nicolas. How did you know I was in Paimpol?'

'I see Etienne from time to time in Rennes. I asked him how his Irish exchange student was doing last time I saw him. He was a little cagey, but he said you were coming back in the summer. I presumed you were maybe together...'

'Me and Etienne? No way! We didn't get on exactly. He wooed my sister over a poppy wreath though...' Hannah hesitated, realising she didn't know anything about Aodhán. She looked at the letter again and his Irish name with its Irish spelling.

'He wooed her with a symbol of death and bloodshed?' Aodhán asked, his eyes raised.

'It's a long story, but Shelley was a victim of the Shankill bomb. She lost her foot. Etienne came to Belfast looking for war stories and he fell for Shelley. I guess she had a good story for him for a while. Shelley was all caught up in the romance of it.'

'I see,' said Aodhán, his eyes lowered. 'It's sad about the bomb and your sister. Sorry to hear that.'

'It was a long time ago, and we don't think about any of that stuff anymore. Sure look at us here in France setting the world alight,' she laughed. 'And me from the Shankill and you with a name with all those fada accents. I imagine we're poles apart.'

'You're right about us setting the world alight, but I'd say we lived in pretty close proximity. I grew up near the Falls Road so we were only minutes away from you. We also lived in Paimpol during the holidays.'

'Why Paimpol?' Hannah asked.

'My mother loved it there.'

'Is she still there?'

'No, she died when I was twelve.'

'Oh, sorry.' Hannah said and set down her knife and fork.

'I miss her, but anyway, let's not talk about that. If you're going to travel with Nicolas, then we'd better get you over there.'

They walked back to the centre of town and Hannah became aware of a shift. The essence of the night had been tempered, and she started to think over what she had done. She should have been elated, and she had felt that way in the morning when Aidan's breath was on her back, but now she felt cold in the shade outside Nicolas' flat.

Nicolas lived on the attic floor of a topsy turvy building that was clad in latticed wood. It had an ancient staircase that wound its way up four flights. Hannah climbed with lead in her gait, unable to recapture the night.

Hannah had trusted Aodhán with her body: she had trusted him based on some loose kinship of place. There was no sense of belonging, just the tug of music and night and the endless, almost swaddling warmth.

She knew that there had not been love and she had hoped in the past that there would be love when the time came. Nor would there be a chance for love to grow. She might never see Aodhán again.

***

Aodhán was still by Hannah's side when she peered around the corner of the room to find the outline of bodies in sleeping bags at various angles across the floor. He watched her tip-toe through semi-darkness. She lifted a small rucksack and pulled on her jeans and top. They descended the four flights of stairs from the attic studio and made her way back out into the brightness of the market.

'I think they might be a while.' said Hannah. 'Fancy sharing a coffee with me while they sleep?'

'It would be a pleasure,' said Aodhán.

The Saturday market on *la Place des Lices* in Rennes was bustling with fruit and vegetable stalls, and the vibrant multi-coloured spectacle of flowers. Aodhán was pleased that Hannah didn't have to rush off and he led her towards a café on the market place. Hannah had intrigued him from the moment he'd heard that an Irish girl was coming to stay with the Ollivier family in Paimpol, but now he was concerned. He was concerned that they had been liberated from their inhibitions and from any sense of caution, and he felt responsible because of his age and because of an overwhelming sense that he should have looked out for Hannah. He watched her across the table of the café. She had emerged from the shower after breakfast with wet hair and a peach face filled with freckles. Her dark hair was dry now and lay in natural curls on her shoulders.

Hannah was silhouetted against the half-timbered, lop-sided dwellings of medieval Rennes. The rest of Rennes was like any other French city, a marriage of old and new, quaint and ugly, but here in the medieval centre, with its sloped roofs and narrow streets, Aodhán felt connected to the past, and his past hit him when he saw that the beauty of Hannah was like that of his mother. He recalled sitting in cafés in Brittany with her and drawing lines in his imagination over the dots on her face. His mother's hair and been long and red, but her eyes and her skin were like Hannah's.

He hadn't known as a boy why his mother's face was so different from his own, and he still longed for the innocent days when he had two parents, one as free as a bird, and the other locked up in a cell. He'd loved them both, and that was all he had needed to know.

'How long will you stay in France?' asked Hannah.

'I don't know. I haven't figured out what I want to do when I grow up yet,' he smiled.

'What do you do now?'

'I teach maths at a college here in Rennes.'

'Will you ever come home to Belfast, do you think?'

'I don't know. I haven't figured out where home is either! Me and my dad...we don't speak. He was in prison when my mum died. I suppose I've been punishing him for a long time.'

Aodhán had spent his life hiding who he was, and couldn't understand why he was suddenly revealing anything at all about his past to this young woman from the Shankill, this young woman whose family had suffered at the hands of an illegal army to which his father belonged.

Hannah spoke softly and carefully, 'We both have something in common then. My dad was in prison too. He got home last summer and I punished him a little too. Now I kind of feel proud of him for how he managed to turn his life around.'

Aodhán thought about what Hannah had said as they placed their orders for coffee. His father had also turned his life around. He was a pillar of the community, but there was one lie that hung over Aodhán and made every crime his father had committed so much more painful. He needed to change the subject, to push the dilemma of his father away.

'Hannah, you know, what you told me this morning, I'm not sure I reacted the way I should have. I panicked that you had entrusted me with something so special.'

'It's okay. Look, sitting here having this cup of coffee has made it all feel a little bit less...I don't know...incomplete. It doesn't feel like you're so much of a stranger, I suppose.'

Aodhán looked at Hannah and felt a draught cross his neck as a shadow drifted over the terrace. He realised what one night with a stranger could mean for Hannah, just as he had often thought about what one night with a stranger may have meant for his birth mother.

Knowing that he was adopted had been a relief at first; an escape from the resentment for his father. Then, after he had contacted the agency, and after he'd realised that his birth certificate had been lost in a fire, he had run away from the search and returned to France. He'd assumed the loss of the birth certificate to be a sign, a sign that he was unwanted by this woman who had given him life.

As the shadow drifted, and the morning lit up the freckles on Hannah's face, he realised that his birth mother could have been young and that she could have been as lost as Hannah now seemed.

He and Hannah hadn't used contraception. He had never been so careless, so inebriated and foolish, and now he had a feeling of responsibility for the beautiful woman lighting up the shadows of *La Place des Lices*.

Aodhán thought of his father, his biological father. He had grown to distrust the man in his head. All he had known since the age of eighteen was that his biological father was a man who had let down his mother. Otherwise, why would his mother have had to give birth in a mother and baby home? Aodhán thought about the meaning of two bodies coming together as one, and he saw that the pleasure he had always taken had been without boundaries. Now, he was bridled by the caution that he should have exercised over the past ten hours of his life. Perhaps he was no different from the man who had let down his birth mother, after all.

He looked into Hannah's wide blue eyes and spoke softly, 'Hannah, we didn't take precautions and I'm sorry. I didn't once think of you or that this might be your first time. It was wrong of me and...'

'Please don't. I told you it was nice and I'm a little embarrassed to talk about it like this in a public place.' she said, her cheeks glowing as she looked from left to right.

'Trust me, no one can hear us and I have to tell you this. When you leave here today, you will leave knowing where you can find me. I'm going to give you my contact details and I want you to stay in touch with me if anything...' He hesitated, recognising the faded colour of fear on Hannah's face. 'Look, I realise that you're off to university in Scotland in September, but please keep my details safe and if you ever have any problems at university or on your year abroad in France and Spain, then remember that I'm here. And I need to add this...Your body...share it with someone you love and trust, someone who will never let you down. I want you to know that you can trust me.'

Aodhán could see how uncomfortable his words had made Hannah feel. Her face was now white and her lips were trembling as she sipped her coffee. She set it down and cleared her throat as the tint of peach returned.

'I know that what you said came from a good place,' she said, 'but I feel a wee bit embarrassed. Can we move on? I hope my friend Rachael's Aidan is as nice as you.'

'My mother told me that Aodhán means bringer of fire,' he smiled. 'Is your friend seeing someone called Aodhán? You should warn her about the fire.'

'No, she's trying to find her brother. She recently discovered that her mum had a baby when she was at Trinity College, but his name is spelt the English way. He's called Aidan Rodgers.'

'I see,' said Aodhán, the market now spinning behind Hannah in a blur of colours. He felt the fire and tried to extinguish its flames on his face. He responded after a pause, 'The English spelling is more common. And Rachael, your friend, did she study French with you?'

Aodhán watched Hannah's face light up as she began to narrate her world, 'No, she hated it. She dropped out and stuck to science, but her mum, Catriona, studied French. She was the one who told me about the French exchange. She's lovely. She let me live in her house for a while when my dad came home. It's on Windsor Park. It was like staying in a hotel.'

Catriona. Windsor Park. Those words stayed. The others swirled in his mind.

From the moment Aodhán had seen Hannah dancing the previous summer, he had felt a magnetic pull towards her. Now, he had uncovered the reason. Hannah had a link to his past. After years in a wilderness, he'd finally met someone with a link to his past.

Hannah's phone buzzed. She read the text.

'It's Nicolas. He's up. He says we're leaving in half an hour', she said, still firmly grounded in the present and unaware of the bridge of past, present and future that Aodhán was now building in his mind.

'I don't want you to leave,' Aodhán said, surprising himself. 'I want to take you back home and make love to you all over again.'

Hannah's eyes widened, 'But you said that I should be careful. And now you're...'

'Now I've realised that someone truly special has walked into my life.' Aodhán's words were breaking up, and he realised that he was confusing Hannah. He leant over the table and kissed her on the lips. He then searched in his wallet for a card. 'Here, these are my details at the college. I'll write my home number down too. Remember. Please stay in touch.'

Hannah took another card from the pocket of his wallet and wrote on it, '6a Snugville Street...when you come home.'

***

'What's she up to?' asked Shelley as she rounded the corner into Snugville Street, nodding towards Mrs McAdam.

'She's cleaning her window,' replied Nathan.

Shelley moved slowly at first, fighting an intangible weight around her.

Mrs McAdam was in her red dress and high heels, her diminutive body framed by an inky sky. A feeling like noise shattered the quiet of Snugville Street as though the silent sky was shrieking a warning.

'She's in high heels...what on earth?' Shelley said, quickening her pace.

Mrs McAdam was staring up at the sky.

Shelley ran. She was six years old again and she was running across the

Shankill Road. She raised her hands to her ears to push back the noise. She could hear it. For the first time, she could hear the noise. She swallowed back fear and looked around for Hannah and Robert. It was Nathan. She removed her hands from her head and shook away the memory of the sound.

She turned to Mrs McAdam. Shelley was afraid to call out or to make any noise as she approached, but still, the step ladder trembled.

Shelley arrived at the foot of the ladder in time to receive Mrs McAdam into her open arms. Nathan supported Mrs McAdam's weight as Shelley slowly lowered her to the ground. She looked up, increasingly conscious of a heavy mass of cool air.

'Mrs McAdam, Mrs McAdam. Can you hear me?' Shelley said, knowing, yet denying what she knew. Shelley saw Nathan's kind blue eyes resting on Mrs McAdam as his hand moved to her neck. Shelley was on her knees with Mrs McAdam's head on her lap. Nathan lifted a limp arm and checked for a pulse on her wrist. His eyes now met Shelley's. Shelley shook her head, 'No, Nathan, no. She can't be.'

Nathan placed an arm around Shelley, 'I'm sorry. Let me take her inside. I'll call an ambulance.'

Shelley followed Nathan, her feet now hovering above the footpath. She looked down Snugville Street. It was empty, and the sky was rolling with clouds. Shelley raised her eyes and thought of Hannah, the stillborn baby who was denied a breath under a moonlit sky filled with fire and bombs. The clouds were moving fast and Shelley knew that there was a change, a shift of nature.

Death settled on her skin and made her shiver.

Mrs McAdam was on the sofa, propped up on two velvet cushions, her eyes still opened. Shelley sat on the floor beside her. She looked around. The house was spotless. There was a fresh vase of flowers in the window and the Royal Doulton tea set was laid out on the coffee table.

She had known, Shelley realised. Mrs McAdam had somehow known.

It was the last day of July. Less than three weeks ago, Mrs McAdam had walked in her eighty third twelfth of July parade. As Nathan called an ambulance, Shelley placed her hands over Mrs McAdam's eyelids and kissed her cheek, 'Sleep now,' she whispered.

Shelley looked at her fine white hair woven tightly around curlers. She moved her hands over them and took a deep breath. She removed the first curler as tears floated in circles under her eyes. She then removed the second and third. Tears dripped onto Mrs McAdam's pale face. Shelley savoured the scent of setting lotion as she unfastened each pink plastic sponge, and she realised that she would never spend another evening putting curlers in Mrs McAdam's hair. She moved her fingers through the silky hair fixing it into place. Tears continued to seep from her eyes, but there was no pain in her stomach, no crushing weight on her shoulders that she had felt when her brother, Robert, had died. Shelley knew at heart that Mrs McAdam was at peace. She felt the pain in her throat and in her eyes, her eyes that were now spilling sadness all over her cheeks.

Nathan came back into the room as Shelley began to remove the curlers from the back of Mrs McAdam's head. He had only known Mrs McAdam since Christmas, yet Shelley saw that he too had eyes like drizzle. He moved to the side of the sofa and lifted Mrs McAdam's head so that Shelley could unfasten the final two rollers at the back. Shelley was aware that his eyes were on her face as she worked.

Nathan moved out of the way when the doctor arrived. Shelley followed him to the back yard, 'Nathan, are you okay?'

'I'm fine. Seeing you there fixing her hair. You looked...never mind.'

'No, tell me. What was it?'

'Nothing. It was a nice thing to do. That's all.'

'Nathan,' Shelley took his hand. 'Will you stay here at the house with me? I don't want to be alone. Mum and dad aren't back until tomorrow.'

'Of course, of course. I wouldn't have thought of leaving.'

Shelley dreaded the call to Holland. She sensed that it was going to be a difficult trip for both of her parents. And now she was calling with heart-breaking news.

'Mum,' she said gravely.

'It's Mrs McAdam, isn't it?' replied Jean.

'How did you...yes, it's Mrs McAdam.'

Shelley heard a deep intake of breath.

'What happened?'

'Her heart stopped beating and she fell into my arms,' said Shelley.

There was another sound of breath.

'I knew it. I just knew it would happen when we were away. I'm glad you were there.'

'How did you know?'

'I knew she would wait until I was out of the way,' Jean replied.

Shelley could hear Jean's voice break.

'Mum, she was wearing her new red dress and high heels.' Shelley didn't mention the ladder. She knew Mrs McAdam wouldn't want Jean to know she was up a ladder. 'She had the house all perfect. It's like she knew too.'

'Did you take her curlers out?'

Shelley laughed tears of sadness, 'Yes, mum. I fixed her hair. She is beautiful.'

'Did you see her last night?'

'Yes, she had all the old ladies round for tea and buns. I helped her clean up, but she must have got up early this morning and done it all properly. She was washing windows when she collapsed.'

'I told her long ago she wasn't to be washing windows again,' said Jean.

'She made me promise one time that her windows would be clean and her hair would be fixed.'

'Same here. How do the windows look then?' Jean laughed through throaty tears.

'Nathan helped me. He sorted all the other stuff too. He went to see the minister at the church and he contacted the undertakers. They said they can bury her on Tuesday. Would that be okay?'

'Yes, tell Nathan thank you. I'll sort the rest out when I get home. I'd better go and tell your dad.'

'Mum, wait, did you have a nice time in Holland?'

'Yes, it was happy and it was sad.'

'Isn't that how it always is with us? I think Mrs McAdam wanted to die, so I was happy for her. I was sad though. I'll miss her.'

'We all will. See you soon.'

'Bye, Mum.'

***

Hannah was ready to say goodbye to Gildas and to France. Gildas had insisted on driving Hannah from Paimpol to Rosscoff. The flights from Paris to Belfast were infrequent, and Hannah calculated that the only way she could get to Ireland on time for Mrs McAdam's funeral was to take the overnight ferry. It would be a long sea journey of fourteen hours, followed by a five hour drive home by hire car, but she needed to keep moving. Sitting still made her more and more anxious for home.

Guilt had wracked her with each moment that had passed in Gildas' company. When she had seen him for the first time after her visit to Rennes, she realised what a rash thing she had done. She had given her body to a relative stranger and here was Gildas, who she had seen almost every day throughout July, looking longingly into her eyes.

'I will miss you. I will remember our summer. And when you come again, please call me,' he said.

'Gildas, it was lovely. Thank you.'

Hannah felt unworthy of Gildas' kindness and his presence, but she knew that the gap between them was more than just years. Gildas was a man who had lived through disappointments; a cancelled engagement and a long-term relationship that hadn't work out. She knew that she was a distraction for him throughout the weeks they had spent together and that she had helped him heal.

In so many ways, Gildas was the man that Hannah had dreamed of for a future time, but for now their lives were not aligned. She smiled as she thought of him lining up the shells to explain the spring tide. Hannah was soon going to be spending time with young people at university who would be investing their efforts in the greedy consumption of life and learning, a hedonistic lifestyle that centred around drink. Gildas, meanwhile would live out his existence slowly and carefully in tune with the tide.

Gildas hadn't tried to make love to Hannah. He had taken her on walks and kissed her goodnight. It was simple and it was patient.

'You missed the spring tide this weekend.' he said.

Hannah didn't answer. She sensed that the spring tide had impacted her life, the life of Mrs McAdam and the lives of many other people.

'I'll pay more attention to the moon,' she smiled.

'Your neighbour will always be with you. I was thinking when you told me about her little baby...I was thinking that she might be happy now, to be with her baby again.'

'That's a nice thing to say, Gildas. You're right. They've been apart for so many years. It was time for Mrs McAdam to see her little Hannah again.'

Hannah stood on the deck and thought of Aodhán and the inflamed passions spent in one heated night. She wanted to see him and be with him and feel the touch of his skin. She pressed her jacket pocket that contained his address. She would contact him. Anything might be possible. And she thought of Gildas and of her desires shored up in a memory of summer. She was at peace thinking of him and of leaving him behind.

THE SLAP

The seething rage, that had shackled Catriona's mind since she'd uncovered the truth, was sitting in the car like a bleak passenger between her and Terence. She hated what she had done as a young woman; she hated Séamus Mac Ruaidhrí for putting his politics before his son; and she hated the fact that she had been so close to happiness when Terence had touched her hand. Terence was pained by the rejection over the past two weeks, but her distance from him was her only attrition for the choices she had made.

'Have you thought about looking up Anne's name in Irish?'

A simple suggestion from Rachael had unraveled a story that Catriona could never have imagined.

Inspired by their trips to Brittany in France, James and Anne Rodgers had changed their own names, and that of their son, renaming him Aodhán Mac Ruaidhrí. Séamus and Áine Mac Ruaidhrí had then immersed themselves in the gaelic language, using it at home and in work.

The family had not disappeared from Belfast: they had become entrenched in its politics and James served his long prison sentence under the name Séamus. When Áine died in 1990, her adopted son Aodhán was twelve years old. When Séamus was released from prison eight years later, Aodhán had already graduated from a line of foster homes and had escaped to university in France.

Catriona and Terence hadn't found Aidan, but they had found his only remaining relative, Séamus Mac Ruaidhrí, a revolutionary who wanted to change the world at the same time as achieving a united Ireland. He was once a Maths professor who had given up his post for 'the cause.'

Catriona knew exactly what she wanted to say when she arrived, but she had to contain herself until tea was laid out in the *Gaelcholáiste*, the Irish medium school, in which Séamus worked. He was, as she had seen him in the photograph, tall and broad, with a full head of fluffy white hair, and completely incompatible with the image that the word 'terrorist' transmitted from her brain.

'What do you do here?'

Catriona was the first to speak after the introductions were made.

'I teach maths and science and anything else in between,' he replied, in a voice so graceful and engaging that Catriona had to stifle her natural impulse to respond in kind.

'Do we call you James or Séamus?' asked Catriona, knowing the answer, but determined to make her point.

'I've been Séamus since 1983.'

Catriona was aware that Terence hadn't spoken. Terence worked for a political party that now had to cooperate with former terrorists in the name of peace, but Catriona understood how difficult this was for him. Knowing that their son had been adopted by a terrorist had brought the romance of summer to its knees.

'I'm sorry but I can't go on with this without saying what I have to say. I can't pretend that this is a social visit,' said Catriona.

'*Please.* Say what you have to. I deserve to hear it,' said Séamus.

Catriona composed herself. She wanted to lash out or throw coffee over him, but she knew how to behave.

'I gave my son up for adoption,' she began, 'and it was painful.' She looked down and pressed her hands into her legs. 'I gave him up because I knew that I couldn't care for him in the way that a married couple with jobs and security might.' She looked Séamus in the eye. 'To learn that my son was raised by someone who abandoned him; to learn that he had been passed from one foster home to another because his father cared more about politics and guns than my flesh and blood...' Catriona's voice was now strained and knotted, but she continued, 'to learn that I had made the biggest mistake of my life, I can tell you now, that was more agonising than giving up my son. I would rather not have known, but now I do know and I need to understand why you didn't love my son.'

Séamus bowed his head and turned to the window. 'I did...I do love Aodhán, but I didn't know that he would end up in care. I couldn't have predicted it. I can't tell you how sorry I am. I can't tell Aodhán how sorry I am.'

'You could start by looking me in the eye,' said Catriona.

Séamus looked at Catriona, 'I won't say that I am ashamed of my politics. My wife was at home with Aodhán here and in France and she had no part in this. Áine was an amazing mother. I failed as a father, but Áine made up for it. Until I was arrested, I can assure you that I did everything that a normal father does. Aodhán wasn't exposed in any way to my activities. He spent much of his life in France in the countryside and he was a happy, well-cared for child. Like any other child who loses a mother, he was devastated when Áine died.'

'But he didn't only lose a mother. He lost a father and a mother, and he was on his own from the age of twelve. What were you thinking? How could you abuse the trust I'd granted you in that way? I wanted a family to care for my son who would have been better than me.'

'I'm sorry for letting you down, both of you. As you can imagine,' Séamus added gently, 'I was surprised to learn that Terence Craig was the father. Can I ask why you two didn't keep the baby?' His warm southern lilt disguised the weight of the question.

Catriona felt the blood rise through her neck, 'What has that got to... We were students. We didn't think that...' Catriona stopped speaking, aware suddenly that this man did not deserve to know anything about her personal life.

'We were young and unprepared to bring up a child,' Terence explained gently. 'The circumstances were difficult. All of that is in the past now. I know that this is more difficult for a mother and I know that if your wife were still here, this conversation would be different. What we are here for is to find out if we can meet our son. Roderick explained to you that Aodhán contacted the adoption agency when he finished university...'

'Yes, he explained.' Séamus replied. 'Aodhán is probably in France. He realised that he was adopted by accident when he had to apply for copies of his birth certificate for his resident's permit for France. His mother had always taken care of things like that. He was eighteen at the time and he was angry with me because I hadn't been there for Áine. He said he always knew that I wasn't his father. When I was released he came to see me to tell me to my face what a failure I'd been. I haven't seen him since.'

'Where in France did he live?' Terence asked.

'Rennes. He studied in Rennes. When he was a child, he moved around France with his mother, mainly in Brittany. Catriona, I know I let you down. I realise that now. I'll be honest...I didn't think about you. All I knew was that you'd given up a child. Now that I've met you, I'm sorry for the pain and I'm sorry that I let you down. I will do all that I can to find Aodhán.'

Catriona left the school with a feeling of despair despite the words or remorse from Séamus. Finding Aidan had always been an adventure. Each small piece of information was a celebration that she and Terence had shared. Reality had now dawned like a blustery morning and she couldn't have imagined a worse scenario for her son. She hoped and prayed that Áine was indeed the mother that Séamus had described.

***

They were in the Ulster museum. A scene of confessions, thought Hannah, as she consumed the open space. Breathing through the adrenaline, she quietly addressed her friend. 'I've got something to tell you.'

'Again?' smiled Rachael.

'It's serious this time.'

'It was pretty serious last time too, as I remember it.'

Hannah placed her hand on her chest to steady her breathing. 'Can you remember what you asked me last time?'

'What I asked you?'

'Yes, we were here on this very spot and you made a joke,' continued Hannah. 'It was almost a funny joke back then.'

'Oh yes,' Rachael smiled, 'I asked you if you were up the...No, Hannah, no no no.' Rachael's green eyes were wide and her slim arms were now on her cheeks, doing nothing to contain the shock on her face.

Hannah couldn't find an expression to suit how she felt. She thought back to the previous day. Her body had burned from head to toe when she'd seen the blue line. Leaning hard on the sink, she'd tried to expel the fear that had gripped her, but her stomach had been empty.

After that, she'd felt nothing.

Her feet had guided her to the the doctor's surgery, where she made the first appointment she had ever booked without Jean. Her eyes had been dry when the doctor explained that she didn't need to do a test, and that the pregnancy kit she'd purchased was highly accurate. She'd listened calmly to the brief instructions on what not to eat, a witness in someone else's appointment.

'But you're so calm,' observed Rachael.

'I know. I don't really know what to think or what to do. When I'm alone, it's okay and I can handle it all. Then I think of home and of people and I am so scared of home right now.'

'What are you going to do? Are you planning to...Sorry, I shouldn't make it more difficult for you, but are...'

'I don't want any choices.'

Since the visit to the doctor, one phrase played over and over in Hannah's mind: *Créature inconnue.* Unknown Creature. Rational thoughts pointed towards abortion as the only solution, yet something in her making must have compelled her to know the unknown.

She turned to Rachael and spoke with in resolute whispers, 'I can't take that on. My mum always did say I had a simple mind. Well, she's right. I can't turn away from this baby.'

'Who was...I didn't even know you'd...'

Hannah contained a smile. She knew that it would be a long time before the world would grant her a smile. 'I met a guy in France. Two guys, in fact.'

Rachael gasped, 'You didn't tell me any of this.'

'I haven't seen you.'

'Yes, sorry, I've been a bad friend. I've been spending too much time with my boyfriend and then there's the issue of Aidan too. We found where he works, but never mind any of that. Tell me about this French guy. Or guys. Which one...'

'There was only one...Oh I'm not as good as you at being open about this kind of thing. The first was innocent. We just kissed, but we saw each other almost every day. Then, on my last weekend, I met this other guy in Rennes.'

'Rennes, that's where...sorry, please continue.'

'He's from here. His name is also Aidan but it's spelt the Irish way.'

Rachael's eyes flickered and a feeling of foreboding eclipsed the light in Hannah's. It suddenly didn't feel right sharing this with Rachael. She shook the thought away. She had to trust Rachael.

'Anyway, I have his details. He was kind and he spoke to me the next day as though...as though he knew that something like this might happen. We didn't...Sorry, I really can't do this.'

Hannah realised that Rachael too was uncomfortable with the detail. Her face was tinted red with embarrassment.

'I don't know what to do, Rachael. One decision is simple...I keep the baby. The other is...should I contact him? He's older than me. He probably already thinks I'm a stupid girl. He teaches at a college, you see. I'm the same age as his students.'

Rachael was in a daze. She turned away from Hannah.

'Are you in shock?' asked Hannah.

'Yes, a bit. I suppose. I'm just thinking...' She looked up. 'Hannah, I'm so sorry that you're going through all of this and I will be here for you. I'm a little distracted right now, but I'll talk to you properly later, I promise. I'll have a good think about what you should do. Honesty might be the best thing, if you think he's nice...he is nice isn't he?'

'Yes, yes, of course, I kind of feel that I can trust him. I don't know if I'll ever find the courage to speak to him, though. It's hard to believe that one night will change his life in such a fundamental way. He'll wish he'd never met me.'

'Hey, don't say that. It takes two and all that. Look, I need to head home now to catch my mum before she leaves. She's flying to...She's going away and there's something I forgot. I need to go.'

'Wait,' Hannah reached for Rachael's arm. 'You won't tell your mum will you?'

Rachael paused and spoke slowly, 'Hannah, I want to tell my mum. I know you'll be surprised by that, but if there's one person in the world who knows what you're going through right now, it's my mum.'

'I hadn't even thought of that,' Hannah replied. 'You can tell her, but

I'm not ready to face anyone yet. I'm so terrified of telling my mum and dad. Be careful that your mum doesn't tell them first.'

'I know Jean and she'll be okay.'

Rachael squeezed Hannah's hand and jumped up anxiously. She searched in her bag for her phone, tripping over the mat at the doorway. She held her phone to her ear and called back to Hannah. 'I'll come and see you later. Promise. Bye.'

Hannah was alone. She looked up into the white space and tears started to trickle down her face. She wanted Rachael to come back. She placed her hand on her stomach and heard a voice in her head telling her that everything was going to be fine. She wiped the stray tears away, breathed in and picked up her phone, 'Shelley, meet me at the park in an hour.'

***

Shelley walked into the kitchen from the back yard with look of bewilderment. Hannah followed sheepishly. Something was troubling both of his daughters. Harry was laying the plates on the table as Jean arrived.

'Well, chef Adams, what's for tea tonight?' she asked rubbing her hands together.

'It's a lasagne. I'm glad you're in good form. Look at these two wet blankets.'

Hannah looked up and Harry instantly regretted his comment. Her eyes that had always been so calm, were now wild and filled with fire.

They ate in silence. Hannah's lips were drooped downwards and she finally laid down her knife and fork and pushed her plate away.

'What's up with you?' asked Jean. 'Are you too nervous to eat?' Jean was seated at the end of the table with Hannah on her left side. 'Don't be nervous love, you'll do great. You'll fail spectacularly with a string of As.'

'Don't say that. It's too much pressure,' said Hannah. 'And anyway, that's not the prob...that's not what's wrong. It's something else.'

Hannah's eyes were now filled with tears and Shelley was looking at her with a worried expression.

'What is it?' said Jean with kindness in her voice. 'What's happened? Shelley, do you know. What is it, love? Tell me.'

'I'm pregnant.' Hannah blurted out the words with a flood of tears and saliva. She looked at Jean.

Harry coughed and spoke softly, 'Hannah, did you say you're pregnant?'

'Yes,' she confirmed, still looking at Jean.

Harry felt a shock through his body. His muscles tensed and his mind blackened. Then there was a sound. Cutlery on a plate. A plate moving across the table. It was Jean. She stood up, her head twitching, her bottom lip encased in her teeth. She stared at Hannah for a moment and then spoke slowly. 'This is some kind of joke. You're getting your results tomorrow. Tell me this is a joke.'

Hannah's head remained bowed towards the table. She was pulling and twisting at the tablecloth with her hands. Harry watched in amazement as Jean bent over and grabbed Hannah by the chin. 'Hannah, answer me, is this a joke?'

Hannah shook her head, her chin still locked in Jean's grip. 'No, it's not a joke. It's not a joke.' Hannah said, her voice trembling.

Jean's hand flashed swiftly to the right and came down hard on Hannah's face with a loud smack.

A throttling yelp followed. Shelley moved her seat back and gasped. Harry blinked. What had occurred? Hannah held her cheek and looked up at Jean with terror in her eyes.

Harry stood up. 'Jean, what the hell are you doing?'

'What am I doing? I'm trying to get her to tell me that it's a joke, Harry. She said she's pregnant. She's not pregnant.'

'For god's sake, can you not see that that girl is terrified. Sit down, Jean.'

'No, I won't sit down. I can't sit down.'

'You will sit down,' said Harry, his voice stronger. 'Come on. Let Hannah speak.'

Hannah had turned her face away from her mother and Jean was now massaging and stroking the hand that had struck Hannah on the face.

Shelley spoke for her sister, 'Hannah got pregnant in France. He...the guy is called Aodhán. She has his contact details.'

'Well, that's wonderful,' said Jean. 'She can call him up then when the baby needs fed. Perfect.'

'Why are you behaving like this?' asked Harry. Jean and Hannah had always been close and he couldn't understand why Jean was turning on her daughter when she needed her most. He thought about the man in France and clenched his fist as he sat back down.

'*Why?* Why am I behaving like this? I'll tell you Harry, because you won't know.' Jean was standing again. 'Raising a child is bloody hard. Hannah isn't married and she isn't ready. I want her to go to university. I want her to find a decent job and get out of this shithole we've all been trapped in for years. Hannah could have made it. Can you not see that?'

'Sit down.' Harry said firmly and powerfully, 'Hannah will make it and we will help her. When you've calmed down, you'll realise that. This *shithole* hasn't been too bad to our family and if Hannah chooses to leave it one day, it won't be because this community didn't care for her. When she gets her results tomorrow, we'll figure it all out.'

'Oh, that's nice Harry. We'll all figure it out, will we?' Jean turned to Hannah. 'How many times did you and this fella see each other?'

'One time,' said Hannah faintly, still holding onto her cheek.

'Did you hear that Harry? One time.' She leaned over the table, 'Hannah, in the world we're living in and with all the brains you've been given, did you not think of using a bloody condom? You're as simple as your father.'

'Mum, stop it! Please stop it!' It was Shelley. She stood up and walked out of the kitchen.

Hannah placed her head in her hands and cried feverishly. Jean followed Shelley and slammed the kitchen door. The silence rolled on until it was broken by the sound of a hoover droning upstairs.

'Hannah, love, she'll come round. She's angry,' said Harry.

Hannah's tormented face was red with water dripping from her nose and eyes. Harry remembered Hannah crying as a child. She had tripped and fallen and her squeals twisted and turned through the kitchen as a fine line of blood trickled from her knee. Harry moved to the seat that Jean had been in. He placed his arm around Hannah and spoke carefully, 'Hannah, you have a little baby growing inside you and you need to take care of yourself. I'll take care of Jean and you take care of my grandchild. It'll be okay. We'll sort it out.'

Hannah raised her head and wiped her face with her hand. 'Dad, tomorrow, I don't want to go by myself. Will you come with me?'

'To school?'

'Yes, will you come with me to collect my results?'

'Of course. I can't think of anything that would make me more proud.'

Harry held his daughter in his arms as she sobbed, soaking his shirt and filling him with love and remorse for a childhood that had passed her by.

'Now, go and lie down on the sofa. I'll talk to Jean.'

Harry found Jean hoovering the inside of the wardrobe.

'Did you finally run out of floor?,' he asked.

'You think everything's so funny, don't you. Can you not see what is happening here?'

'I can and I know how much you wanted Hannah to do well. She will. She's determined. She won't let her education slip away.'

'It's not even about that, Harry. It's about losing her youth. She's entitled to some freedom. All she's ever done is work and she needed some time to enjoy herself,' said Jean, her voice breaking at the seams between anger and peace.

'But you had your brother Robert to look after at fifteen. You've only ever been a mother and it was okay back then, wasn't it?'

'No, it wasn't. I resented it. I saw my friends running around partying and I felt sorry for myself and then he died and the guilt was...the guilt still hurts. I don't want Hannah to go through all those adult things. I don't want her to have a baby that she resents. I want her to be married and have some security when the time comes for all of that. And for now, I just want her to be free.'

'None of us is really ever free, Jean. You know that. And she will have security. She has a dad who owes her nine and a half years of security. I'll provide for Hannah, whatever it takes. And if we have a baby in our house, you'll fall in love all over again. You know that too.'

'I love babies, yes, and I know all of that, but I can't help but grieve what Hannah has lost.'

'She never knew she had it. She never got to taste it. She hasn't lost anything.'

'But she has. This summer in France, she got to be young and enjoy herself. How could she have been so stupid?'

'You're forgetting there were two people involved.'

'Yes, the French guy. And what are you planning to do, Harry, welcome him into your home with open arms or punch him in the face?'

Harry stared at Jean in disbelief. How could she move so easily from sympathy to what felt like hatred.

'That was below the belt. Don't ever say something like that again,' he said calmly before walking to the door.

Jean pulled him back. 'Wait, wait, Harry. I'm sorry. I shouldn't have said that. I didn't mean a word of it. I am in complete shock. Let me speak to Hannah.'

'You might be in shock, Jean, but sometimes you can be cruel.'

***

Jean rubbed her temples and walked around the room when Harry left, his words creeping into corners of the walls like unearthed ghosts. She waited. The front door clicked closed. She took a deep breath and tried to collect her thoughts. Hannah was pregnant. Her little girl, who had the world in her grasp, was now grounded to the place they were in.

She walked to Shelley's room and looked around. The wallpaper and carpet had been changed, but Jean could still catch a glimpse of Robert there. It was either real or imagined, but comforting nonetheless. What would Robert have said about his sister? He'd always looked out for Hannah, a gift in a soft blanket handed to him at the age of four. He would have helped Hannah. Jean knew that.

She looked at the sewing machine table. Was she behaving like Anna? Harry had said she was cruel. Did she carry the spirit of her mother, after all? Anna would have wanted Hannah to do well too. There was always that crushing sense that Anna didn't belong as a mother, although she sometimes looked and sounded like one. Then there was Granny Sally, who'd never had a husband, but who was maternal to the bone. Would she be looking down on Jean with her tender eyes, telling Jean to go easy on Hannah, reminding her that she too had once been that girl?

But Sally hadn't been that girl. She was a millworker, a millie, from the Shankill, born in a world where chances were torn like a rip along the selvage the minute a woman gave birth.

Hannah was asleep on the sofa when Jean entered the living room.

'I'm sorry, love.' she whispered, placing a blanket around her and kissing her red cheek. 'We'll figure it out. I'm sorry for hurting your face.'

Hannah's eyes flickered and she looked up. 'I'm scared,' she said.

Jean sat on the floor and looked at her daughter's pale face. She could see her own reflection, the fear of a young girl whose mother had died, and she could see her mother in Hannah's eyes.

'I always wondered what I would do if this happened,' Jean said. 'When you told me about Catriona, I even thought of it. I swore that no child of mine would ever need to give up a child. And you won't. I'm still shocked, but I promise this, I will love my grandson.

'Grandson?'

'Or granddaughter,' Jean added nervously.

'But mainly grandson.'

'I could get used to the idea of another girl,' Jean replied.

'But you'd prefer a boy.'

'I'd love a boy.'

'Mum, you do know that most people wouldn't say that?'

'I'm not most people.'

'No, you're not most people,' said Hannah with a suppressed smile, 'Anyway, I can't even think that far ahead. I was shocked too you know.'

'What about this boy? Do you like him?'

'I don't know. Yes, maybe, but he lives in France. I don't know what to do about that bit. Should I tell him?'

'What does he do?' asked Jean.

'Maths lecturer.'

It was strange to hear it twice in one week, thought Jean. Catriona had also said that her son's dad had been a maths lecturer.

'What did you say his name was?'

'Aodhán...with a funny spelling.'

'What's his surname?' asked Jean, her mind now alive with concern.

'It's on a card in my bag. It was an Irish name. Mac something with fadas'

'Oh shit,' said Jean too swiftly.

'The fadas are the least of my worries,' said Hannah. 'He said his father had been in prison in Belfast. Oh god this child's granda was in the...never mind. Mum, what is it? Why are you looking all around the room?'

'It's something Catriona said. Remember she was looking for Aidan?'

'Yes, but the names aren't the...'

'Wait. Wait. Hannah. There's a story. When did you last speak to Rachael?'

'Yesterday,' said Hannah.

'And she didn't say anything?'

'No. Why?'

'I wonder why she didn't say anything,' said Jean, searching around the room for an easy way to tell Hannah what she knew.

'She didn't have a chance to speak. I was telling her my problems.'

'Oh shit,' repeated Jean as she fumbled through the vocabulary in her mind.

'Mum, you're worrying me. Why do you keep saying "oh shit?"'

'Aidan, Rachael's brother...' She took a deep breath. 'His mother and father changed his name to an Irish one years ago. He studied maths at university. I'm sure the place he went to sounded like Rennes.'

A faint croak came from Hannah. 'Oh god,' she said.

This can't get any worse, thought Jean. She tracked back to a concurrent thread in her mind, that had been cut off in the confusion. What was it that Hannah had said about prison?

'Hang on a second.' Jean stood up. She watched tears flow down her daughter's cheek, yet still she needed to confirm what she now suspected Hannah was going to reveal.

'What. What is it?' asked Hannah.

'When you said his father was in prison, were you about to say he was in the IRA?'

There was silence. Jean looked at her daughter's face that was now red on both sides.

'Hannah, this can't be. You can't have a son whose grandfather was...Oh god, this is bad. Shit. I thought the pregnancy was the problem five minutes ago and now all this. Oh shit. What will your dad say?'

'What will Catriona say? Oh Mum, have I made a mess of things between them all?'

'That's not your problem. You've probably done them all a favour. We'll figure it all out, love. Don't worry.'

Jean stared at the fireplace and tried to make sense of it all. If Hannah had met Catriona's son, Catriona might find him because of a mistake that he had made with a young girl, Jean's young girl, who was too immature and helpless to take on a child. Jean understood something for the first time. She understood why Catriona had made a decision that had been so foreign in Jean's eyes until that day.

DEEPER SHADES OF COLOUR

Hannah watched her dad from from a distance as he shook hands with teachers and pointed to his daughter. She smiled at the way he was so dressed up when the other fathers wore jogging bottoms and jeans; she was touched by the pride that was clearly emanating from his expanded chest; and she was confused as to why he was trying so hard to speak without his Shankill accent. She laughed inwardly as the last raindrops of shame dispersed into a light mist of embarrassment. Whilst jubilant students jumped and posed for photographs on the lawn, it was Harry Adams who was graduating with three A grades from the penal institution of shame to which his daughter had assigned him. Hannah's smile broadened each time she heard the words, 'Hannah is my daughter.' She walked over to him as he approached another parent.

'Dad, I think it's time to go home now.'

'Just a minute, there's Stephen Simple, a prison officer. His son is in your year. Do you know him?'

Hannah didn't have time to respond. Her dad was shaking hands with Conor Simple, whose eyes crashed to the ground when Hannah approached.

'Pleased to meet you, Mr Simple,' Hannah said with confidence, taking strength from the awareness that the origins of the rumour had come from Conor and not a close friend.

'I never got to thank you for letting people know that my dad was coming home, Conor.' The words slipped from Hannah, invincible now in the knowledge of what secret was contained within her own body.

Conor's father glared at his son and glanced back to Harry with a look of concern. He turned to Hannah, 'Congratulations,' he said. 'I hear you're going to the University of Edinburgh.'

'Actually, I'm thinking of staying at home. I'd like to spend more time in Belfast now that my dad is back.' Hannah's eyes didn't leave Conor's face as she addressed his father. Conor looked up finally and reached an arm out towards Hannah. He pulled her to the side.

'I'm sorry,' he said at a distance from his father.

'I didn't expect any less. You told the whole school your cousin was pregnant. I always remembered that,' Hannah said.

'I'm an idiot. I'm sorry.'

'Conor, you have been an idiot, but you need to grow up.'

Conor kicked a stone and looked up timidly, 'Are you going to Queen's?'

'I have to make some phone calls today, but maybe.'

'If I see you there, I'll buy you a pint,' he said with an apologetic smile.

'A sparkling water would do,' said Hannah.

Her words stumbled from her mouth with a clumsy confidence, the insinuation that she wouldn't be drinking alcohol made in haste and with poor judgement. It was too early to think about telling anyone about a pregnancy that had confounded her and that had thrown her future into disarray. Three A grades had given her a temporary reprieve from the internal wrestling in her mind, but soon enough, the sickening fear would return.

Hannah was tired. She rested on the steps of the School of Modern Languages after she and her dad had made a quick tour of the university. Harry joined her and they both looked towards the red-brick gothic castle set on the trim green lawn opposite them. Hannah had never wanted to go to Queen's University, although she had selected it as her second choice. She thought about why she had done so; a lack of conviction perhaps in her own ability to leave home. Queen's was right beside her school and she hadn't been inspired by the thoughts of going to the same place for a further three to four years. When she had completed her university application, life seemed more compelling beyond the Irish sea. Now, as she sat on the periphery of her old school and on the steps of the university that complied with her current circumstances, the thoughts of boarding a ferry to Scotland filled her with nausea and an overwhelming sense of lethargy. It was a lethargy that had tracked each step she had taken that morning, and that was now pulling her home to Snugville Street.

'You could be happy here,' Harry said.

'I could,' Hannah replied.

It was true. Perhaps the lure of Scotland was more about what her friends were doing than what she wanted herself. She tried to imagine herself sitting on the same step outside the tall Victorian terrace surrounded by friends, but as the image progressed to one with friends staring at her stomach in disbelief, she was reminded again of what lay ahead.

Hannah wondered if the acidic feeling of pending sickness that was now building was invented in her head as the enormity of what was occurring pressed down on her, or if it was the result of some physiological change in her body. Harry was removing something from his pocket that glimmered in the sunshine and caught her eye.

'This is for you,' he said, and handed Hannah the shiny gift bag. 'Congratulations. Your mum has something from both of us at the house, but this is from me.'

Hannah's eyes started to fill with tears. She blinked and tried to focus on the bag, but her hand was shaking as she lifted out a small box.

'Come here, I'll open it,' said Harry. He turned it towards Hannah.

Hannah ran her hand along a gold chain with an intricately cut pendant that clutched a small, luminous stone. She held it up to the light and looked more closely at the stone. It was almost colourless like a diamond, but the light of the sky revealed a tint of pale blue.

'It's beautiful,' she said. 'I've never owned anything like this before.'

'I know you prefer silver, but it's an antique and I wanted to buy you something gold,' Harry said as he unravelled the necklace and tied it around Hannah's neck. 'The stone is aquamarine,' he added, 'to protect those who travel by sea.'

'Travel. I don't think I'll be...'

'You will. One day. You're only nineteen. You've got years ahead of you to do what you want to do.'

'Thanks dad. I like it. It's lovely. I really do like it.'

'Everything will be okay, Hannah. A baby isn't a burden. You could still live in France or Spain or in any other country your heart desires. Can I ask you something?'

'What is it?'

'This guy in France, do you think about him?'

Hannah blushed, 'Yes, I do. When we were at school this morning, I saw someone from the back and actually thought it was him. I'd like to see him again.'

'I think you need to tell him.'

'But Jean said to wait.'

'She isn't always right,' smiled Harry

'But what about his dad?'

'Only Jean has a problem with his dad.'

'So, you're okay with your grandson having an IRA grandfather.'

'I wouldn't say I'm thrilled about the fact, but let's deal with one thing at a time. I'm amazed that I'm going to be a granda. By the way, why did you say grandson?'

'Mum has pretty much declared that it has to be a boy.'

'Oh right, I see,' laughed Harry.

'I think she actually came around to the idea based on it being a boy.'

'Well, in that case, I should champion the idea of a girl.'

'Would you bet this necklace that it's a girl?'

Harry looked up and held a smile between his lips. 'No,' he said finally. 'That necklace cost me a lot of overtime! I think it's a boy too, Hannah. It's just a feeling.'

'We'll see. God, I can't believe I'm actually talking about this now. I thought I'd be in shock for another few weeks.'

'The human spirit is pretty amazing. Somehow we get on with things. For some reason, Robert lost the fight. I'll never understand why.'

'Maybe it's time to start celebrating the life he had.'

Harry turned to Hannah with eyes so steamed up with emotion that she had to look away. 'Yes,' he said calmly. 'It's time to celebrate the life he had. When he was a little boy, he was mad about the bands. One night we had to let him sleep with the drum tied around his neck.'

'Mum told me that story,' smiled Hannah.

'He was good too. He could have been a drummer if he'd stuck at it. He drifted and got in with the wrong crowd.'

'Did he though? Do you really think that's what happened? Did it have to be someone else's fault? I was thinking about this, and Robert was given every opportunity. He got to go to America for three summers as a kid, he survived the Shankill Bomb and he even got sent to Holland when he was in trouble. We can't blame anyone for what happened to him just as we can't blame anyone for the path Nathan chose. Look at Aodhán. His dad was in prison too, he lost his mother, and he went into care at the age of twelve. He survived. No one was helping him.'

'And then he found out he was adopted,' added Harry.

'I know,' replied Hannah. 'I was trying not to think about that. That's why I went so late to get the results. I was scared of bumping into Catriona and Rachael.'

'You'll have to face them eventually.'

'I know. I'm going to go there this afternoon.'

'Do you want me to come with you?'

'No, I'll need Jean for that. Dad, I'm sorry for the way I...'

'It's in the past. No need to apologise.'

'I wasn't nice.'

'You were stressed,' Harry replied.

'I resented you.'

'I know.'

'Anyway, I'm sorry.'

'Thank you,' said Harry, pressing his hand on Hannah's knee as he did when she was a child. 'Now, let's get back home. Jean will be having a canary.'

'I fancy a fry,' said Hannah, realising that the nausea could have had hunger at its source. 'Ring her and tell her to get the sausages on.'

'You don't eat fried food,' said Harry.

'I could murder a sausage right now. And some bacon and fried potato bread.'

'I thought you said you felt sick?'

'I did,' Hannah smiled, and reached out her hand to her dad. 'That was five minutes ago. Keep up! I'm carrying a hungry boy!'

***

Belfast called Aodhán home. The town of his youth was like a cousin he'd played with as a boy, and up close he could remember its smiles and its fights as it carried him to a place where the memories had no faces, sculpted as they were from feelings like comfort and hostility. If France contained his mother's red hair flying like red wool around dance halls, or if it reflected her smiling freckles through streams of sun in cafés, then the streets of Belfast filled Aodhán's throat with an aching for the soft voice of his father.

There was an irony set in the concrete memories of Aodhán's past: Belfast was his father's borrowed home and his mother's place of birth, but his mother had never seemed particularly attached to the apron strings that had once pulled her home to the Falls Road.

It was Séamus who had proclaimed Belfast as home. It was the same soil as Ashbourne in County Meath, he'd often said, and he'd dug his heels into it and tried to unearth the plantation of Ulster and burrow his way to a United Ireland through his politics of war.

Aodhán understood the romance and the passion that led his father to believe that guns were the only way to take him there, but the metal of a gun left Aodhán cold, and the life he had led in France had transported him far from the microscopic lens through which his father viewed Belfast. Aodhán's classrooms were filled with students from North Africa, and he'd started to see the patterns of post-colonialism at close range. France, Ireland's sister republic and the land of liberty, egality and fraternity, had once set a fence around those founding principles with its colonial prowess, so that decades after the freedom of those colonial countries had been won, the mistrust continued to leak through the hearts and minds of immigrants who sought an education in his classroom in France. Aodhán was proud of the Republic of Ireland's freedom, but conscious that it too had a border, not the political border that divided the earth into two countries, but the religious border that kept the government of the Republic in check and the people in line. His father fought not only to unite Ireland, but also to free the people from the Catholic Church: he was an atheist, a Marxist and a Republican and his kind of freedom had its own restrictions on religion, capitalism and monarchy. Freedom, Aodhán had come to learn, was never exempt from its own oppressive confines, and was a choice as much as an imposition.

Here in the leafy avenues of South Belfast, Aodhán was far removed from the voice of his father. He had walked past Methodist College, where students assembled with their parents on the lawn. At first, he hadn't understood why they were there in August, but he soon recognised the expressions of students huddled with small brown envelopes, and memories of his own educational experience revisited him.

It was in the third foster home that he had chosen to end the constant igniting of anger at his mother's death. Cynthia and Colin Andrews lived on the North Circular Road, at the foot of Cave Hill and in the midst of detached dwellings, bowling lawns and tennis courts, a part of Belfast not dissimilar to the tree-lined road he was now on. Cynthia and Colin were doctors and devout Catholics who had a family of five children. They believed that bringing children into their home and caring for them as their own, was the most charitable offering they could give to God. Aodhán had admired them from the moment he met them; the hostility towards foster carers that had raged in the other two foster homes, tempered by his intrigue of the couple who were willing to risk the safety of their own children by having a foster child among them. The first week hadn't passed without him testing their resolve: he had set the children's tree-house alight and had waited by its side until Colin had appeared with a hose. Colin had made a deal with Aodhán: he had said that he would keep Aodhán safe if Aodhán kept his family safe. It had seemed like a fair exchange and Aodhán had complied without speaking, eventually fitting in around the family and forming a bond with the housekeeper and the three year-old boy that would never be severed. The Andrews children all went to university and Aodhán was no exception to the academic success that was nurtured within the walls of the detached home. Later, when he learned of his adoption, the fire that Colin Andrews had extinguished was rekindled once again.

Aodhán took a deep breath and turned into a white detached home on Windsor Park. He looked at the land around it and wondered how long it would be before it too was pulled down and replaced with an apartment block, a fate to which the other houses on the road up until that point had clearly fallen. He rang the bell, conscious that it was early, resolute in the determination that, like Colin Andrews, Hannah had been sent to him to provide clarity and reason.

Hannah. He could see her pale face again filled with shadows and light. And he could see two words set in blue ink: *Snugville Street.*

'Hello.'

The door had opened and a man in a suit was speaking. He repeated. 'Hello. Are you looking for Helena?'

'No, I'm...I'm looking for Rachael. She's... I'm trying to find her house,' said Aodhán, unprepared for the prompt answer at the door.

'Rachael. She lives two doors up in the red-bricked house,' he pointed. I'm going to see her mum if you want to follow me.'

Her mum. Aodhán's feet were anchored to the tarmac. He wasn't ready to move. What was he doing here? He only wanted to know which house. He took a deep breath. What was he planning to do anyway? Stand outside the front door like a stalker? Now things were moving too fast. This man with his confident smile and energetic gait was taking him to see his mother. He was closing his door and walking now and Aodhán was beside him with feet falling on a gap of air each time they tried to reach the ground. How well did this man know Rachael and Catriona?

'Are you at school with Rachael?' the neighbour asked Aodhán at the front door.

'No, I... It's actually Rachael's mum...I, I was looking for...'

The man was now staring at Aodhán and Aodhán sensed a movement in the sky that grasped at the breezy sway of the fir trees and strangled their vacillating branches. Every flower was stationary, from the whimsical blue *love-in-a-mist* with their feathery pointed edges, to the purple iris with their crepe-like petals. It was a calm that held its own breath, following the swift flight of Aodhán and this stranger from one home to the next.

'I'm Terence,' the man said, holding out his hand, 'I'm a close friend of Catriona.'

'I'm Aodhán,' Aodhán replied quietly, and with a sense that his name now controlled the motion around them. Terence's hand remained joined to his in a close and patient handshake.

'Aodhán,' Terence repeated, staring, and then dropping his hand by his side. He looked up at the door and rang the bell, attempting to twist the door knob, investing energy in a handle that had never turned.

A girl appeared, tall and tanned with a buoyant ponytail and wide smile. She looked at Terence first, 'Terence, why didn't you come round the back? We're in the kitchen. You should have come on in.'

Terence didn't speak, but motioned his head towards Aodhán. Aodhán tried to understand the unsaid conversation between Terence and this girl. *This girl.* He looked at her again and caught her familiar green eyes at the same time as she stole something from his. She turned back to Terence. 'You haven't asked me yet,' she said, smiling.

'Your results, yes, I didn't need to. Your mum texted me first thing. Well done!' He reached out and kissed Rachael on the cheek. Aodhán sensed that tight feeling again, like a knot closing around his neck. He was looking at apartments on the road camouflaged by moving trees, and now he was here at his mother's home and standing before his sister. He hadn't planned it this way: he hadn't planned anything. Now he was caught in this vortex of stillness and he needed to keep moving.

They were walking through a hall, following the long limbs of Rachael. A yellow light gleamed off the walls and Aodhán's heart was beating fast in the awareness that the bright, inviting colours were created by his mother working in tandem with the sky. He looked to the left where a living room caught his eye, a blurred kaleidoscope bouncing off the intense golden hues.

He was in a sparkling kitchen and could hear a dishwasher swish as his eyes followed the bounding light. His peripheral vision was taking in gloss and whiteness and refusing to move towards the colour and shapes at the table by the window.

His eyes focused, his breathing slowed, his throat filled with a pain, and the blurred edges of colour became his mother.

She had been reading a magazine, and her hand was clutching a mug when she turned to the three people and smiled. She squinted and looked again. 'Terence, good morning. I didn't expect to see you,' she said, her voice warm and rising and falling like Aodhán's stride that could now feel the earthy tiles beneath his feet. He took in the hard edges of a marble table and the soft edges of a beautiful woman. He stopped and Terence walked by him. There were looks from Rachael and there was a tilted head from Catriona towards Terence.

'Catriona,' he said, gently lifting her hand and raising her from the table. 'I was outside and I...' He turned towards Aodhán to indicate the words he couldn't assemble. 'This is Aodhán. He knocked on my door.'

Catriona moved her hand to her mouth. Aodhán looked at her and saw again the familiar green eyes. He was aware of movement to his right as Rachael gasped and she too was there with her hand at her face, staring.

'How did you find...' Aodhán understood that she was talking to him, but her head was turned to Terence in confusion.

Aodhán found his voice. 'It was Hannah. I met Hannah in France.'

They all looked at him.

'Yes, yes, of course,' said Catriona. Her voice was shaking and the vitality that had greeted them all in a stream of colour diluted as she swallowed hard and appeared to be unsteady on her feet. Aodhán stepped forward and reached out his arms. Catriona fell against him. He sucked in tears as a woman's arms encircled his; a stranger whose body was a tremor of light bones and fine skin; a stranger who was his mother.

Mother. The word steadied him, despite the unrest. Tears were flowing down his sister's face; his cheek was lightly touching the soft hair of his mother; and the neighbour, who had walked to the door with him, and who had rung the bell, was holding onto the kitchen bench with ashen eyes and a strong, muscular jawline that was tensed and afflicted.

Moments passed by and Aodhán couldn't let go of his mother. He wanted to stand back and look at her face again, check the green eyes, learn the colour of her cheeks. He hadn't seen her mouth or her neck. He recalled her smile, and it was welcoming, and he needed to pull away and see her, but he was holding the woman who had given him life and he didn't want to let go of the present and the memory of it. The neighbour's eyes were seeping small tears now and Rachael was moving towards him and taking his hand. They were both there waiting and Aodhán knew he had to stop. He let go.

He let go, and looked in the eyes of his mother again, and could see the likeness he had imagined for so long. He breathed deeply and sniffed back the tears that were bottled up inside him. Catriona smiled, her face red and covered in small blotches where water had settled and deposited a salty residue.

Terence stepped forward, 'Aodhán,' he said, looking to Catriona for reassurance. 'I don't know how to...'

'Wait, wait,' said Catriona. 'I think we need to sit down.'

Rachael came towards him then and hesitated, looking at her mother, 'Can we sit down after I have hugged my only brother?' She smiled and Aodhán reached towards her and held her, glimpsing over her shoulder at two sets of glistening eyes.

Rachael stood back and Terence unexpectedly reached towards Aodhán. Aodhán briefly hugged his mother's neighbour and was surprised by the raw sound that emerged from Terence's chest. Terence pulled away, seemingly unable to look at anyone or to confess his tears. Aodhán's eyes were fixed on the neighbour, and he wondered at his reaction and the reason for the swift hug. Was he merely caught up in the emotion of his friend and her search for her son? Aodhán was at the table now beside Catriona and opposite Rachael, who moved up a seat when Terence approached. Catriona was fumbling her hands and Aodhán sensed a heightened stress about something unsaid. Society had yet to dictate the etiquette for a reunion between a mother and a son, and so they all sat in silence.

It was Terence who took the first breath, and it came in a throaty cough, an after-tremor of the strangulated noise that had emitted from his body as he'd embraced a stranger. Aodhán studied this man's face and started to see something. There was his muscular jaw, his neck, shoulders and chest, all following the same pattern. His eyes were strangers looking back, but there was something else: an expression, a reflection. Aodhán flinched and stemmed the thoughts that were preposterous.

'Aodhán,' said the familiar voice. Why a familiar voice? Aodhán breathed deeply in the realisation that he now knew this man.

'Aren't you Terence Craig?' Aodhán asked.

Catriona and Rachael both looked up at the same time.

'I am,' said Terence.

'I thought I'd seen you somewhere before. I recognise your face from my childhood...from TV.'

'Aodhán, actually, I...I don't know how to say this.'

Catriona held out her hand to Terence, and Rachael made a sudden movement with her head, swishing away the air of confusion with her long pony tail. 'Oh, you don't know, do you? Of course you don't know. You met Terence at the door. Aodhán, Terence is my mum's boyfriend from university. Terence is your dad.'

Catriona stared at Rachael and then softened when she looked back to Aodhán, 'Sorry Aodhán. I didn't know when was a good time to say. We were all just standing there and I couldn't figure out if you knew...if you'd spoken to Terence outside or...'

'No,' said Terence, 'No, we hadn't spoken. We'd walked from my house to yours and Rachael answered the door after Aodhán told me his name.' Terence looked deeply into Aodhán's eyes, 'Aodhán, I'm sorry to deliver so many shocks in one day, but we...we've been looking for you for four years.'

Aodhán listened to Terence and dissected his face bit by bit, matching it up with his own: two dimples, two defined cheekbones, and a strong muscular neck. He heard a voice, and it was the voice that had reverberated around a lecture hall in France, a voice that had told his father he hated him, and a voice that had been soft and caring when it had considered the plight of his mother as a young girl in the presence of Hannah. Aodhán pieced together his face, his body and his voice, and as he saw Rachael's eyes sparkle across the table, he could see himself. All of him was here at this table of strangers. All of him except the fire and Áine. He looked up and wondered what she would think of this meeting. She would have been talking by now and making everyone feel okay. Aodhán borrowed the spirit of Áine and smiled, 'I hadn't bargained for a full family unit. This is unexpected.'

'Actually, Aodhán,' said Terence. 'There's more. I also have a daughter. She's called Helena. She's in England this weekend at a job interview. She'll want to come straight home when she finds out you're here.'

Rachael spoke before Aodhán had time to register the additional information. 'Helena and I are your half sisters. My dad was married to mum. He'll be amazed when I tell him this.'

'I'm surprised you're not already on the phone to him,' smiled Catriona.

'Actually, the first person I'm going to call is Hannah.'

The taut silence came again at the mention of Hannah's name, and Aodhán tried one more time to think of Áine.

'I think we need to thank Hannah,' he said. 'She made this all happen by mentioning in passing that her friend was looking for her brother Aidan, spelled the English way, she stressed.'

'Ah yes,' said Catriona. 'That name thing caused us all a bit of confusion.'

'My mum will be looking down from heaven with a smile on her face,' said Aodhán, eager now to include Áine in the moment. The instant her name passed, the atmosphere changed. Aodhán could feel her presence as shoulders fell and arms spread and the people around him relaxed.

'She will indeed,' said Catriona as she lightly touched Aodhán's arm, 'and your mum would want me to make you a nice cup of coffee after all the shocks this morning.' Catriona stood up and busied herself in the kitchen, watching over her shoulder as she worked.

'You didn't expect to find another dad, did you?' It was Terence and his demeanour had softened, his eyes more blue than grey.

'No, I didn't and I don't really know what to say. You guys live on the same street, then?'

'Yes, Catriona moved here five years ago. My wife, Norma, she passed away last year.' Terence's voice faltered. 'She wanted to meet you too.'

'I'm sorry to hear that,' Aodhán said. 'My mum died when I was twelve. It's hard.'

Terence spoke hesitantly, 'We hired a private detective to find you, and last week...last week we met your dad.'

Aodhán's cheeks burned. He had visited strangers before he had gone to see his dad.

Terence continued with a smile, 'You've quite a unique Northern Ireland family.'

'So it seems,' smiled Aodhán, still enveloped in the guilt. 'How...how was he?'

It was Catriona who answered, as she returned with a coffee pot and cups. 'Aodhán, he wants to see you.'

'I know...it's time. I'll visit him tonight.'

'What are your plans for today?' asked Catriona.

'I don't have any.'

'Can you spend the morning with us? Hannah and her mum are...'

Catriona looked down and stopped speaking. Rachael's eyes flashed towards Aodhán. 'What mum is saying is that you can stay here and talk to us and maybe catch up with Hannah later. It might be a good idea to catch up with Hannah. You two could maybe go for a walk or something when she gets here. We can take care of Jean.'

Aodhán wondered what Hannah had said to her friend. His cheeks flamed again as he thought about what he'd done, and the possibility that Hannah had discussed it with Rachael made him feel uneasy. But he was here in his mother's home and he needed to learn his story. He turned to Catriona and looked back at Terence. 'I need to ask you,' he said. 'Why did you...why the adoption?'

Rachael stood up and reached for Aodhán's hand. 'Aodhán, I'll leave you with Terence and mum. Before I go, I want you to...you need to know that my mother always loved you.'

Aodhán's eyes spilled this time with the tears he had been holding in. Tender eyes brushed his skin from the man across the table, and the soft hand of Catriona eased his accelerated breath. He propped up his head with one hand and blinked to control the water that had stopped flowing when he had chosen hatred against a father he once loved.

He would listen to the story of Catriona and Terence, a story that he had already retraced in a café when Hannah's embarrassed eyes had revealed his birth mother to him. His mother had been a young woman who had allowed passions to dictate her fate.

He controlled his breathing and looked into Catriona's eyes, 'I understand what might have happened, and you don't need to tell me your story.'

'But I will,' said Catriona. 'I will tell you because you need to know that we live in a different world today, and that the restrictions of religion and society no longer apply. An unmarried mother can access an education today. I could have married Terence.' She stopped and looked up before continuing. 'I did have choices and I could have chosen family. I didn't and I'm sorry. I chose my own education. I'm sorry, Aodhán.'

Aodhán was silent, taking in the words of Catriona and trying hard to remember them. She was confessing something, and he had a sense that she was doing so not to clear her own conscience, but to warn him of something unsaid.

Everything that morning, from the girls on the lawn huddled in groups assessing their results, to the fidgeting trees that had stopped moving in the dense air, had felt like a warning. The reunion with his mother and his father had passed so peacefully, that he was consumed by a feeling that the walk into Windsor Park was the beginning of a journey and not the end. His jacket contained a card with neat words that he could see clearly now, *'6a Snugville Street... when you come home.'*

***

'Mum, what are you doing?' asked Shelley, her lungs filled with the compelling scent of liquid fumes and her legs dangling off the end of the sofa as she looked through some documents she had found on the French Huguenots.

'Just touching up the floor,' said Jean

'You're varnishing the floor?'

'Could you not move up stairs? Jean complained. 'I'm trying to get this finished.'

'Mum, why on earth are you painting the floor?'

'Catriona and Aodhán are coming tonight.'

'Mum!' exclaimed Shelley. 'Have you not learned your lesson after last time?'

Shelley recalled how all the door frames were repainted white the night before Catriona's last visit. Her woollen scarf had clung to the tacky paint on her route to the kitchen and the champ had tasted of toxic fumes. 'You'll be lucky if it dries out by tonight! You'll be ruining Catriona's expensive shoes this time. Anyway, why the big fuss about Catriona and Aodhán? You don't repaint for Nathan coming to visit.'

'Nathan isn't the father of my grandchild, is he?' said Jean, returning to work, pausing and then popping back up again. 'Is he?' she repeated with eyes roving around Shelley's face.

'Mum, you can rest assured that you only have one pregnant teenage daughter and that I have never so much as kissed Nathan. I told you before, we just meet for coffee the odd time.' Shelley's body softened at his name. Ever since Mrs McAdam had died, she and Nathan had met for coffee in town on Friday afternoons. There wasn't a chance of a pregnancy, since Nathan continued to treat Shelley as a child, seemingly oblivious to the fact that she couldn't stop looking into his eyes. She blushed and shook away the thoughts, 'Mum, could you not do what a normal person does and fluff some cushions?'

'Your grandmother would turn in her grave by your domestic standards. Maybe the stork brought you after all. You don't seem to follow the accomplishments of my fine French line.'

Jean stopped and looked up from the floor with a smile that had been etched in her face since the previous day when Shelley had laid all the photocopies of her findings on the kitchen table. 'I always did have a petite French nose, like those French women in the movies. Do you not think I look a bit like Catherine Deneuve?'

'Haven't a clue who she is.'

'What the...? Did you learn nothing at all in school? All those bloody exams and you don't know the best actresses of the twentieth century!'

Shelley smiled. Her impressive exam results had taken them all by surprise. 'Funny enough mum, her name didn't come up in the History of the Great War.'

'Remind me of the story again so that I can tell Catriona. I need to get it right.'

'Why are you so determined to impress Catriona?' Shelley asked.

'I'm not trying to impress her. She's a woman after my own heart, and she would not appreciate a scruffy floor. Here, by the way, she's offered to give up work and mind the baby when it's born!'

'No way!' said Shelley, conscious of the potential for controversy given Jean's territorial claim to the baby. Two weeks had passed since the slap that had shaken Snugville Street, and suddenly Jean was the most caring grandmother in Belfast.

"I told Hannah that she needn't bother,' said Jean. 'I'll be taking care of the baby.'

'But what about work?' asked Shelley.

'I'm retiring,' she said proudly. 'I'm gonna get a big sign that says "No more bling" and turn the lights out for the last time.'

'But why?' asked Shelley, relieved and bemused by Jean's decision.

'I want to raise my grandchild.'

'Surely that's Hannah and Aodhán's job?'

'What use are those two going with be to a baby?' scoffed Jean. 'He lives in France and she's going to be studying. Hannah wouldn't know what to do with a baby. The boy will need Granny Jean.'

'Granny Jean and Granny Catriona,' smiled Shelley.

Jean pouted her lips in Shelley's direction. 'Tell me the French story again.'

'You're like a child,' Shelley laughed. 'Here goes. In 1690, Soloman Le Blanc served under Schomburg in the Battle of Boyne.'

'And that's King Billy's side?'

'Yes. We've been through this, *yes*,' said Shelley impatiently.

'Just making sure. I'll have to tell Mrs McAdam about that in heaven! Please continue with my story!'

'Alright. Soloman Le Blanc married the lovely Marie Barault in 1712 in Dublin town.'

'And she was French too?'

'Yes.'

'And Huga-no?'

'Huguenot, yes. Soloman was a merchant, but I can't find where he died. There's no record of it anywhere. Anyway, his great great grandson, John, or perhaps it was Jean le Blanc, married a Belfast girl in 1791. He changed the name that year to White.'

'I wonder why?'

'Maybe he didn't want anyone to know that he was French during the French Revolution. Well, that's what dad said.'

'Your dad's a right know-it-all. Go on!'

'John's eldest son, John, inherited the family's linen mill in Lisburn, but his younger brother, Herbert, set up his own mill here in Belfast in 1805. Herbert's great grandson was our Herbert, Mary's husband and Sally's dad.'

'Can you imagine the house they would have had?' said Jean with misty eyes.

Ever since Shelley had told her the family history, Jean's obsession had been the house and the style they had lived in.

'And the sewing machine upstairs,' said Jean. 'Granny always said it was expensive. I wonder if Herbert bought it for Mary before he died.'

'Possibly.'

'It's a pity the house was pulled down,' sighed Jean.

Shelley smiled at the twist in her family history. Her Protestant Huguenot ancestors had travelled to Ireland to escape religious persecution in France, and two hundred years after an ancestor served in a war against a Catholic king, the land on which Herbert White lived with Mary, was acquired by the Catholic Church.

'I think it's lovely that we can visit the church, though. It's a beautiful building to have on the land,' said Shelley.

'It's hard to believe Granny Sally lived in a big fancy house for the first few months of her life. Yes, at least it's a church and not a factory or something that'll get pulled down eventually. Imagine a Catholic Church in the middle of all those wee Protestant streets. Do you think Herbert is laughing from the grave?'

'I bet he is. I like to think of him as both happy and sad,' said Shelley.

'I think so too,' said Jean, her eyes wandering into the distance.

Shelley bounded off the seat as one of her pages floated through the air.

'Shit, Mum, what the f…?'

'Were you going to use the F word?'

'Yes! Yes, I was! My bloody foot is all covered in varnish!'

'Ach don't worry love. Sure, it matches the other one now.'

Shelley swiftly moved her foot away, 'Mum!' she screamed.

Jean's hand moved to her mouth. She looked up to Shelley with pleading eyes as a smirk expanded her petite nose. Shelley tried to quell the tiny muscles at the edge of her mouth, but she lost control and hysterics filtered through her body. She was face to face with Jean, who was mocking her prosthetic foot whilst brandishing a varnish-splayed paintbrush that was now oozing dollops of varnish over the floor.

'You're not normal, Mum!' Shelley laughed.

'I know, love. I know, but I'm what God gave to you. Where's Hannah by the way?'

'Where do you think?' smiled Shelley. 'It's Aodhán's last day.

'Oh god, those two think they're in love, don't they?' said Jean.

'What makes you think they're not?' asked Shelley.

'Oh, they maybe are, love, but a baby changes everything. Aodhán said he'll move over when the baby comes. We'll all be one big happy family then. Can you imagine?'

'Flip me, will we have to have Séamus Mac Ruaidhrí round for tea?'

'Not on my life,' said Jean. 'No, love, the white chair at the window couldn't hold the bullets that Séamus Mac Ruaidhrí would take around this street.'

'Right enough. He wouldn't be too popular on the Shankill, would he? What has Hannah done to the dynamics of this town? Mum, how would you feel about having an IRA man as your grandson's grandfather, an ex-con as a husband and a peeler as a daughter?'

'A peeler?'

'Yes, I'm thinking of doing two more years at school and then signing up to the PSNI.'

'Holy shit! Could you not do something normal like...' Jean looked around the room, 'make cushions?'

'No,' Shelley laughed. 'No, I want to join the police. Oh, and one more thing.'

'What?' said Jean, returning to work on the floor.

'I'm thinking of writing to the church on Herbert's land to ask them if we can plant a tree.'

'A tree?'

'In memory of the young people who have lost the battle of depression.'

Jean looked up and smiled tenderly. 'That's a really lovely idea. Thank you.'

'I....' Shelley hesitated.

Here was Shelley's chance to tell her mother about the blackness that had crept into her mind, but she couldn't do it. Not now. There was too much going on with Hannah and the baby. Shelley would manage the sadness on her own.

'What is it, love? Is there something wrong,' asked Jean.

'No, no, it's okay.'

'If it's that. If it's...Shelley, love, if you ever feel sad, you need to control it. To touch a nettle...'

'with soft fingers is to welcome its bite,' said Shelley, finishing her mother's sentence. 'I know. You've said it a hundred times.'

'I have?'

'Yes.'

'And did you take heed?'

'Yes, I will grasp the nettle,' she said moving towards the stairs. She looked back at her mum and smiled. 'Shout on me when you need the spuds peeled. They'll taste good with a garnish of varnish.'

Shelley walked up the stairs and realised that she had been grasping the nettle through sleep. Ever since Etienne had given her the memory of those who had died in the bomb, she knew where to go to escape, and it always started with a vision of a pillow covered with soft red petals. *Les pavots* were flowers that looked after her sleep, and Shelley knew she would survive as long as she could drift away from her world with her eyes closed and her mind on a place of peace.

***

Jean's backyard was no more than three metres wide by five metres long, and it was brimming with blossoms and blooms. Catriona had only been

180

to Jean's house in winter and hadn't seen the contents of her yard on a summer's night. It was one of those late August evenings where the sun reaps what the rain has sown, imbuing the world with deeper shades of colour. Purple bellflowers spilled from cracks in the white-washed walls, whilst a row of painted tins containing reds, yellows and pinks occupied the length of the window sill like a rainbow. A wrought iron ship's wheel was painted white and black and stood against the opposite wall as proud as the family portrait in the living room, its weight imprinting two dents in the concrete from the supporting handles. Most striking of all was the thick ship's rope that was hooked around blue wooden balusters at the edge of the four walls. Catriona had noted the other front gardens on Snugville Street, lavished with the same pride that was here on the deck of this moored vessel of a home.

She was alone with Hannah, who must have observed Catriona taking it all in.

'Do you like Jean's new garden?' asked Hannah, ending Catriona's journey around the space.

'I can't take my eyes off it,' said Catriona from the vantage point of the small bistro table near the window, 'Jean is walking proof that small is beautiful.' Catriona looked around and then recognised her error, 'Oh Hannah, I didn't mean small in the sense of height. I meant small like the yard.' Catriona felt her cheeks glow.

Hannah smiled a reassuring smile, 'Small is beautiful. Look at me!'

'Of course,' smiled Catriona, relieved that Hannah had not been offended.

'And Aodhán isn't so tall either,' Hannah added with glimmering eyes, eyes that were permeated by the same light that transforms a rain-drenched landscape into a soulful shade. Catriona knew that Hannah had cried many tears, but Aodhán was shining now in Hannah's eyes like the sun. Catriona, meanwhile, who'd held back tears for so many years, and whose eyes had been set in the sun to deflect her internal shame, now found herself crying like heavy rain at the mere mention of her son's name.

Catriona could hear Aodhán's voice from the kitchen laughing at Jean. He'd offered to do the dishes. Catriona had escaped the chores with a glass of French wine and the company of Hannah. It was the first time she had been alone with Hannah since she'd found Aodhán, and she felt a compelling urge to apologise for something. She did not know how to define the basis of the apology. Hannah broke the silence.

'I'm sorry,' said Hannah, her words mirroring Catriona's thoughts like a card facing the wrong way in a deck.

'You're sorry? Why are you apologising?' Catriona asked gently. 'You haven't done anything wrong.'

Hannah looked at her hands, 'But you waited all these years to find your son, and then this all happens and it's made things so confusing.'

'Hannah, stop right there, now. Nothing could be farther from the truth. You brought my son back to me. Yes, I found what college he was teaching in, and I was halfway to the airport to find him, but who knows what would've happened if I'd gone there alone? I'll never forget that you...' Catriona found her words melting into water again. Almost two weeks had passed since she'd found her son, yet she was still unable to complete a sentence without the rain dispelling the affected sunshine of her eyes, 'I'll never forget that you brought him to me. That means so much. He came to find me.'

'He said it means a lot that you were looking for him too,' whispered Hannah, glancing towards the kitchen to verify that eavesdroppers could not hear her.

'I need to tell you this,' replied Catriona. 'No matter what happens between you and my son, I will always be here for you. We will always have our own connection. Always.' Catriona's voice faltered as she spoke with tears rattling in her throat. She swallowed and marvelled at how she had descended into sleet.

'Oh, don't cry,' said Hannah, her face now brimming. 'If you go, you'll make me go and I've cried enough tears lately.'

Catriona sipped her wine in the quiet of Snugville Street and looked in the eyes of her friend. 'You'll still go to France, you know?'

'You think so?' said Hannah with surprised eyes.

'I know so. It's what you want, isn't it?'

'Yes, and I don't even know why.'

'To speak French,' Catriona said flatly. 'That's why.'

Catriona understood the nineteen year-old before her like she understood herself, and for that reason alone she feared the affection Hannah held for her son.

'Yes,' smiled Hannah, 'All that effort to speak French, eh? It seems silly.'

'It seems sensible to me. I would have loved to have had the chance.'

'You still have,' said Hannah.

'I'm too old now for a year abroad,' smiled Catriona.

'No, you're not!'

'I'll have a grandson to look after.'

'Not you too!' Hannah said, rolling her eyes.

Catriona awaited an explanation.

'Mum's convinced it's going to be a boy.'

Catriona watched as Hannah's face tipped to the side in thought, and smiled with the realisation that the invigorated movement of Hannah's head was like a shadow of that of Jean's.

'Catriona?' she asked in the shy tones of the fourteen year-old that Rachael had once brought into their home.

'Yes,' replied Catriona, recalling the timid girl with affection.

'Rachael said that you called your baby Etienne before the adoption.'

'Yes, that's right,' said Catriona. 'I always liked the name. I was reading a book at university at the time. It's called *Germinal*.'

'It's on the list,' beamed Hannah. 'I mean, it's on the list of the books I have to read for Queen's.'

Catriona smiled at Hannah's ceaseless enthusiasm for her education. Rachael had no notion of what she would be studying, her chief interests remaining in the tight circumference of a rugby player and his evangelical family.

'Well, there was this character,' Catriona explained. 'I barely remember him now, but I must have liked him. I remember his spirit, but nothing else really. There were miners I think...and a bit of socialism. Your dad would like that book.'

Catriona watched Hannah's eyes light up again.

'I could buy him the English translation,' she said. 'I want to get him something. Did you see the necklace he got me?'

Catriona reached out and touched the stone Hannah was holding in her hand, 'Aquamarine,' Catriona observed. 'Lovely. I'm glad you made friends with him.'

'He's been okay about the baby stuff,' said Hannah.

'What about Jean?' It was Catriona who was now whispering and ducking under the sill of the high kitchen window.

'She's been great since she found out you offered to look after the baby. She never stops talking about it all, and I'm only one month in. It's a bit early for her enthusiasm.'

'Ah, I see,' Catriona said in softer whispers, 'Am I stepping on some dainty toes?'

'No no, not at all,' laughed Hannah.

Catriona could foresee the future there and then, and she realised that Jean was put on the earth to raise her little grandchild. Maybe it would be a boy and maybe Jean had been waiting for a little boy since she lost her own.

'That was a nice dinner,' said Catriona after a pause. 'Jean makes the best dinners.'

'You sound like Rachael,' said Hannah.

Catriona watched Hannah's eyes move into the distance towards an imagined sea at the end of the yard.

'Catriona?' she asked finally.

'Yes?'

'If the baby is a boy, can we call him Etienne?'

Catriona's body pulsated. She looked up to blue sky and breathed deeply to wash away the rain. 'I can't think of a better gift you could give to me, than to call the baby Etienne. Thank you, Hannah. It's perfect.

CONWAY STREET

Etienne emerged from the sludgy earth with dark sand glued to him from his shoes to his bony knees.

'Watch out! It's dangerous,' called a distant voice in English. 'The tide is turning.'

Hannah panicked. She realised that the water was rising fast on what Etienne had called his Treasure Island. It was a lump of rock covered in luminous gold seaweed, and she and her pirate son were busy picking shells near a rock pool when Etienne had tripped and sunk. The voice travelled like a whistle. Hannah looked up as she lifted her son and carried Etienne across the expanse of watery sand towards it.

A black labrador rushed across the sand, flicking up grey mud and wagging its tail furiously. Etienne jolted and whimpered at first, and then insisted on getting down to pet the dog. The dog's owner approached them, 'The dog is very friendly, sorry.' he said in French, pulling at the dog's collar.

Hannah stopped and looked. She had wondered when she would meet him. It was one week into her stay in Paimpol, and here he was in front of her, warning her about the tide. He was looking back at her with puzzled eyes.

'Thank you, Gildas. I think my son likes your dog.'

'Hannah' he said, with an effort to pronounce the first letter of her name. 'You're in France,' he added in English.

'Yes, I'm here,' she smiled.

He reached forward and Hannah prepared to kiss him, *faire la bise.* Gildas' arms encircled her and she found her cheek against his and her body enfolded in his arms. He moved his arms back, his hands still touching her shoulders and looked at her again.

'I can't believe it,' he said with errant vowel sounds that made him sound almost childlike, unexpected sounds from someone Hannah had only ever thought of as grounded and wise.

'And you've learned some English, I see,' said Hannah, switching to French to recover the man she had remembered.

'It's not good. I had to. I am working with some Irishmen who refuse to learn French.'

'That doesn't surprise me,' smiled Hannah.

'What are you doing here in Paimpol?' he asked.

'I'm here with my mum and my...Gildas, this is my son. He's called Etienne.'

'Etienne, pleased to meet you.,' Gildas said, shaking the young boy's hand. He looked up to Hannah, 'After Etienne Ollivier?'

'No, it's a long story. He's called Etienne after another little boy.'

It had been four years since Hannah had seen Gildas. She hadn't been tied to Gildas in any way, yet the guilt was there as she realised that everything about that summer would be revealed in a swift calculation of Etienne's age. The walks and the boat rides and the sharing of time with Gildas before she had met Aodhán were clearer in her mind now than the night she had spent in Rennes. She had danced with Aodhán at the Fest Noz, but there had been no dancing in Belfast.

'Where are you staying?' asked Gildas.

'I'm in an apartment in the centre of Paimpol. Etienne's dad has been staying with us. My mum is with the Ollivier family. Etienne Ollivier is coming back from Paris tonight to meet us. His family thinks Etienne is named after him too. We've never corrected them.'

'I won't tell your secret,' smiled Gildas. 'How long are you here for?'

'I'm going to be working here,' Hannah smiled, 'I have a job in the mornings teaching English for the British Council. At the weekends, Etienne will go to his dad in Rennes. They're going there this afternoon, in fact.'

'You aren't...you won't be...'

'We won't be living together. We aren't together, his father and I.'

'Come, sit here,' Gildas said, leading Hannah to the rocks where his bag and jacket lay. 'I walked here, otherwise I would take you for a coffee. Sit and talk a while, if you aren't in a hurry.'

'I'm not in a hurry, no.'

'How old is your son?' asked Gildas.

'He's four.' Hannah looked up at Gildas with apologetic eyes. 'Gildas, the summer I was here, I met someone. It's a long story, but Aodhán is from Belfast. We met in Rennes where he now lives. We tried to be together in Belfast, but it didn't work out.'

Hannah bowed her head. They had tried. In the beginning, there was a rush of love and passion that seemed to be guided by the fate of the situation they were in. Hannah had retreated into Aodhán's world, and had completed her degree in Belfast, dipping in and out of the student life that she could never wholly embrace. She knew that she didn't need to tell Gildas anything about her life, but she wanted to explain something to him.

'Aodhán... he had never settled in one place for long as a child. He and his mother moved around. I think that Aodhán has her nature. He doesn't like people being too close. We're different. My family is part of Belfast. My mum and dad help a lot with Etienne. They'll never move from Belfast and Aodhán needed to keep moving.' Hannah circled the ring on her right hand. It was simple gold band that Aodhán had given to her after Etienne was born.

'But why France? You'll miss your family.'

'Yes, I will, but I didn't go to France and Spain when I did my degree. I stayed at home to look after this boy.' Hannah ruffled Etienne's hair. He looked up up with a wide smile. She looked at Gildas. 'I could see that Aodhán was unsettled in Belfast and I told him he should move back to Rennes,' she explained, recalling the tight walls of the terraced house near the university where they had lived for three years. 'Anyway, we're here,' she added. 'I'm spending a year in Paimpol. Then I'll go home to look for a job. I did want to send you an email, but I felt bad about...'

'Please. I had no expectations that you would stay in touch. I knew you were young.'

'You never did tell me your age,' smiled Hannah.

'I am ten years older than you. That much, I remember. It kept running through my mind. You were only nineteen and I was worried you might think I was...I was just careful. I felt I was too old for you.'

Hannah thought of Aodhán. He was seven years older than her, yet age had never mattered. 'You know, I've been here for a week already', she said, 'and I wondered if I'd meet you. I even took my mum to the Ile-de-Bréhat. We got completely soaked. We could barely see a metre in front of us. My mum didn't think much of the island.'

Gildas laughed, 'You didn't check the forecast?'

'I told my mum I had checked the tide and I explained the thing about the moon. She said I was a bloody lunatic,' Hannah smiled.

'Perhaps you are,' laughed Gildas. 'Could I take her out on the boat before she leaves?'

'She's leaving tomorrow morning, but you should meet her. It's her last dinner at the Ollivier house. I'd like that, but maybe you've got...you could bring...' Hannah's face felt warm as she tried in vain to find the best way to ask Gildas if he was married.

'I am alone,' he smiled, his eyes resting on Hannah's face. 'I should walk back to Ploubazlanec if I'm going to make it on time for dinner. It's getting late and it will take me an hour. I will call Elen and arrange to meet you all. She won't mind me inviting myself. She never turns down fresh seafood.'

'That would be good. I'd like to see Jean cooking lobster.'

'You should go now too. The tide is coming in fast.'

'I will, yes, I'll go. Thank you.'

Gildas placed his hand on Hannah's, 'Thank you for coming back.' He turned to Etienne and brushed his hand over his dog, 'Goodbye Etienne, I will bring your friend to you later.'

***

Jean's eyes were still red and swollen from the tears that had flowed. She looked in the mirror and applied some makeup to cover up the stains. *Etienne Harold Adams* had gone to Rennes, and tomorrow would be the first full day since he was born that she wouldn't hold his little hand. The thoughts of a full year without him in her daily life was more crushing than the memories of her own son. Mourning for the living was more exhausting than mourning for the dead, and Jean had started to mourn three months ago, when she had learned that her home and her heart were to be torn apart.

She and Catriona had immediately booked six Easyjet flights to Paris. Jean knew that Hannah was doing the right thing for herself, but it was the wrong thing for Etienne.

Harry, in his wisdom, had said that they would all have to learn to trust Hannah, but Jean didn't know if she could trust Hannah. She never seemed to keep Etienne warm enough. She'd run from one place to the next, always forgetting his coat. She was in too much of a hurry to raise a child.

And then there was Harry with his simple mind. He was always on Hannah's side. They would work in tandem to overrule Jean, and they had conspired together about this ridiculous move to France, uprooting the boy from the family who had raised him.

Aodhán would already be halfway to Rennes with Jean's boy.

Jean took a deep breath. She would be meeting Etienne Ollivier for the first time since the summer he'd spent in Belfast, and she needed to put on her best face for him after six years. She'd already made a fool of herself by collapsing into Elen's arms in tears over her grandson. She finished her face and heard a familiar voice call her name with that soft J sound that had made her smile for a summer. *Etienne.* He was here. She walked to the top of the stairs and looked down. She grabbed the banister and stared. Her voice came to, 'Good lord, Etienne, son, what have you done with your hair?'

Etienne smiled and stepped forward as she neared the bottom of the stairs. 'Wait, stay there.' He kissed her four times, whilst Jean remained on the third step. 'Ah, still so romantic, Jean. Your kisses are forever beautiful.'

Jean lifted her hand and moved it across his cropped hair, 'What the...?' she began. She stood back and took in the smart black suit and red tie, 'What have they done to you, son? Your hair and your...' She caressed his earlobe, 'Your ear. What's happened to your ear?'

'Ah, you've noticed, said Etienne, touching his earlobe. 'Painful surgery. That's what happened. It didn't look good at the bank.'

'Yes, I heard about the bank. I didn't think, to be honest, being a financier would be your cup of tea, but look at you! You look very handsome.'

Etienne held out his suit jacket, 'Do you think so? I'm glad you approve,' he smiled.

A voice came from the dining area. 'He has sold himself to the devil,' said Kristen. 'His master is money. He will fall soon enough.'

'Oh, my little sister, who is always happy to say this until she needs a loan from her big brother,' Etienne said, moving towards her and tugging at her multi-coloured headscarf.

'He looks a little bourgeois, don't you think?' added Hannah.

Etienne looked to Hannah with cool eyes, 'I would take offence, but ever since you called your son after me, I will allow you to say it.'

'Gildas is coming too,' said Elen. 'In fact, he's bringing us dinner. He said he'd met Hannah earlier.'

Jean turned towards Hannah and whispered, 'Gildas, what kind of name's that for a fella?'

Hannah rolled her eyes and spoke firmly, 'Mum, he's a lovely fella for your information. And an excellent cook!'

'All these great cooks! What ever happened to real men?' asked Jean.

'Oh, Gildas is a real man, Jean,' Elen grinned. 'He runs a fishery and volunteers with the local coast guard. I think you'll like him.'

'Is he the one who put ideas in my daughter's head about the moon? It's just I have a bone to pick with him and his forecasts. Your woman there was babbling on about the moon meeting up with the stars or something, while the wean nearly caught his death of cold.'

'The child.' said Hannah to a confused Elen. 'Wean is child.'

Elen laughed, 'Jean, sit down please. Have some wine.'

Jean was drinking her wine in the living area. It was her last night in Elen's home and, as much as she had enjoyed the easy friendship with Elen, Jean was looking forward to a soft seat on Snugville Street. She wondered how Elen coped always being so far away from Mathieu. Her sentence was fixed until Mathieu's retirement.

She looked towards Hannah, who was busy helping Gildas at the stove. The image of Hannah by a stove was the first anomaly in her line of sight. The second was the smile on Hannah's face. It had been a long time since

Jean had seen her daughter smile like that. Who was this Gildas, Jean wondered? Yet another older man, it seemed, although Jean understood Elen's reference to his looks. He was an incredibly handsome man, so tall and with dark eyes that had lived several lives. Etienne sat down beside her.

'Tell me this, son. How well do Hannah and Gildas know each other?' Jean stared at his head as she spoke. It was like a shrub that had been clipped back too far. Jean missed the hair on his chin and on flowing over his shoulders and could not acclimatise to Etienne without it. He had lost his poetry, although his soul remained in his eyes.

'They dated when Hannah was here the second time, when she worked at the school,' he said.

'They did what?' said Jean.

'Sorry, maybe Hannah didn't want anyone to know, but I think Gildas liked Hannah a lot.'

'But she met Aodhán that summer.'

'I know and I'm sorry about that. I did try to keep them apart,' said Etienne.

'You did? Why was that?'

'I remembered hearing about Aodhán before Hannah came here. My parents were talking and they had said that his father was in the IRA. Then you told me about the IRA when we were in Belfast and I realised that Harry would be angry. Aodhán asked me a couple of times about Hannah. I ignored him.'

'Does Hannah know that?'

'No. What did Harry say about it?' asked Etienne.

'Oh, Harry wasn't the problem, son. I nearly had heart failure when I found out. I couldn't get my head around the fact that my grandson's grandfather was in the IRA. That was an even bigger shock than Hannah coming home pregnant.'

'I feel responsible for that. I'm sorry.'

'What on earth do you have to be sorry about? Aodhán's a nice lad. I couldn't blame him for what his father had done.'

'I had a girlfriend that summer. I stayed away from Hannah. I wasn't very welcoming, but she seemed happy with Gildas.'

'Did she now?'

'Yes. Gildas' father was a good friend of my father,' Etienne continued. 'I've known Gildas all my life. He is a good person.'

'Is that right?'

Jean's voice was responding to Etienne but her mind was now on her grandson. She pushed the selfish thoughts away. The idea that Hannah might be happy with this Frenchman filled her with fear and dread. Yet, she looked up and saw her daughter smile. Aodhán had made her smile in the beginning too. It was Harry who had seen the danger signs. 'He'll never settle,' Harry had said. 'He has never known home.'

Jean thought back to the meeting of three grandfathers; a triumvirate of Northern Ireland's sins and passions. There was Terence Craig, the gentle politician who wanted to keep the union safe, Séamus Mac Ruaidhrí who had actively fought to pull it apart, and Harry Adams, who was more concerned with trades unions than the union with Britain. Young Etienne had a heritage that crossed boundaries that few people would have believed. And now he was in France. Jean's throat began to ache again.

'So, Etienne,' she said. 'What's with the new look?'

'I thought you'd like it,' said Etienne.

'I do. It's lovely. But tell me this, is there a woman behind all of this?'

Etienne smiled, 'There is.'

Jean sighed, 'Ach son, you should never change yourself for a woman or for a bank. I'd have loved you the way you were. Except for the ear, of course. Yes, the ear really was a bad job.'

'Thank you, Jean. I love you as you are too. Tell me, how is Shelley?'

'She's okay. Shelley is okay,' smiled Jean.

Jean often wondered if Shelley was okay. She had no idea what ever occurred any more in Shelley's mind. While Hannah shed thoughts from her mind like bullets, Shelley stored hers up in a secret arsenal.

***

Harry awoke with sweat dripping down his face. His body clung to the sheets as dawn fractured the darkness, a merciless reminder of the burden of life.

He peeled the sheets from his body and walked to the bathroom. Filling the sink with ice cold water, he plunged his face into it and gasped. He reached for a towel and took a deep breath. 'Live, Harry. Keep on living.' He looked around the bathroom. Etienne's toys were still there on the side of the bath; Etienne, who carried the hope of his grandfathers on his tiny shoulders. It was the right thing for Etienne and Hannah to be in France. Jean would never understand because her mind was always in conflict with her heart.

Harry turned the dial on the shower and a spray of lukewarm water covered his chest. He increased the power and the heat. A spray of blood beat against him. He lifted the soap and wiped it away. There was no blood. Harry looked up at the water. It ran clear.

He moved to the bedroom in his towel and looked out towards the Benefits Office, as he had done every day for four years. He leaned his head against the window. Down below, the memory of his daughter's fall. Her legs hadn't worked, she'd said. She'd tripped on the kerb and her legs had turned to rubber.

The sun had cut through sulphurous clouds and glistened off the blacked out windows of a brand new jeep. Harry had known instinctively that his time had come.

He had been wrong.

Four years on, Harry could see the silent screams that were etched on Shelley's face as she looked up to the window where he now stood. The curtains were wide open and he could see Nathan buckled over on the road. Harry's legs had worked, but it was too late. Nathan was dead. Neither Harry nor Shelley would have been able to catch Nathan as he fell.

Etienne had been born like a gift of spring, but Harry had stood by the side of a grave with his heart torn between the earth that was falling onto a wooden coffin and the earth that would lead them to a hospital where his grandson was sleeping.

As they had all stood side by side at the grave, unfamiliar cries ripped the air and shattered Harry. All that he had built up since leaving prison, all the resolve and the strength he had gathered, was drowned out in the tears of two parents who had turned their back on their son.

But it was not just the wretched tears of Nathan's family that tormented Harry. It was not just the memory of Nathan's wet clothes against his chest as he held his seeping body. Harry had looked across the street where Shelley remained motionless on the footpath outside their home, and he could see one thing clearly on his daughter's face: Shelley had loved Nathan.

Sliced up with his own grief was the guilt of knowing that he preferred Nathan to be dead than to be within reach of his daughter's heart.

Harry had bowed his head as Nathan's body was lowered to the ground, sad for the destruction of a young life; relieved that Shelley had escaped the darkness of Nathan's world.

***

The metrical rhythm of two feet striking the pavement in tandem was the one thing that Shelley would miss about walking the beat. Her new role as trainee detective constable beckoned as the two year probationary period came to an end. It was the last time she would walk through the city centre on a Saturday night, policing the thriving Cathedral quarter that had emerged triumphantly humble from peace.

The Cathedral quarter was a world apart from the Shankill. The buildings were the same, but the simmering darkness was merely a rumour of another place and time, and not the reality that continually pounded at her front door. Men kept their politics hidden under long shirt sleeves, contained, yet ready to emerge again if the tide of peace turned.

Shelley stopped with her colleague at the Duke of York bar and watched. Plump, pink geraniums spilled from hanging baskets whilst more than one hundred people talked and laughed under gas heaters; smoking and drinking, unattentive to the underworld that Shelley had come to know.

She looked at the bench outside where Nathan had stopped to light a cigarette on that winter's day more than four years ago. Shelley had contentedly inhaled the scent of smoke, blowing circles of breath into the frosty air.

There had been a wedding reception in the back bar of the Duke of York. A bride in a flowery summer dress had smiled as plates of sandwiches were handed around three small tables of guests. Shelley hadn't understood, at first, that they were at a private wedding party. Nathan had then pointed to the little reserved sign on the table where they were comfortably seated with two pints. They'd got up to leave, but the father of the bride had told them to stay where they were. They had been offered sandwiches and a slice of cake and they'd stayed in the Duke of York for the rest of the afternoon, close in the commune of strangers.

'I'd like a wedding like that one day,' Shelley had said.

Nathan was silent. He'd then taken her hand, 'I'd marry you like that.'

'You'd marry me?' Shelley had laughed.

'Yes. I would marry you.'

Shelley, who hadn't so much as held hands with Nathan, looked him in the eye. 'Should you not kiss a girl before you make an offer like that?' she'd said.

He'd kissed her then. A bluster of cold wind had arrived through the door of the pub, as the memorabilia of an old Belfast swayed. Shelley had looked around and had created her own memory, and she carried it now with her on her last night. Shelley had loved Nathan. She wondered how long she would hold that memory. She knew she would meet someone some day, a better match in circumstance, perhaps, but she would never replace Nathan.

'I love you.' He'd said it casually, before sipping his pint.

He didn't need to say it any other way. Shelley had already known that Nathan's love was there.

'I loved you when I saw you fixing Mrs McAdam's hair. You were beautiful. You are beautiful here,' he'd added, touching her heart.

Shelley replayed his words as her feet picked up rhythm again after the short pause on the cobbled stones. She looked up to the sky as she walked. It was the clear blue of a late summer night. The sky had been a mass of brooding movement with a glimmer of sunshine on the day that Belfast had taken Nathan away. The same Belfast sky that had claimed the girl on the bed of poppies, the sky that had taken a baby to safety in the clouds as German rain fell on Belfast's soil, and the sky that had covered Mrs McAdam in its blanket of cool air as she fell, had swept Nathan away.

Nathan hadn't chosen death.

He'd lived in fear of reprisal from a group of people whose bodies were fixed on response and whose minds did not know how to react. They had been watching Nathan. They'd said he owed them money, but money had not been the issue. Nathan had already paid them what they were due. It was his desire to part company with the people who had protected him throughout his youth, the people who had formed his family when his parents had walked away, that had led to his end. His wish to be free was a death wish.

It was only now as her career aspirations unfolded, that Shelley could see how Nathan's past would have come into conflict with her present. She wondered sometimes if Nathan had been taken from her so that she could live her life free of his struggles. She looked up again and whispered a silent thank you to her friend.

She recalled what her dad had said about suffering. She had always known she was lucky, and as she thought of all the people who had passed from her world, she understood that their suffering had filled her life with meaning.

***

'Is there something bothering you?' asked Jean, as she tried to keep apace with her daughter's hasty stride.

'Yes,' said Hannah.

'What is it?'

'I wanted to buy Etienne his Santa presents.'

'I already bought them,' said Jean.

'That's the point!'

'What's the point?'

'You bought them!' exclaimed Hannah.

'It's December. Someone had to think about it.'

'I wanted to think about it!'

'You're too late.'

'What do you mean I'm too late? I've got two weeks to sort it all out.'

'Exactly!'

'We've plenty of time to buy presents.'

'You're disorganised.'

'There was no way I could have carried a load of stuff back from France.'

'Look,' smiled Jean. 'You're on holy ground now. Behave yourself in case that nice priest comes along.'

Hannah and Jean were standing in front of the Holy Cross Church, just over a mile from their home on Snugville Street. Hannah didn't really care about who bought the Christmas presents, but she needed to make her point, and now that Jean was laughing at her, she found herself repressing her own childish remonstrances and listening to the music trickling down the steps.

Jean had heard the music too. Hannah could see her mother's face turn towards it.

The Holy Cross Church sat contentedly in celestial peace at an intersection of two unsilenced populations: a Catholic one and a Protestant one, and Hannah was there with Jean to see the memorial that Shelley had arranged with the help of an interfaith charity. The church was a surprise from every angle, a raised juxtaposition from the urban reality surrounding it. Two fairytale towers topped with green copper roofs were unified by a square facade in pale stone. Steps ran up the centre where floodlights lifted the stone to burnished white.

'The plaque is this way,' said Jean. 'Come over here.'

They climbed the grassy hill to the left of the steps. It was late afternoon and the light had already deepened the grass to black in the shifting darknesses. A fledgling tree stood naked of its foliage, and Jean shone a torch towards the simple white stone adjacent to it.

Hannah reached out and touched the marble and the memory of her brother. She kneeled by the brass plaque and read the inscription.

In memory of His children
Whose minds were clouded with despair:
God will provide for them.

Hannah's eyes fell on the word 'despair.' She breathed deeply and dabbed at hot tears with her cold hand. 'Shelley did this,' she said, her voice faint.

'Shelley did this,' repeated Jean.

'Did she write it?' asked Hannah, after a pause.

'The priest helped her.'

'It's lovely,' said Hannah.

'It is.'

'She's an angel.' Hannah spoke in a murmur, her attention drifting again to the rising music.

Jean placed her hands on her daughter's shoulders, 'Hannah, Shelley's going to be okay.'

Hannah looked at the plaque again, the word 'despair' harsh against the glistening purity of the marble. 'I know, but sometimes it seems that she's so alone. Losing Mrs McAdam and then Nathan… it was all too much. And then I went to France with Etienne…'

Hannah looked up and hesitated before a whisper of a voice stole her own words, 'Mum, I'm sorry.'

'What for? Going to France?'

'No, I was supposed to be looking after her.'

'Who?'

'Shelley.'

Hannah placed her hand over the torch. 'It's too noisy... I mean it's too bright.'

Jean dipped it to the ground. They were in semi-darkness again as Hannah spoke, 'I wasn't holding her hand.'

'When?' Jean's arms were folded across her body against the cold. They dropped to her side. 'Do you mean?'

'Yes,' said Hannah, 'The day of the bomb. You told us we weren't allowed on the Shankill Road and I took her there.'

'Hannah, come here.'

Hannah followed Jean to the steps of the Holy Cross church. She sat down and huddled into her woollen coat.

'You did nothing wrong,' Jean said sternly. 'You were just a child. Do you still remember?'

'Every detail,' said Hannah. 'You know a silly thing that I kept thinking about afterwards? I wet myself and I was embarrassed. All the dust and the blood, and I was embarrassed about that! I was eight and I kept thinking that nobody wets themselves at eight.'

Hannah felt the touch of Jean's cold hand on hers and watched her breath smoke through the air. They remained silent on the steps of the church, ambivalent to the cars and headlights on the road before them, focused on a distant place in their unsheltered memories.

'It's nice here, isn't it?' said Jean, her words soothing against the bite of the cool air. 'Herbert and Mary would've had a good view over Belfast, wouldn't they?'

'They would,' said Hannah. 'They'd have seen the hills and those houses wouldn't have been there.'

The music continued to amplify behind them. 'It sounds like a carol, doesn't it?' said Hannah.

'Have you ever been inside the church?' asked Jean.

'No, I've only ever been to Catholic churches in France.'

Jean took Hannah's hand. 'Time we changed that. Come with me.'

They reached the top step and the song became clearer. Jean pulled back the door of the church and looked inside. She smiled and turned to Hannah. 'Come here, love. Come and see this.'

Hannah's eyes adjusted to a new darkness and she saw the outline of a choir of nuns serenading a constellation of golden candles. The nuns were facing the altar and their song cantered over the darkness, the gravitational pull and swell of their vocal symphony harmonious with the movement of the flames.

Divergent breaths ascended and descended, *Sleep in Heavenly peace.* Unified voices exalted and depressed, *Sleep in Heavenly peace.*

Hannah breathed deeply and followed Jean back down steps in

contented serenity, the music gliding behind them.

They walked home in uniform short strides. Old mills and new apartments passed them by as they consumed shared memories without speaking, both listening out for the rested voices of their past.

The light was warm on Snugville Street. As neighbours competed with each other for the greatest number of garden illuminations, their efforts bestowed the street with streams and ribbons of moving colour. Hannah looked in windows, and smiled at house-proud women perched on their leather sofas watching titantic TVs that had been attached to the walls above their mantelpieces. 6a Snugville Street would never have a TV in that location. 'The light would fade Robert if we moved the portrait,' Jean had said.

Jean's front garden was bright with a fluorescent snowman and a flashing sleigh. Harry had complained that Jean had made him buy them and install them two hours before Etienne's arrival. No amount of spending and effort was too much for Etienne's return after six months away.

'Wait til I tell your dad about the nuns,' Jean said, filled with the electric enthusiasm of her Christmas display.

Hannah opened the front door and a rush of heat struck her from the fire and the depth of colour. The white chair had undergone a transformation to cranberry velvet; the sofa had been upgraded to brown leather, in keeping with fashions; the chair by the fire was its own unique shock of rambling roses; and the room was once again overflowing with Jean. Family photos in a medley of brass frames were placed at angles on every surface, Mrs McAdam's Royal Doulton tea set shone like nostalgia from its position on her old oak dresser, and there on the white sheepskin rug by the fire guard was Etienne, concentrating hard on plucking his lego from the long threads of fleecy wool. He looked up when they entered the room.

'Santa's coming,' he said.

'Fourteen days, son. Come here and look at the advent calendar.' Jean lifted the calendar by the side of the TV and feigned astonishment, 'My goodness. Santa must be coming tonight! All the chocolates are away!'

Etienne's blue eyes lit up as he wiped the chocolate from his lips with the back of his hand, 'Granny, don't be silly. Santa's not coming. Maybe Granda ate the chocolates.'

'Granda. Hmm, is that so, Etienne?' Jean said with her hand on her hip. 'Where is Granda anyway?'

Shelley's head peered around the kitchen door. She whispered over Etienne's head, 'Mum, come here. Dad wants his old work boots.'

'In the house?' flinched Jean.

'It's for the...you know...' said Shelley, pulling at an imaginary beard with her hand and mouthing, 'Santa.'

Jean located the errant boots, approached the kitchen, and was pushed back by Shelley. 'No, no, wait,' Shelley said.

'Granda's an eejit,' Jean mumbled as she sat down on her roses.

'Which Granda?' Etienne asked without looking up. 'I have four Grandas.'

Hannah laughed. It was Etienne's profession of fortune that he had four grandfathers. In addition to Harry, Terence and Séamus, Etienne had laid claim to Colin Andrews, Aodhán's foster dad.

'The Granda in the kitchen, silly', said Jean.

'I have two Grandas in the kitchen. *You* are the silly billy, Granny.'

'What's Terence doing here?'

'Granda Terence is away with Nanny Trina to Merica. He's getting me a cowboy hat.'

'Well, who the...' Jean's hand was raised to her head. 'It's like *Guess who's coming to bloody-well-dinner* in this house!' Jean turned to Shelley, 'Did your man bring...?'

'Shush,' said Shelley.

The front doorbell rang and Etienne bounded up, 'Maybe it is Santa,' he said, racing to the door.

Hannah followed him and caught the weight of the small child as he moved backwards in breathless astonishment. She smiled, the white head of fluffy hair of the apparition at the door, unmistakable.

Séamus and Harry had formed an unlikely friendship and worked together once a month at an interface project, trying to improve the lot of young men who'd been to prison. Harry had yet to bring Séamus home to Snugville Street.

Hannah was impressed by the outfit that was now passing through the room. Séamus was the most authentic Santa Claus she'd ever seen. He had a real beard to match his white hair and his growing stature was ideal for the role. Hannah watched as Etienne cocked his head to the side and moved confidently towards the familiar shape. Hannah stepped in quickly, 'We'll have to call round to Granda Mac tomorrow and tell him about this, won't we?' she said excitedly.

Etienne looked her in the eye like a child who'd chosen to believe, 'Yes,' he said, and quietly moved away from Santa. Hannah stood in the doorway and looked around the living room. Etienne was shyly hovering around Jean's legs, Shelley was on the sofa smiling nervously, Jean was hugging Etienne and averting her eyes from everyone, and Santa was now seated by the window below a Christmas tree enveloped in thick, silver tinsel.

It was time to stop waiting for bullets on Snugville Street, but there was still a tension in the room as each person took in the sight of Séamus in a festive mix of red and cranberry velvet.

Harry was shaking Santa's hand when Hannah stepped outside and pulled the door behind her. She looked to her right and followed a long line of red-bricked houses on Conway Street. She continued in her mind for less than a mile until she reached a peace-line of aluminium and barbed wire. There was a sewing unit that had once belonged to Jean, and in its window sparkled a blinding bling-encrusted orange dancing dress. She smiled as she roamed over the barrier near the shop, where Martin Luther King, Nelson Mandela and John Lennon met in literary and artistic unity in murals painted on either side of a gate. *Imagine* was etched in large, bold letters.

Hannah moved beyond the gate towards a curtailed strip of houses, a remnant of Conway Street, that had once run from the Shankill Road to the Falls Road. Just by the corner of the Falls Road was a large concrete Benefits office opposite a row of red-bricked terrace houses. Hannah wondered if a French exchange student would have carried the same sense of difference as he had stood stoically consuming *le peuple* under a Falls Road sky.

And was there a girl on Conway Street who could tell the same story that she had told? Perhaps the girl had a brother like Robert, or a friend like Nathan. Perhaps there were secrets hidden behind elaborate vases, secrets of mothers who had gone to homes to give up their children and find their freedom, and of men who'd wondered what had become of their sons. Perhaps there was a father like Harry, with a name like Séamus, who had left the next generation to question why.

Was there a Jean on Conway Street? Was there a mother holding the life and soul of her family in her small bleach-toughened hands, a woman who had attacked the living and the dead on her skirting boards, and who had, one day, taken down the faded posters on her son's wall? Maybe she too had had a picnic with sandwiches wrapped up in cling film to celebrate a peace that was waxing and waning and waiting for change like the dawn of a new spring tide.

ABOUT THE AUTHOR

Angeline King was born in 1975 in Northern Ireland. She graduated from Queen's University of Belfast, where she studied Modern History and French. She went on to complete a Master's Degree in Applied Languages and Business and had a successful career in international business for fifteen years. Angeline now lives in her beloved home town of Larne with her husband and children.

Angeline's blog can be found at:
www.angelineking.com

61008098R00124

Made in the USA
Charleston, SC
14 September 2016